POLLARD

Laura Beatty lives in the middle of Salcey, one of the very few remaining medieval hunting forests in England. The forest, she says, has provided us with food, forage, fuel, materials for building and transport – yet it is also the place where we keep our bogeymen, where witches live, and where characters go in and 'come out wiser or sadder or dead or different'.

Laura Beatty is married with three children. She is the author of two biographies: a book about Anne Boleyn, written for children, and Lillie Langtry described as 'unputdownable' (*Express*), 'vastly entertaining' (*Observer*), 'fresh and revealing' (*Literary Review*) and 'irresistibly enjoyable' (*Sunday Telegraph*).

ALSO BY LAURA BEATTY

Anne Boleyn
Lillie Langtry

LAURA BEATTY

Pollard

VINTAGE BOOKS
London

Published by Vintage 2009

6 8 10 9 7 5

Copyright © Laura Beatty 2008

Laura Beatty has asserted her right under the Copyright, Designs and
Patents Act 1988 to be identified as the author of this work

First published in Great Britain in 2008 by Chatto & Windus

Vintage
Random House, 20 Vauxhall Bridge Road,
London SW1V 2SA

www.vintage-books.co.uk

Addresses for companies within The Random House Group Limited
can be found at: www.randomhouse.co.uk/offices.htm

The Random House Group Limited Reg. No. 954009

A CIP catalogue record for this book
is available from the British Library

ISBN 9780099516941

The Random House Group Limited supports The Forest Stewardship
Council® (FSC®), the leading international forest-certification organisation.
Our books carrying the FSC label are printed on FSC®-certified paper.
FSC is the only forest-certification scheme supported by the leading
environmental organisations, including Greenpeace. Our
paper procurement policy can be found at
www.randomhouse.co.uk/environment

Printed and bound in Great Britain by Clays Ltd, St Ives plc

CONTENTS

For Emily

I moved on, looking neither way,
Trying to hear
The outcry that must go with all
Those upflung maidenly gestures, that arrested
   humpback rout
Stumbling in blackberries and bracken –

Silence.

Trees, it is your own strangeness, in the dank
   wood,
Makes me so horrifying
I dare not hear my own footfall.

From 'Trees'
by Ted Hughes
Collected Poems (Recklings)

PROLOGUE

There was a wood once.

Just itself to begin with, turned inwards, filtering light and meditating on the seeds spinning down from its twigs to the tangle of its floor. Birds, wildlife.

Later, someone found it, defined it. 'Wood for 800 swine.' '3 shillings for the custom of the wood.' Used it. Gridded out, like a town, and its quarters named. Then it was cut into rides, hunted, managed, grazed, chopped about, foraged, felled, filled in again.

Now it's a country park. Paintballing, archery. Rabbits, rats, squirrels, vermin mostly. And it's where the runaways go. They run patrols every now and then, of course, and the Ranger's pretty vigilant, but it's a big place and if a kid doesn't want to be found . . .

And the town's right there, playing grandmother's footsteps with the wood. There's a scrubby path now, to the nearest housing estate. It's meant to be an up-and-coming area, industry parks, logistics, 120,000 houses over the next twenty years. But it makes no difference. It's like a bucket's leaking. They pour out everywhere, the homeless, the misfits, the drifters. You can't plug the holes fast enough. Riffraff. Bums. For every house they build there's someone who can't live in a building, a new person on the street, or that's how it seems. If you took a bird's-eye view, you'd see them blowing about the streets like litter, the same lost faces in the same places, moving around to rules of their own, rules that are difficult to understand. My patch. My pitch. Move it. You could mark them on a map if you wanted. They are as constant as the Eleanor Cross or the shoe factory.

Have a look round.

By the precinct, 10.30 p.m., boys from the estate. Just bad boys some of them but you can't tell, who's staying out tonight, who's going home, who's going down the plug faster than whoever else. That was Lola once, with the long legs and the sideways smile – someone else now – over by Marks, with a local policeman, giving it a bit of mouth. You'll end up shagged, bagged and binned if you don't look out, I'm just telling you, I'm not shouting. And she did. All three. So that was a short story.

Under the colonnade, Reuben taking over from Bucky. Tom, Dick and Harry on the bench by the canal, their chaos of cans, their glazed and bursting faces.

Or this one, always round the church somewhere, on the benches in the little bit of green at the back, part park, part graveyard. Anne, they call her, no family name known, age uncertain. She served a prison sentence once. Caught religion, like a cold, off the prison chaplain. Take no notice. Just walk quickly past. She mouths things, some strange words sometimes, from the Bible or off the billboards, and then there's all the bags she lumps around. Useful for litter collection. She's good at that. Otherwise no one at home.

Meanwhile, at the bottom of its hill the wood waits, and watches the town's bulging advance. It accepts the tides of people who pulse to and fro under its branches. It has little choice. Witness, it whispers, its leaves interlocking, witness the change. On the cut timber, stacked in pyramids down the felled rides, you can count the years. Trees keep time inside out, and in circles. But the wood's older than that.

We are still growing, the trees tell each other. Despite everything. We are still working with water and with light. Breathing with many mouths. Balancing with exactness, and without thinking, the ratio of roots to shoots, calculating dieback.

Witness, the trees say, as the years go by. There are no similarities between a man and a tree. As far as we can see.

And separate from both the town and the wood, aware of nothing, except her own dark limbo, Anne shuffles about the churchyard, under the scabby planes. Straining inwards, to where she holds her history, in time-rings of her own. She knows it's there. She can feel it, though she has forgotten its detail.

So, no light for Anne, except what comes from a coloured plastic lighter that she holds up in moments of distress, depressing the gas flow and flicking the flint with practised ease. Her fingers are hooked like roots, purplish most days. It is amazing that she can operate something as finicky as the little cog on the front of the lighter, the cog that controls the flame. She is worried obviously that the lighter will run out, so she adjusts and adjusts. She only has the one. Lighten our darkness. She is a religious person and it seems to give her comfort, the flame.

Otherwise how much of it do you believe, what she mouths or mutters to the volunteers in the soup kitchen? I lived in a ditch for three months, she says. They can't keep her indoors, that much is certain. She leaves every flat, every room she's been given. Slept in someone else's hut on the allotments until she was turfed out.

Three months in a ditch and I never felt a thing, she says. Who knows if it is true.

Suffer the little children, that's another of her sayings.

Don't even ask.

I can't see the wood for the trees, Anne says, picking up a cigarette butt off the pavement outside Caffè Nero, gathering up her bags again. Not often lucid.

What have you got in your bags, Anne?

The sins of the world, she says, ramming the butt down into this bag or that.

Now that's a heavy thing to carry.

And then she's up and off again, lolloping down the main street, past Marks. She has a characteristic walk, raising her knees a little, as though her feet were catching in something all the time, as though she was walking through a bog. At Top Shop she stops by the window and looks at the mannequins, dressed for the beach and the disco, bare belly buttons and blue eyelashes. She stops and she rummages again and she holds up the lighter.

She speaks bird. She does speak bird. If you were to catch her on one of her bird days you'd be surprised. She must have all of a dozen different calls, whistled out between the teeth, or lips pursed, or somewhere weird near the back of God knows where.

So maybe.

Beyond Marks she trundles across the road, slow, in front of a blaring bus. There were words once, Anne says unruffled, on the far side. Standing still, among pedestrians, who swivel to look. She can't remember now. But there was a language once, before the dark came down, before they left her, with the glimmerings of memory and only the lighter to see by. Stumbling about among a jumble of catchphrases.

The world was alive then. You could put your feet down on something solid. You could depend on things to mean something after all.

So that's what Anne's doing, as she rootles in the bins, or stops with her lighter aloft, outfacing the commuter traffic. She's waiting in a blizzard of words, for something to click to a fit. In the beginning, she says to herself, rummaging again, examining every scrap that floats wind-borne down the shabby streets. *Blair, Going Going Gone*, she reads. *Back to School*, and *Over the Hedge*. She makes her way down the gravel path to the church door. Leave not a stone unturned. So she doesn't. But it's not here, whatever she's hunting. It's gone, she knows that.

Then, one day, while it was still dark, there was a fox. Just a fox licking like a stinking flame around the bins behind the bakery. And it flicked something matching in her head. So she followed it, although it was quicker than her and was soon out of sight, and she has been going ever since. Slow going, because she has her bags with her, six bags, all from Mothercare. She leaves the churches, St Giles and St Peter's, and she lopes on flat feet, down the painted residential streets, taking a foxy direction, through back alleys of setts, scrubby with buddleia, round corners, out along a roaring dual carriageway. Over the bridge, and she's never been this far before, and over a river and all the bad boys lounging on the bridge call out to her as she passes. Give us a light, Annie. Go on give us a light. We know you've got one. She puts her head down and pulls the bags tight and scuttles past.

Through the new estates. So many houses, so hard and so blank, and further out, the industry parks, brick and tarmac acres with familiar names. Foxhill, so that's hopeful, the Willows, Sedge Mere. And as she walks, reading the signs, the dawn suggests itself to the urban sky, which has its own lights and doesn't mind either way. Whatever, it says, shrugging in-turned shoulders. But Anne sees and somewhere inside her something lifts reciprocally and in gratitude. A connection of sorts. And it is in the murk of this, that she makes out, at last, a shape more like herself, where it could be she belongs. A shape that isn't flat or square or angled, but like that for instance! – as she comes to a mile of chain-link fencing, broken down in part, behind which heave up the forms of something sloped, a curve, a rise. Hill, she says to herself, out loud and with conviction. That's definite. So she slips through the fence to the foot of the hill and she climbs, toiling upwards, with her bags tearing because the ground is sharp after all, though it doesn't matter because the dawn has begun, and when it breaks, at last, all will be mended.

She helps herself up with her hands. The ground is so many sided, so hard-edged, so metal and strange, and pools of sludge to surprise you, and meanwhile, the sun has one leg over the horizon now and all is waking to its light. The sky lightest blue and, Anne sees, filled with gulls, and on every side, as far as the eye can see, the ground is grey and whitish and rust-coloured. Hills of no colour and, beyond the hills, houses. Winter, she remembers, although the sun says summer, which is puzzling. And then, she thinks, be sure the green will come at last. She's seen the ground dead before, she remembers that too, only that was under a dead sky, and the green still came. She'd never known the green not to come at last. On top of the hill, she settles as best she can, on the side of a fridge, with her back against the hillock of a filing cabinet. She arranges the mangled bags around her and looks out over the hills of rubbish, and the gulls scream and pick, as if they too were blown litter, and she waits.

Any minute now, Anne. Any bloody minute.

The wood sees the lights of the town go out with the dawn, the dull sunset glow that hangs in its sky all night replaced by immediate morning. It could see Anne too – on top of her rubbish mountain, her back half turned, looking at her salvation only peripherally – if it wanted. It could see the toy cars drive up and the people get out, see Anne strain towards its outline, turning her head like an owl to ask herself, what's that, while a pin man with a megaphone burps instruction and two others mount the rubbish matter-of-fact, as the law always is. It could see Anne, struggling with her darkness, face the wood now, looking at its furred edges at the suggestion of its own dark, which she almost recognises, almost names. It could watch her inevitable and forcible removal, undignified, eyes still on the wood, until the rubbish rises against her sightline.

The wood does see, but its concern is with life, not the individual. It doesn't matter. There's always another time, for someone else, if not for you.

We just witness, witness, witness.

GROWING UP

Hands were a problem. She couldn't look at her hands. She just practised making petite gestures like the ones her sister made, but with her eyes shut. What are you doing Anne? Nothing. I'm not doing anything. Well you look daft with your eyes shut feeling up your own face. So, keep it to yourself, Anne would think. Keep your mouth shut Anne, she said to herself. And she opened her eyes and shut her mouth and sat still to avoid drawing attention to herself. Which was impossible.

Suzie's hands though, Suzie's hands were pretty like little birds. Never still, always fluttering up and down, nestling in her hair, skimming her brand-new bosoms, sucking and sipping at the corners of her mouth. Up and down, up and down, they had lives quite of their own, so busy. Anne wanted hands like that, hands like little bald birds, tippety-tapping like that with their lacquer beaks. But hands weren't her only problem. The shared bedroom was a problem because it was never far before Anne bumped into the bed or the dressing table, or knocked the lamp or barged the wardrobe.

Anne get your big bum out of that bleeding window you're making the room freezing, for instance. What do you want looking out of the window at this time of the morning?

She wanted to watch things. She wanted to watch her father for a start. She wouldn't have minded if he'd looked up and seen her but he was too busy wobbling with the first turn of the pedals, shoving his dinner in the bag over his shoulder. Everything was always difficult for her dad. Everything was against him – balancing the bike at the top of the hill, and the bag, whose flap was always the wrong way, fumbling at it in the stingy half-light, on his way to the poultry plant. The back of his neck was plucked chicken-raw and he moved his head with the motion of the bike forward and back, forward and back, the bike zigzagging just like a chicken did, till he got under way. She was a big girl now, boy was she a big girl. She shouldn't have needed a father any more. She knew that. Bye Annie. Bye Dad. Be a good girl.

Nothing, not even that any more.

But if her father offered no companionship, that was not the case with the moon. The moon kept an eye on Anne. She would have settled for the moon, if Suzie hadn't complained. She liked the moon because it had a white face like she did and because it knew how to make itself small. Bye moon. Bye Anne, have a nice day.

So she sat in the window, filling it right up, and she watched things and Suzie slept, not like a little bird but like a little pig. That was Anne's secret, how horrible Suzie looked when she was asleep. Her mouth round and glistening and sometimes there was dribble on the pillow. And the noise that came out of it. Pig noise. Anne adjusted her shoulders in the frame and watched. She watched the red eye of her dad's back light close in the fog. She watched the sky yawn itself wide awake over the wood at a pace she recognised and she breathed, because there wasn't enough air to go round in the little room once Suzie had had her fill – or she would have breathed if Suzie hadn't interrupted. What are you doing Anne? Nothing Suzie. Sorry Suzie. Well do nothing somewhere else. So she pulled in her head and backed into the room like every morning just about and like every morning she knocked something, inevitably, off the crowded bedside table, or the dressing table, or the shelf; nail polish probably. Clumsy tart.

Suzie had bad language when they were by themselves. She had a big mouth for a small person Suzie did. Anne did not like bad language. She found it offensive. When Suzie had gone, Anne sat by herself at the dressing table and opened out her big hands and put her head on one side like she'd seen Suzie do and mouthed the names of the nail polish. She had no idea whether she pronounced them right but she liked the sound, her private litany. Pink Two Timer, Gilty Party, Dusky Plum, S Cherry Zade. That's a nice colour Suzie. That's what she would say, one day, very matter-of-fact. Paint my nails for me Suzie. Holding out her hand again, the fingers extended, like now. Although when it came to it she never actually asked, although she still could, one day.

One day was Anne's favourite day. One day I'll have Bitter Chocolate, Moroccan Moon, Hi Ho Silver Lining. What are you doing Anne? You look like a goldfish, opening and shutting your mouth. Someone had sneaked up on her, propping up the doorway with their hands in their pockets. Mr Smartypants. Michael or John or Connor. They fancied themselves. She had God knows how many brothers and sisters and they all fancied themselves. Nothing, any of the above. Nothing, everyone else who's asking. Anne wasn't doing anything.

Bath the baby for me Anne wash the pots don't just sit there. Get out the way are you listening to me do something useful do the tatties for me get the pizza out the freezer if I have to tell you one more time.

Couldn't Suzie do something for a change?

No Suzie couldn't. Suzie was busy for chrissake. She was on the phone. She was watching her nails dry. Get Anne to do it; Anne's just parked in front of the telly box. She's doing nothing as usual.

That was how Anne's life went. One day after another and when her dad came back from work in the evening, that was the same too, pretty much. They talked about the new abattoir, mostly, when they did talk. He worried he should shift over. Karen's Lewis was starting at the abattoir, did they know, or Paul's Mary or Richard and Judy's Joseph, Pat and Sarah's Julie, Tim and Rita's Michael. It was always a matter of interest and surprise to her parents when someone joined the abattoir and every day just about there was someone new; whole battalions of people setting out in white wellingtons with steel toecaps and chemical-warfare boiler suits eager to cut throats and chop meat and hose down concrete with disinfectant. In Anne's mind the abattoir stretched to a distant horizon busy like an ant heap with the children of her parents' friends. She imagined it like Christmas, all noise and white and red. Must have been a party.

Then there would be no conversation except for the telly. Then her dad would say – it's a small world. This made Anne feel uncomfortable so she sat very still and tried not to feel things pressing on her. She did not doubt her father. She was a trusting person and besides you couldn't say the house was anything but small. Why would the world be any different?

But when she put her head out of the window, which she did as often as she could, then she felt hopeful. It could well be that a small world was still big enough. The sky was big if you like, but then the sky wasn't the world. The clouds, the wind. The sun up there. That was big.

Oi! Mooning about up there, open the door.

That was the Parcel Force man. Anne hated the Parcel Force man. He gave her the willies. Will you open the door or won't you? She never answered him. She just stared down from the window, went down the stairs as slow as she liked, stood in the doorway, blocking it up so he had to lean to see round her. Where's the pretty one? Sexy Suzie, Anne's big sister, geddit? He fancied her sister. She'd seen him, licking his hand with his rude tongue, sticking up his hair at the front in the driving mirror before getting out. He called Suzie sweetheart not open the door. When is she going to stop growing? he said, cocking his head towards Anne. He smelt of spit and aftershave. Have to get a ladder to get to her, and he jerked his hips forward and gave a wink to Suzie. Anne didn't like the shiny front of his trousers. At all. He put the parcel into Suzie's arms with his hand on her waist and his face glistening and all his spit and aftershave breathing at her. Steady now mind how you go and he slid his hand, Anne saw, from her waist, down over her backside. Suzie was disgusting. She did mail order nearly every week so the Parcel Force man could slide his hand on her backside and call Anne open the door.

Anne liked words. She learnt to read very early, although she never achieved full understanding, or so they said. It was just that she liked the words by themselves too much, had they known. She liked to feel their individual shape in her mouth, berries to be rolled round whole. She liked the separate sounds of them, the weight of them dropping, not crushed all together and lost. So she spoke her sentences slowly, with plenty of room. She spoke like a person packing a shopping bag, with care. For practical reasons, obviously, she said very little.

She can't see the wood for the trees, her dad would say, when she was small. He stopped saying it when she got large and irritation got the better of him. But the wood stayed with her, as a challenge, as something important. It was at the foot of the hill. Seeing it was Anne's first identifiable achievement, in her own eyes.

In the wood Anne saw the connection. There was room for everything to be themselves but still they fitted together, depended on each other even. Sometimes the fit was so tight, so interwound, it was difficult to sort it out, but she was patient; she didn't know their names, but she followed the stems of the old man's beard and the ivy and she knew them to be distinct. She assumed that they were happy like that, grateful for each other's difference and sensible of some similarity.

At home no one was grateful and difference was not a good thing.

Home was small and inwards. It could have been lighter maybe. It was painted red downstairs, the colour of old blood and there was stuff everywhere, piled on everything, magazines and telly guides, sticker books of Connor's, manuals, CDs, computer games, Michael's Xbox, packets of biscuits open and cups half full, cups with mould sometimes. It made you nervous. You were always going to knock something unless you were very careful. Everything had sticky dust on it, ash and dust. Frying fat and cigarette smoke, that's what it smelt of.

All of Anne's family were small, like the house, although there were a lot of them. Visitors would cock their heads at Anne's height and ask her parents, Where d'you get her then? Must've been a tall milkman. Then everyone would laugh, except Anne. By the time she was fourteen she was too high and too wide for most of them to notice.

Meanwhile, the wood drew her. So many tall things and so happy. Inside Anne's head the world was all upwards. It was breezy tops and lower filtered light, and movement. There was no clumsiness in the wood, as far as she could see. She carried the feel of it around with her, as an alternative. It took her over. The slim verticals of its timber-grown trees were her private rhythm. They put their feet down in her dreams at night, sprang up on the table when she set down the glasses for tea, grew out of her fists when she held her knife and fork upright at meals. When she played with the baby she would find herself stopping in the middle of something, colouring for instance, and setting the crayons on end, little wax copses across the floor. She became slower and quieter than before. Her head was so full of their rustling, her eyes barred and spotted with light and shade. She didn't want to spoil it.

But Anne's family was not like the wood, except perhaps in number. They saw no example in the wood, only trees. So Anne turned inwards and tried again. Trees are not people, she said to herself – and it was people that were her problem, or rather one of her problems, because sometimes the problems grew in her head, as thick as the trees.

Anne's mother wasn't much use either. She said, You are as old as you feel and I feel nine hundred. And, They say you are what you eat.

Tomato ketchup then, and toast, Anne thought, moving Suzie's magazines so she could sit on the settee.

Don't you touch them books. Mum – Anne's got my books. Anne get your clumsy hands off of there.

They also say children on diets high in protein grow bigger, taller bodies; but it doesn't have to work that way. It could be that growth operates on a pulley system. You grow as long as your innocence takes to shrink. You go up so long as belief or

19

trust or hope go down. That is how it is for some people, whatever they say. Or that is how it was for Anne.

Whenever she could, while she waited for a world that she would fit, Anne walked to console herself, down the hill from her parents' house and into the hanging wood, for a bit of space, a little quiet and to put her size into perspective.

Mum – Anne's off out again.

But Anne learnt that if she called out something indistinct, over her shoulder, as she left – pushbike, for example, or, mend Michael's flat – they let you alone. After all, it was more room in the house without her.

She walked out quick to get out of sight. You were on top of the world when you started, a folded country of hills and hidden valleys, thickly wooded and then exuberantly open. There were toy churches, farms, villages like handfuls of pebbles put down. All of it was small. Like her dad said, it was a small world after all. From the house, the road plunged into the valley at a crazy gradient, so that, as you descended, the hills at the back heaved the horizon up and over your head with each stride. Walking down the hill with the trees coming up to meet you was the closest thing to shrinking that Anne had ever felt. By the time she reached the bottom, she could imagine she was normal.

She felt fine in the wood. Sometimes she'd just lie down and breathe the loamy air at the trees' feet. She'd close the eye furthest from the ground and with the nearer one watch the toil of the insects heaving themselves over twig and leaf. That's big, she'd say to herself. That's insurmountable.

One day, when all shred of hope was gone and she realised no one else was getting any bigger, Anne stopped growing and decided she would move down to the hanging wood for good.

She walked out quick, like she always did, only she thought they might have heard her heart, it was so loud. Nobody stopped her.

The wood was the same as always. She breathed the air, which there wasn't in the house. She listened to the birds, who didn't shout. She lost herself down the quiet rides and cricked her neck looking up through the trees' green cathedral. She lay down in her usual places, at the trees' feet. And the trees took her in. They opened stiff arms and spread their fingers above her head. They whispered their world of wind and light, the muddy secrets of their roots. They juggled birds for her. They showed her the tiny things that height can produce, the delicate, missable fruits and tassels.

Then the dark fell, at the day's end, and with the dark the wood grew. The trees shot up and away from her as if she had made a mistake. The cold came up through the ground and she was alone. After a while, she told herself that she was having a holiday. She'd gone for a chill-out, as Suzie would say, just for a few days and then she'd probably go back. Well, she'd go back once she'd got a job in the new abattoir, that's what she'd do.

Among the ferns and last year's dead leaves, in the ditch that she had selected to sleep in, Anne hugged her knees and told herself stories. Wait till she'd got sorted. She'd walk back into the house, in her white suit and the white boots with steel toecaps; orange the toecaps were. They had a proper uniform at the abattoir, not like the poultry plant, where it was all old and cruddy and you wore your own painting overalls pretty much, like her dad. And when she walked in they'd say, What you wearing Anne, where you been? Look, everyone, Anne's back. They'd all be clustered round her looking and she'd walk over to the table and sit down because she'd be tired, and someone would have to fix her tea instead. John and Michael and Suzie, they'd be all mouths open, and she'd just shrug cool as anything and say, Oh working at the abattoir, and she'd look at her dad, who hadn't shifted over, had he, because she was no fool and he'd never do it, not till it was too late, not till the abattoir was full.

But it was hard to keep your mind on a story, when everywhere there were rustlings and crackings. Little ferreting things scuttled where Anne couldn't see them. In the dark the quiet wood was alive with noise. She heard cars stopping and starting. She thought she saw a man once and lay flat in the ditch, her heart bulging against the twigs and leaves beneath her. She couldn't remember when she'd last been afraid. She was big, wasn't she? She was never afraid in the day.

The trees could have told her. Sound is what takes over in a wood, in the dark. Shufflings, things dropping, knocking. The piglike muntjac yelping in the undergrowth. Somewhere to her left, one of the pines mewing like a cat.

There are voices outside that you don't hear until you are alone. Don't attempt the wood on a night as dark as this, unless you know it like the back of your hand. There's too much of your own mind out there.

Down in the ditch Anne's head swivelled, swivelled. Listen. Wood and a riding wind.

We won't help, say the trees. We are miles up at night, hooking our fingers into the sky, in league with all you most fear. We snag and whip. If you try moving, deafened with your own heartbeat and your breath booming, we jab and prod, sudden and out of nowhere. We are long silhouettes that reach to the sky. Married to formlessness, knocking branches at the night, tattling tales.

Into a wind that spooks and bolts, they are talking.

And inside the wood, where Anne crouched, the dark roared, although below the canopy nothing moved. Chilly for summer. Not a night for standing around.

While Anne shivered and panicked the moon opened its cold eye beyond the trees, and in its glimmer a bird crossed one of the far fields, just the black outline of it, could be an owl, could be a late crow, hard to see. On the bank above the road a weasel paused upright and the white of his chest flashed in the headlights of a passing car. Then down and away into the deeps of the wood, his small sound, scurrying through Anne's consciousness nightmare size. She couldn't help whimpering. A weak, animal noise, but it shocked her, it seemed so loud. Her throat dry. Had she given herself away?

Not a hand's distance visible, in the wood, only where the moon opened a slip of sky between treetops, a nail-width of light, or a star, the dog star for instance, flared minute.

How long does a night last? Anne lay in her ditch and locked her shoulders and strained her eyes and willed the light to break. Please God. Please God. And stretching away down the ride, the limes that stood head and shoulders above the other trees shivered alone in reach of the moon and watched the horizon and said nothing, while an aeroplane blinked, blinked. And the wind rode the wood, mercilessly, all night long.

Wobbly, in the dawn Anne crawled to the roadside. She thought she'd watch her father going to work, just for reassurance. She waited a long time. She told herself that if she called out to him perhaps he would help her. He would get off his bike and not mind if he was late. Give her a swig of his tea, let her eat his dinner. Anne hadn't made up her mind what she'd do, when he came scooting round the corner. He whisked past. Lack of sleep had made her slow. She opened her mouth to call. And then she didn't call. He was gone in a moment. Anne stood on the bank with her mouth still wide and her mind calling, still seeing his back, the shirt stretched over his chicken-bone shoulders, even after the corner had swallowed him up.

She had never seen her dad like that before. He had looked almost young, hooped over the handlebars, leaning into the corner, speeding away into the summer morning. He must look like that every day, the separateness of her father's existence hitting her suddenly and for the first time. He could have been anyone's dad, or no one's. He didn't look like he belonged to anyone, just a man in painting overalls, taking his secret self off to work.

But Anne felt better when she'd seen him. It wasn't that different from watching him from the house. Bye Annie. Bye Dad. Be a good girl.

Anne's mum never walked anywhere. If she wanted to go to the village she got the car out, even on a day like today. She was a lazy cow if you like, not that Anne would have used the word cow. That was Suzie, or her brothers, cow was. When Anne saw the car go past, with Leanne strapped in her baby seat, she headed back up the hill. She would have waved at Leanne but the car was going too fast.

Anne still had her latchkey.

On the side, when she got in, there were someone's cold chips and mayonnaise, still in their paper. Anne ate them first, wolfing them down with the chip fork. Then she ate toast, cereal, smoked turkey ham and two packets of crisps from the cupboard.

What are you doing, Anne? Connor was in the doorway, mouth open, with his duvet round him. They stared at each other. Nothing, Anne said, by instinct. Nothing. Then, after a while, she said, I've left home, but with a note of appeal in her voice, as if she was trying it out, as if she wanted it verifying. She wanted to say, Did you notice? Or, Did anyone ask? But somehow she didn't.

Connor gathered the duvet round himself and moved into the room. Doesn't look like it, was all he said, and then, I'm watching telly.

Connor wasn't so bad. He was only seven. Anne didn't mind Connor, so long as Michael or John weren't around. I'll watch it with you, then. Any excuse, and it was warm in the kitchen, compared to the wood. She thought she'd make tea. She made Connor tea too and took it over to the settee. What was up with him anyway? Why wasn't he at school?

Poorly.

They watched *Chancers*, *This Teen Life* and *Pingu*. After a while Anne felt uneasy. She didn't want to be there when her mother came back. She got up and went upstairs. She went into the boys' room and took one of Michael's fleeces so she wouldn't be cold at night. Then she went in hers and Suzie's room. Thank you very much. Suzie had put cushions on Anne's bed and a pink drape, like it was hers already. I've only been gone a night, Anne said out loud. Then she wondered why she'd been surprised. Suzie was a cow, if you were looking for one. Anne knew that. She knelt on her bed and looked out of her window, at her old view – the road to the wood and the poultry plant, the fields, the big sky – to remind herself what it looked like from inside, to see if it looked different.

But she couldn't see anything. However she faced her eyes

25

forward they looked back, through the back of her head, at the bottles and jars, the make-up remover, shampoo, styling spray. At Suzie's clothes spread out luxuriating, easing their shoulders into the extra space. She couldn't see her old view, only Suzie's room. That was hurtful. She wanted to smash everything in that room. She took three pots of nail polish. That would teach Suzie. Not Dusky Plum because that made your nails look like you'd missed with the hammer. Hi Ho Silver Lining, Gilty Party and Moody Blues. Then she went back and took In the Pink as well, for good measure. Paint her own nails if she felt like it. Then she went downstairs and filled her pockets with food.

Ta-ra Connor.

Where you going?

Nowhere. I'll be in the woods if you want me. If Mum and Dad start going into one, come and find me in the woods. I'm getting a job.

Connor was still pale under the duvet. He never took his eyes off the telly. Alright, Anne. See you. Is there jobs in the woods?

Yes. See you, then.

Can you make me another piece of toast?

She went back into the kitchen. She made him the toast and another piece for herself, because if you're putting on the toaster you might as well do two.

When she gave it to him he looked round her to see the telly.

Ta-ra.

Ta-ra.

It was summer but Anne got cold. She had no shelter. She got wet like she'd never known. Water has no manners, Anne discovered. Whatever shape you make, it finds a way. She was bent over like a boulder the first time it rained, with her nose, for warmth, inside her shirt. She could see water in the folds of her belly and how did it ever get there? Oh Jesus, she said to it. Give us a break. Get lost, can't you? But Anne was good at enduring. She sat like that and watched it rain inside her shirt and waited for it to stop. Was it funny or sad that she had rain inside her shirt? Look, she said to herself, it was so sad that her hair was crying. The water was running off her hair ends, down her chest and in her bra and over her belly as if she was her old windowpane.

From where she was sitting, on the far edge of the wood, she could see out to the fields. All the fields gone milky with rain and the cows lying, blinking it off their eyelashes, still chewing. There was no time when you weren't eating, if you were a cow. Inside a wood, rain is sound first and wet second. Patter, patter, patter and the smells came right up out of the ground and the birds just sat, shaking themselves like dogs every now and again.

If she was a windowpane, Anne would be able to see her insides, like the clock Michael had, the alarm clock from the jeweller's he got where you could see all the bits in different colours. She used to sit and watch the little wheels clicking round when he wasn't in, didn't she? Sneak in his room and look. What are you doing Anne? Nothing. She wasn't doing anything. Well don't do nothing in here see. Now she put her nose back in her shirt and watched herself, as if she had little red and blue cogs and springs, small electric green rods whirring, a primrose pale, half-moon with wires, that shuffled back and forth. Do nothing if I want to, she thought. Do nothing all day. Then she studied the hairs, the fine pale hairs on her belly, the wet, white slab of her and the little shiver pimples. More like a chicken than a clock. A great plucked chicken.

Imagine that, if you could grow feathers; if you could ball yourself out like the birds and shake the rain off. She would love feathers. What do you want for Christmas, Anne? I want feathers, mainly. Please. Any particular colour? Anne removed her face from her shirt and looked up at the falling rain, at the trees above her, layer after layer of leaves, like feathers themselves, finding their own space against the sky. Accepting the rain. Coping, weren't they? Quiet, each leaf itself but the same as the others. Yellow was the colour of the sun, if only. Blue was the colour the sky should be. Red was the colour of the Parcel Force van. Red was the last thing she wanted. She didn't want red, she wanted green. Green feathers all over like an ash tree, and she could move around the woods invisible then. Invisible, warm and dry. Curl up in a ball and sleep like a bird, her face in the softness of her own feathers.

But you don't die of wet. You can get wringing, river-soaked and you survive. That was the first thing Anne learnt. The second was how not to be seen, even without the feathers. She had learnt that if you turn your back and look purposeful people don't stare, or at least you don't see them staring, and if you walk away they can't ask questions. It was her instinct to hide, even if no one was looking for her. She already knew how to sit still and be quiet. She learnt to go out more at night than in the day. She got canny, like an animal; she had to. But she didn't steal. She emphasised that to herself. She didn't steal, she borrowed. It wasn't stealing if you took from your dad. How was that stealing?

The night after she got wet, her fourth night in the woods, Anne went back up the hill in the moonlight. She was big and strong striding up the hill. She felt herself rise out of the feathered woods like a giant. She'd survived. Back in the small house the walls pressed up against her. The ceiling sat on her head like a hat. There was washing out on the drying rack, over the chairs, all over the kitchen. It smelt of pizza and onions. Your regular detergent – *New Pizza and Onions. Mrs Tarbot says she will never go back.* Anne remembered advertisements. She had loved the advertisements, a world where every problem had a solution that you could buy, simple as that. On the table there was Leanne's dummy, a bottle of tomato ketchup. There was butter and crumbs on the newspaper and on Connor's schoolwork. Anne took some bread and some cheese. She took a pot of jam. Cereal, that was something she hadn't had for a long time; Loops or Wheetos? She poured herself a mixing bowl of both. She put the telly on mute.

Lovely telly, all the colours and the separate world of it. The people who brushed their teeth under waterfalls using electric toothbrushes, who drove shiny cars up and down stairs and smiled their shiny smiles; they'd never sat under a tree and had it rain inside their clothes. They knew about hospitals and murder and doing sex and they opened their eyes and their mouths in great big silent screams and carried guns and betrayed their husbands all inside a box even smaller than her house. Anne ate her cereal and watched the telly. She went to the toilet and took a roll of paper with her for the woods. She stood on the bottom step of the stairs and listened to her family breathing in the dark. Maybe she'd go up and get Leanne, she thought. But then she thought she'd wait – maybe when she'd built a shelter. Then she'd get her and they'd live happily in the wood, and when Leanne cried, she'd comfort her, like she could have done the only time they'd stayed out before, if she'd had a light to see what was the matter.

Then Anne left it tidy and went out to the shed. She took the best saw, a mallet, a hand axe. She filled her pockets with nails and staples. She took a garden fork and some vegetable seeds, cabbages, onions, carrots, broccoli, everything she could lay her hands on. String. She went back into the house and rootled in the drawers for matches, a kitchen knife, a spoon. She took her brother's sleeping bag, the travelling rug, a saucepan, a cup, a plate. Then she piled everything into the wheelbarrow and went back down the hill. Survival changes your character.

Only now, huddling and hurrying, glancing back at the home that hadn't been one, did she realise she was leaving. In the moon-splashed road the light was so bright, the shadows so strong, that she looked over her shoulder constantly. Was she afraid of being seen? Or was it that she wanted someone to see her, to shout at her from the window, Oi! Anne what are you doing with that barrow you get back here this minute. But there was no one at the window. Only the ghost of her old self, leaning sad on the sill, the great big shoulders crammed into the frame waiting for one day.

Anne's feelings came and went like the weather. Long ago she had learnt that they were of no consequence, so although she was crying when she left with her haul she took no notice. She pushed as well as the shudderings of her body allowed and waited for them to pass. Down the hill in the moonlight with the small explosions, the pops and gutturals of sorrow like an engine for the barrow. It was as if her body was voiding itself of something, childhood perhaps, belonging; she couldn't have told you which.

The wood was the wrong way round with light, a world in photographic negative. Down the wide rides the moon watched her go, the barrow heavier now the ground was uneven. She had to lift it over roots or rock it back and forth. She had to mind where brambles snatched at the precious load, where ruts or sudden dips made the sleeping bag slide off, or the barrow tip. She should have stopped to rest, taken her time, but she hurried as though there was someone behind her, as if she could feel their breath on her neck, their hand hovering at her shoulder to snatch her back. Who on earth? she asked herself as she pushed on. Who'd follow you, are you daft or something? She struggled forwards, pushing, rocking, lifting the jumble of her future – who would have thought a life could weigh so much? – heading for the deepest part, where the paths didn't go, down ways that were impassable even without a barrow bellied with possessions. Across her shoulders and up her neck there was a coat hanger of pain.

The trees bent over her, craned their tops down, whispered, what's she got what's she got, but she kept her head down. She didn't stop until the moon showed her a pollard ash the same shape as herself with a small stream at its feet. Then she put down the barrow. You have to have water for survival. Thanks, moon.

At the foot of the ash Anne took out the sleeping bag, squeezed herself into it and sat against the trunk. When the pain in her shoulders was less and she began to feel sleepy she slumped sideways, her cheek on one of the ash tree's mossed feet, her body a question mark for all the questions her temperament hadn't fitted her to frame; the whys, the hows, the how much longers that she never thought herself important enough to ask. She slept.

GROWING ROOTS

The trees in the wood did nothing, or nothing that you could see anyway. In the morning the sun got up and lit their leaves and the breeze, if there was one that is, ruffled and shook them, and the little animals burrowed around them or scurried over them. Then the dark came up and swallowed them.

We are rooted, say the trees. Rocking, lifting, shifting, fluttering. Tangling their tops above Anne's head. Always moving, going nowhere.

Wood is a circle, that's all. Standing, springing, dropping, shedding, a constant flux of up and down, and in and out, and wider and wider. And birds, like leaves, that rise and fall, arriving in wide ellipses, from elsewhere, to clothe the branches and leave again.

We have some secrets, say the trees. Worn lightly. Shed, if you like, each autumn, from twigs that are stiff with forgetting. The secret of transformation, for example, turning by multiplication the sealed scales of the bud into fistfuls of leaves, or the soft green necks of spring shoots into building materials.

We produce tassel or blossom, like that, when you least expect.

Bending in a sudden breeze. Pigeons clapping up out of them, for no reason you could see, or jackdaws spiralling down, to sit and argue in the branches.

We keep ourselves to ourselves, they say. Whispering water, creased with a slow current, should you look. We filter light. Our heads billow like smoke though we try not to think of fire.

But they never lay down, Anne thought, or got up, or moved around. They just were, and that was what Anne thought she'd do too, just be. For the moment.

On still days, thin and far away she heard snatches of conversation, if there were walkers or joggers on the paths. Anyway I've told her, she heard. And, They've no idea how to manage. And, Have you thought about changing? We had a super time. It isn't what I wanted. Do you find he responds . . . She never saw them because of the leaves. She just let the words fall into her mind and rest there. Sometimes days would go by between phrases. She didn't think about them at all. She didn't try to guess or understand.

When she was really hungry she ate the food she'd brought with her. You don't need to eat much if you sit still all day and she had no will to do more than that yet. She felt drained by her decision, barely able to lift her hand from lap to mouth, barely able even to chew or swallow. Nor did she sleep properly. She dozed irrespective of day or night, her thoughts flicking about her head like bats, her eyes glazed or shut, often she could hardly tell which. Once or twice she squeezed out of her bag and staggered a little way off, to empty herself. Then she climbed back in and continued sitting, a nylon chrysalis, waiting for something to change.

She didn't want to go home again. Was anyone looking for her? She didn't know. You couldn't lose Anne, her father would have said. She blocked out the sun she did. She'd kick a man senseless. She was big enough to look after herself.

No, her parents wouldn't bother looking. The telly would have been on. There was always a noise in the house. There wasn't the space or the quiet to brood. It would have been a relief, to be honest, what with six others to worry about and Anne being a bit of a freak.

Anne leant her head against the ash tree. That's how it would have been. She knew.

When her food ran out Anne went through the bins in the woodland car park. People throw a lot away. The end of a bag of lamb-and-mint crisps, half a chicken tikka sandwich, apple cores, blobs of spat-out chewing gum that you could resuscitate if you were patient. She ate what she found, tasting it first to see whether it was palatable. As she got hungrier she got more adventurous. She watched the birds, tried the berries and bits that they ate. She saw a wren low down in the dappled dark of the understorey, tail right up. Wrens are such small birds. It had a white worm draped from its beak, the same length both sides as the wren itself. And the worm was waving to and fro, still wondering blind where it was. Imagine finding something to eat that was the same size as you. But Anne didn't want to eat worms thank you.

She took from the fields that lapped the wood, the beans that were cattle fodder, the kale, the turnips and potatoes. If she was hungry, she rubbed the earth off with her sleeve and ate it there and then. If she could wait, she took it back to her place, washed it in the stream and baked it in her fire. You pushed it wet into the ashes. It took a long time. You had to find something to do while you waited or you went mad tweaking it out with a stick, one arm over your face against the heat and smoke. You baked long before the potato.

On the far edge of the wood was a field of cows. She must

37

have passed them a hundred times before she twigged. She stood by the stile amazed. That was so obvious. Babies survived on milk. They didn't need anything else at all. Why hadn't she thought of it before? No one was around. Just the song-filled hedgerows and the long summer grass, still wet, and a whole field of nourishment waiting for her to help herself. Anne was practically singing as she got over the stile.

But it didn't work like that. At all.

She told herself that she'd been too excited. She'd try again and she'd just walk round the field, casually, and she'd talk to the cows to get them used to her. She'd be really calm. She'd take her time. But every time it was the same. The mad look – and cows can look mad. The kicking out. The see-saw bucking run, udders swinging wild, and all the other cows careering round the field in sympathy.

Once Anne was so angry she ran after them, hitting out at whichever cow was nearest, her mug in her hand as she ran. I only want some milk. You stupid cow. Bitch. Sod.

Crying and crying afterwards, among the pats, with the cows eyeing her from the far corner.

The day the milk did come, she was so worn down, it took her by surprise. Spraying out almost rude, and the cow curving her head round, licking her nostril with her tongue on one side and going back to eating as if nothing was happening. And Anne put her head against the giving flank and wept her gratitude and relief. Thank you, cow. Thank you. I'm sorry I called you names.

Milk, as it turned out, wasn't enough. Anne wasn't a baby so food was still a problem. She tried everything. She wrapped her hands in dock leaves bound with cocksfoot because it was the strongest grass, and gathered nettles, thistles, and boiled them up and ate the whole thing including the water they were cooked in. She took eggs irrespective of size. And she could kill. She'd had brothers, after all, so she knew how it was done. She made snares like Michael's out of her dad's wire and she thought she'd catch birds, rabbits, hedgehogs. She watched them so she'd get to know their habits. Like the milking, it took a long time. You think animals are simple but they're inexplicable, especially when you're hungry. She watched rabbit after rabbit nibble, hop, nibble. Go on, she'd say, go in it. And the rabbit would nibble, there's a person over there, hop, look up, oh a snare, no thank you, nibble, hop. How did they know? How did they know what a snare looked like? And Anne would unfold her legs, stiff with waiting and go back, a hole in her tummy big enough for a burrow, and gnaw at another uncooked beet.

And birds were even cleverer.

She lay in the ditch watching the rabbits and smelling stew. She had cramps from nettles and beets and uncooked potatoes. Her breath was fetid. Her belly was tight and balled with wind. How could emptiness have such solidity? Please, she said to the rabbits, please. On the way back, empty-handed again, she saw the fox, gleaming with health, digging for worms. He glanced at her, ears pricked and went back to his digging. So she wasn't a threat obviously. Nothing scary about stupid old Anne. She can't even catch a rabbit. Well, you're stupid, she said to the fox, digging for worms when you could have rabbit. You've got the teeth. You know how to do it.

It was the rain that drummed some sense into her. In the early dawn it woke her, wedged as usual into the sleeping bag. She'd given no proper thought to her shelter. It was just thrown together, a shoddy lean-to against the straight bole of an ash that she crashed in at night, like a burrow. The rain was streaking straight through it. She couldn't believe it at first, how angry it made her. What? Again? All her possessions getting wet. The precious sleeping bag. She hit the ground at her side until her fist hurt. Clumsy tart, she shouted at the rain. Bitch. Stupid sod. It shocked her, maybe she was turning into Suzie after all. Now you're really wild, she told herself. Now you're out of control.

It wasn't just the wet that she was angry with, it was her own stupidity, the lack of foresight. She was a practical person but she thought for the first time that she couldn't cope. She'd never make it. She hadn't even thought about rain. What about snow? What about wind and sleet and winter? She'd spent all this time hunting and she'd caught nothing. What had she been doing, when she should have been so busy?

She was groaning with wind when she got up sodden, her hair plastered to her face. One or two walkers, well water-proofed, looked up in surprise, as she lumbered past them, lowing to herself. She must have looked something else. Get to the bank, she was saying under her breath. Get to the bank and find Dad. It didn't matter to Anne who saw her now, or what they thought. She was past caring pretty much.

All the ditches were talking with water. She jumped and lurched the quickest way. Even so, she got to the bank late. She just saw the flash of him, slicked with wet, as he reached the corner, his brakes squeaking and the water sheeting up either side. You're going to have an accident Dad, one of these days, if you're not careful. I'll bet no one checks your brakes now.

She watched the empty corner for a while, the rain still dropping, dropping, dropping. Well, Dad's gone to work. So I might as well, she thought, turning slowly back into the wood.

Method. You had to have that. You had to have method to

survive. You couldn't just expect rabbits to fall into your lap. You couldn't expect to stay dry and well without proper shelter, and what about the water, what if the stream dried up for instance? What about that? Anne asked herself. You didn't think about that, did you? And she was in a mad rush now, to make up for lost time, to build, to make everything right and tight against the weather, to provide for thinner times, to get the hunting sorted out. Michael managed and he was useless. She couldn't get back to her camp fast enough.

Through the rainy morning, with her dad's saw, Anne coppiced herself a clearing round the ash shelter. Hazel mainly, and anything with a trunk too thick for the saw she left for later, to chip away at with the axe. She cut as close to the ground as she could, pulling the cut stems free of the canopy and laying them in piles as she went. She couldn't believe how quick you could let the sky in, working faster and faster and saving looking up so as to be surprised when she'd finished. Then standing, face upturned, watching the rain fall through a hole in the wood.

After the coppicing Anne trekked round the dripping wood and emptied the litter bins of plastic bags, which she opened out and tacked edge to edge on the sticks of her lean-to. On top of the bags, she threw the brash, dragging it over untrimmed and hoicking it up and over. By early afternoon the rain had stopped and she'd made herself a green burrow. Warmer than before at least, and waterproof. She ferreted about for food, a mugful of squashed raspberries, a pigeon's egg that she broke and tipped down her throat raw, a half-gnawed beet, and she watched a squirrel, across the new clearing and straight up the trunk of a sapling, shaking a shower of drops as it crossed into an oak.

Unable to light a fire with the sodden wood, Anne lay in

her burrow and tried to shiver herself warm and dry. She took off her sodden clothes and wrapped herself in the leftover bags and whatever else she had that wasn't wet. It wasn't a good night, but at least she'd made a start. And it serves you right, she said, shivering and shivering. It serves you right.

The day after, the sun came out and that was enough. Anne put on Michael's fleece and her trainers and went on with the coppicing to warm herself up. She made a washing line and hung up the sleeping bag and the rest of her clothes and at lunchtime, when the sun had done its work, she lit a fire. Then she sat in the fleece, in the sun, by the fire and baked and watched her things steam and admired her shelter. She gave herself the afternoon off and she thought about her next move. Warmth, water and food. That's what you need for survival. Warmth, water and food. She lazed against the pollard ash. What about winter? she allowed herself to think again. How will that be? From the depths of her comfort, she almost luxuriated in it, like not getting out of bed on a cold morning. How bad will the winter be?

The summer lulled her. In the days that followed, even if, at her own instruction and now that she had come to her senses, Anne was busy, still she was busy slowly. Slow was natural to her but it was underlined by warm days, by the way that the sun patterned the wood, by the birds, whose names or songs she didn't know, flicking past, catching her eye in the under-growth. And Anne would stop, now who's that, and follow for a bit, or lie and watch until she knew them, giving them her own names, Brownie, Black-hat, Whipso Wee. In between, she tried to be dogged and systematic. One at a time, she made what she needed. She never looked beyond the project she had in hand, unless it was backwards. She looked backwards to see how far she'd come. She looked back to encourage herself forward. Good job Anne, she said to herself. Good job.

Daily, she'd wake in the first light, get up and cross the wood and lie and watch for her father. She liked the swish of the bicycle and the small freedom that the hoop of his back expressed. It set her up. And when he'd gone she'd start back. Off to work then, Dad. Me too.

At first Anne had filled her cup at the stream wherever it was deep enough. Now she worried constantly that the stream would run dry. She would dam it with wood and stone, she thought, to make a good, clean, shallow pool. Then she'd be safe. She went out looking for stones the right size and shape, down the field edges, where they'd been thrown by the farmers to save the plough, grunting them back to the clearing, sometimes just in her arms, sometimes in the barrow. She always carried more than she could manage but you couldn't leave them in case of never finding them again. Across her back and shoulders the coat hanger of pain was permanent.

She piled the stones where she wanted the dam to be, dug round with her dad's spade, to make a start for the water and to slow it so the building would be easier. The last thing she wanted was for any of the precious stones to dislodge or get swept away. Slow work. Fitting the stones, plugging with wood wrapped in grass, last year's leaves, clay. Got to be tight like a jigsaw puzzle. Only it was easier than a puzzle. Puzzles made your head whizz. So many pieces all the same. Just pointless. The stones were all different and you could see which ones would fit, turning them slow in the flow of water, balancing, your hands freezing purple, till the edges clicked. Then up again with your back creaking and on to the next.

It was a sunny day when she finished the dam. The under-storey of the wood, the hazels and field maples, the ferns and bramble and the plants she couldn't name, the dog's mercury and enchanter's nightshade, everything spotted and splashed with light. It was beautiful to Anne and the filling pool most beautiful of all, sparkling as it swelled. She took off her shoes and waded in and she couldn't stop herself from laughing out loud, she was so excited. She walked round and round, puddling the pool out with her bare feet and then, when her feet were too cold to do it any more, she sat on the edge and hugged her knees and watched the water settle.

From one of the hazels at the back of the clearing, little birds came. Brownie and Black-hat. Hopping, hopping. Cocking their heads. Come on, Anne said to them, help yourselves. I've made a pool. And they sipped and hopped and twittered their find. Water for us all. There's plenty, Anne said, enjoy it.

The success of the pool was invigorating. She spent long times sitting by it and marvelling. She marvelled at its inverted daytime world, at the ink of its night. She marvelled at the moon's wobbly face. She marvelled at the leaves and feathers that coasted lazy on its current, circling and catching. When it rained she marvelled at the drops that fattened it for her. Doesn't matter if it rains now, she would think with pleasure; filling up my pool, isn't it?

After the pool she started with her plan for a better shelter. She already knew the places where the cut timber was stacked. She went down with the barrow and hauled what she needed by night. She set a wall of stakes at one end of her hovel, facing the sunrise, to keep out the wind that she hated most, the one that came cold from the east. She worked on until she had surrounded the tree and her hovel, not worrying too much about the shape, dragging the stakes from the timber pile as she needed them and, on days when it was soft enough, hitting them into the ground, with her dad's mallet. While she made the walls she considered the roof. She tried one or two different things. The stakes wouldn't stay balanced against the trunk of the ash without something to support them so in the end she cut hazel and soaked it in her pool and wove it together to make giant basketwork scales that she fitted over-lapping all the way round. She sat at the foot of the pollard with her legs out straight and her work across her lap. Every now and again she looked across at the stockade round the ash, for encouragement, or up at the pool of sky, fringed with trees above her head. All the birds were going to and fro. We're all busy, she thought.

When enough scales were done she stole a bale of hay from the field and barrowed it back to the clearing, heart thumping. That was stupid. She could easily have been spotted. She pulled off the orange binder twine and laced the scales to each other at the top and down the edges, careful to keep the weave of the basketwork running down not across to let the rain run off it freely. The hay, she shook out inside for a bed. On top of the basketwork she tacked plastic bags again. Then a layer of bracken and on top of the bracken, stakes, raying out from the centre, tied through to the basketwork again and nailed to the top of the palisade. Then she dismantled the lean-to and hauled it out through the door. Another good job.

Spending her first night in the hut, with it right and tight and roofed over, was so exhilarating that she stayed awake until morning just to enjoy it. First she lay down in her bag on the hay, but then the position was not quite right. While she lay close to the side wall, her eye was continually drawn by the lightness at the door. She got out, dragged the bag to where she could lie facing the door but still against the wall, got in again. For a while, until the dark was properly up, that was good enough; but then the square of the door became more attractive again. To lie sheltered but able to see out, that would be the real luxury. So, out again and drag the bag to just inside the door and there – that was perfect. Look at that night sky and the tops of the trees just feathering its edges. It was a starlit loop of dark, cut across by bats. Look at those bats. How did you do that? So quick, it was like electric. You could feel yourself out there with them, up in the clear, with only moths, Anne supposed, for company – or for eating. And then the owl made her jump, racketing into the clearing. He had his legs out like he was crash-landing, very unsteady. He nearly rolled over in mid-flight. Owls can't fly at all. They make a right mess of it, wings everywhere, rocking about. Chaos.

Anne shuffled over onto her back and looked at the slip of sky again. Bats and stars and her shelter. She was bubble-light with elation, floating up, she thought she was, back to the bats, up through the clearing and flipping out through the top and further and further, a dark moon, bowling through the sky towards the humming stars, like she was pulled by a magnet.

Later, she got up again and went out to see what the hut looked like from the outside at night. She walked right the way round, one hand running round the ridges of the pile wall. The fox had his den. The badger had those great big hills and holes. The squirrels had that mess they threw up any old how in the tops of the trees. The birds were the only real competition. They were the only ones with any craftsmanship. They fitted out the inside as well as the out. They made it nice with feathers and moss, and Anne began thinking of

46

improvements she could make. Keep the feathers off the birds she ate. She could do something with them, and they'd keep her warm.

In the dawn, finally, she felt her own weight again. She watched the stars, pale now and almost inaudible, the hum of night nearly gone. And in the trees above her, the birds woke up, in their own constellations of sound and sang the sun up, which had the grace to shine, on this first morning, until it was the ground, not the sky, that was spangled and Anne went out with the stars at last and slept until midday.

Anne opened one eye. Her stomach was making an extraordinary noise. That was what had woken her. Roof. That was the first thing she saw. Roof, walls, sun on the leaves. It was pretty good living in the wood once you had a house. There was a finch in the doorway with its head on one side. Aye-aye. Who asked you in? Cocky. She sat up. She had to find some breakfast. The finch flitted off and Anne got out of the bag. Shoes first and off for a wiss, then we'll see. Coming back she couldn't help singing – it was so nice to see the hut neat and trim with the tree coming out of the top like a chimney. She sang Suzie's old songs. If I was a rich girl, na, na, na, na, na, na, na. I'd have all the money in the world, if I was a wealthy gi-irl.

Normally Anne went out, on her way to the bank, and milked one of the cows in the field at the side of the wood. She'd given them all names now, or not all of them, but the ones she liked most, to differentiate them and for politeness' sake, so she could talk to them properly when she milked them, or sat among them for companionship before the farmer came.

At the field gate she stopped and looked over. See if it's too late or not. Ho, ladies. They were used to her now. They just looked up and one or two lowed and swished their tails and went back to the long business of eating and digesting and producing milk. It was different in bright light. Usually she would have got straight over and gone among them with her mug. They had slow, breathy conversations, Anne and the cows, in the dawn, when the cows were just black bulks, lying or standing, grey mist up to their knees, plopping out their pats and chewing already. She liked to run a hand across their fat flanks. Ruby Tuesday, Dusky Plum, Coco Pops. Or she'd squat down in their midst. Why would you ever keep your milk in a fridge she would ask herself, sipping and refilling in a world of swaying udders. They were all body, cows were. Anne liked them for that, for their accepting eyes and their slowness, and their noisy functions. Breathe, gush, munch, breathe, slop – their tongues out, their wet noses in the beaded cobwebs, loops of drool and their feet splaying.

But she'd never milked as late as midday. The bright field was too exposed. She didn't dare. What instead? She was reflecting on her options when she noticed a cat skulking along the hedge, after the late fledglings no doubt, or the baby game birds. As she watched a gunshot cracked to her right and the cat buckled and fell. Anne's hand flew to her mouth. The cows humped up their backs and skittered away in panic. Anne would have gone too, only she was rooted with amazement, looking now at the cat crumpled by the hedge, now down the field to see where the shot had come from. A big man lumbered up the field edge. He didn't see Anne until he was level with her. He was breathing noisily like the cows and with each out-breath came a stream of barely audible comments and curses. Hmm that's done it. Hmm shot the hmm bloody bugger. He caught sight of Anne as he passed her.

Fox, he said loudly, not stopping. Bloody hmm fox.

Anne climbed the gate and hurried after him.

You shot a cat. That's a cat, that is. Can't you tell the difference?

They stood over the corpse. It was staring, the yellow convexity at its eye's centre empty and flat like a leaf. Like a willow leaf, Anne thought.

That's a cat, she repeated firmly.

The man turned it over with his boot, flicked it up into the hedge. That's a hmm bloody fox that is.

They looked straight at each other, in amusement more than anything else.

He was a big man, but he was more like a cow, Anne thought as she faced him and took him in properly. His shirt was stretched over a ball belly. His hair was rough and grew in whorls like the cows' did, and his eyes were large and liquid and sad and heavily fringed. Just like a cow.

Could you eat it? Anne asked eventually and with evident regret.

Could you what?

Could you eat it? she repeated, nodding towards the cat. I mean after you'd skinned it, obviously. Would it eat alright?

The man laughed at her. He looked amazed. His stomach moved when he laughed. Bit of butter and bloody sugar and it would slip down a treat.

She didn't want to go eating that, he said. What did she want to go eating that for?

I'm very hungry, Anne said. I've built myself a house with a roof and now I'm hungry. I've just woken up.

If she'd just woken up she'd be wanting a bit of bloody breakfast, that's what she'd want. A bit of breakfast – that was better than a old dead cat.

Or a fox.

Or a hmm bloody fox. And he laughed again.

His name was Steve. Slow Steve they called him. He might be slow but he got it done in the end and what was the hurry anyway? Some people were in such a hurry they got to their grave before they'd had time to enjoy themselves. That was what he thought, although his eyes looked inexpressibly sad all the time he was talking, but maybe that was just how they looked. Some animals looked like that, Anne had noticed, doleful, for no particular reason.

They shook hands. He only lived at the dump. Mother would fix her up some breakfast. Mother made the best bloody breakfast. They left the cat and walked up the field to his truck, parked on the track the other side of the hedge. There was an old dog in the cab that made a commotion when they approached, barking and snarling. Give over that bloody racket, Buster.

He was losing it a bit, poor old boy. He couldn't go out with the gun any more. He was blind in one eye and he only had three legs but he was a good dog.

Anne heaved herself into a crampedness of diesel and grease and old metal. She didn't know how to fit her knees. She hadn't been in a car in how long?

The plastic seats creaked as they bumped in and out of the holes on the track. Buster set up a whine. He didn't like the old holes, poor old dog. He put one of his three legs on Anne's thigh and leant on it heavily. His nails needed cutting. The skin on his muzzle was loose at the sides of his mouth so Anne could see his teeth and the milky-looking blind eye, and every time they went over a pothole they bumped shoulders and he dug his foot into her leg. He looked about a hundred. Anne had never seen an animal so old. You didn't often see animals that old in the wild. He would have been dead by now, Anne thought, normally. You died in the wild when you couldn't fend for yourself.

They bumped out onto the main road and then, on the edge of the town, up another track to the dump. *No more than 5 DIY waste items per week. No fly-tipping. No tyres. No barbed wire. No aerosols. £50,000 fine for breach of regulations.*

That was a lot of money.

Bloody right.

Steve cut the corner quite tight. Buster shot onto Anne's lap. Hold tight. There was a chain-link fence all round and a series of sheds that – now that Steve had stopped – Anne could see contained tempting piles of unwanted goods. There were teapots, jugs, jars, small domestic items, soft toys, bicycles and lawnmowers, household appliances, Hoovers, hairdryers, TVs, you name it.

Well, this is us.

Anne was gobsmacked. Released from the truck, she gawped at the sheds full of possessions. All this stuff. What must their houses be like, if this is what they chuck out?

A right sight worse. I tell you what. They go off and buy something else, rubbish, and it's in the dump after a year. I see the same bloody families. Steve hoisted Buster down out of the cab. The dog was nearly the same size as he was for goodness' sake. They wanted their heads examining. Waste of money it was. Waste of bloody money.

It looked pretty good to Anne.

That's what she needed, some things, now she had a house. A jug like that for instance, that would be nice, or a telly. She could have a telly in case they ever got electric in the wood. You never knew. They might.

Twenty pee that jug was, if she was interested. Anne's face fell. Of course, money. How could she have forgotten. She put the jug back quickly, ashamed. She cleared her throat, holding her hands together as though to stop them straying, the temptation being almost too much for her. Just looking at the moment.

Breakfast.

Along the back of the yard there was a bungalow with a little bit of garden, where Steve and Mother lived. There were flowers in colours that made Anne's eyes fizz. Mother loved her flowers. The path to the door was lined with bucket-shaped cement bollards painted gloss green and three game-looking gnomes, chipped and cracked and one of them legless and listing. Who next? Anne wondered, watching Buster's uneven progress ahead. Towering over the bungalow, as though about to crush it in the next stride, a pylon reared up from behind, wires clicking like knitting needles. It gave you the willies. Anne hunched her shoulders up round her head and scuttled after Steve.

Inside it was darkish and smelt close, like a burrow. One bar of the gas fire was on, even though it was summer, and beside it, in an armchair, sat a woman as old as Buster. She leant over the armrest, twisting round to see them as they came in. That you, Steve? On her head there was greasy-looking lilac bonnet, a knitted beret, from which her hair dangled to just below her chin.

That's us. Got your hat on, Mother?

I'm going to have my hair done. She made a girlish gesture with the hand that wasn't leaning, cupping her hair ends briefly. Going into town. Tender Touch are taking me. Who's that you've got there?

This is Anne. Anne, meet Mother.

That was nice, Anne thought, to be introduced like that, like she was someone. Very nice. She put out her hand and then waved doubtfully. She didn't know what else to do.

Anne's come for one of your breakfasts.

Mother nodded. I make a nice breakfast, don't I Steve?

The best.

There was no sign of Mother fixing anything up, so Steve cooked eggs and toast and frankfurters and baked beans. He didn't seem surprised. They ate it in the living room with Mother.

Nothing like one of Mother's bloody breakfasts I tell you. You get that down you.

Anne did.

Nice and quiet in the bungalow. Just the liquid sounds of food being eaten. In and out, slurp, slop and swallow. And breathing; Buster, for instance, snoring under the table.

After a while Mother craned even further forward out of her chair. What's that you're eating? Steve's jaws came to a halt, as though a machine had been switched off. He had both his elbows on the table either side of his plate. His massive shoulders were leant right over, for the purpose of shovelling. It was only his forearm that moved at all, Anne noticed. In fact it was all in the wrist. Also he could fit an entire frankfurter in his mouth at one go. He bent it against the inside of his cheek and just flipped it in.

We're eating your breakfast, Mother.

Steve resumed chewing, swallowed. He even ate like a cow, Anne thought, slow and vacant and contented. She gobbled. She couldn't help it.

I tell you what – Steve pointed at his food with his fork – no one makes a better breakfast than Mother. Do they, Mother?

Mother looked pleased with herself. No, they didn't. She fingered her hair again, shook her hair at Anne. No one did. She would have made them a good breakfast. She would have made them something if they hadn't put that pylon up. She jerked her head in the bonnet towards the back of the bungalow. We had veggies out there before they put that pylon up, before Bill died.

Mother was sensitive to it. It didn't bother Steve. He didn't even notice it. She hadn't been well ever since they'd put up the pylon. That was right, wasn't it? How long was it? – three year?

Makes my head buzz. Mother passed her hand across the top of her eyes, nodding her head to herself as though something had lodged inside it. They put a pylon in your garden yet?

No, Anne said. Not yet. She was going to have veggies too. When she'd planted them. She'd got seeds.

Bring us some when they're up. I like veggies.

I will.

Then there was silence. Anne looked at Steve's empty plate. He might eat slowly but he got through a fair pile. She looked from the plate to the man, and back and forth several times as though unable to believe so much food had been shifted at one sitting. Quantity impressive. Quantity of breakfast very impressive. Steve sat motionless and glazed. Problems with internal traffic. He was busy governing airflow, Anne could see that. The down-thrust and the up-thrust fighting it out. She could hear it even – wheezing sounds, a faint hiss of air escaping or a gurgle as something accelerated past some hidden obstruction. His cheeks puffed out now and then. And sometimes his top half convulsed briefly and with violence. Pardon.

Eventually – did Mother want anything to eat?

She used to eat like a horse, Mother did, when they grew their own. You wouldn't believe it. Anne thought she would believe anything now she'd seen Steve actually do it, eat a week's breakfast in one sitting. Mother had her own teeth then, mind, in those days. Not that she didn't now, Steve said proudly, she had a bridge, didn't she, so there must be something of her own still there. Some of her own bloody teeth for the bridge to fix on to. Pardon.

Mother swivelled her neck like an owl, bared the bridge for Anne to admire. She might have some of them carrots and a piece of white bread, if she had time.

Course she had time. Couldn't do them any harm to wait five minutes while she ate her carrots, could it? You had to eat. Keep your bloody strength up.

He got up and fetched her a tin of carrots that he tipped cold, slop and all, into a bowl. She didn't want them warmed, did she?

As they come, as they come.

On his way back to the table hissing and guffing. Pardon.

Twice Steve had to get up and go out to receive deliveries and Anne was left alone with Mother sucking the carrots across the bridge and down her gullet.

Had he got anything, this morning? she asked Anne in one of their silences.

A cat, Anne said. He shot a cat. She looked up to see Steve in the doorway.

It could have been a fox, Mother. Don't go jumping to conclusions and don't mention it to Smarty when he comes over.

Mother convulsed. The carrots slipped dangerously sideways and something orange and unspeakable flew out of her mouth. She was laughing, evidently.

Don't you let on he shot a cat. He only got paid for the vermin.

Well, cats are bloody vermin if you ask me.

Can't argue with that. Can't argue with that. The carrots became the focus of Mother's attention once more. Steve manoeuvred himself back into his seat at the table and resumed glazedness and fixity. Just the noise of the carrots over the bridge again and the air. Pardon.

When she'd finished Mother looked round at Anne. He's killed men, you know.

Shush, Mother.

He's shot a lot of men. He used to be in the Forklinds. Special Forces.

Anne looked from Mother to Steve and back again. What to say. She had a feeling of recognition about Forklinds, but dim, very dim. Buster dreamed of rabbits and an extra leg. Otherwise silence.

He can't have no furniture round his bed. You watch out, if that's where you think you're headed. He wakes up and tries to strangle you in the night. His wife left him, didn't she, Steve? She left. Take more than that to scare me off. He's not strangling me.

That's enough, Mother. Those speaking, bovine eyes. Anne doesn't want to hear our troubles.

Time to go maybe, although it was hard to tear yourself away from your first friends. That was what they were, wasn't it?

Back down the track on foot, turning it all over in your mind. Cross the road and along and up the field, further than you thought but not too far after all. Past the cat still in the hedge and it must be, what, mid-afternoon? Back to the hut. That was something after all, your own hut and the quiet and no pylon clicking like a cricket above your head yet, just the birds and the leaves and the sweet woodland air.

Anne got into the habit of spending her days away from the clearing. She wandered further afield now and more openly. She would go out first thing, milk, then lie in the ditch and watch her father. He saw her once, blinked like an owl, skidded to a stop.

What are you doing there?

Anne stood up like she'd done something wrong. Nothing, Dad. I'm not doing anything.

She might have said, living, instead. She might have said I'm just living if you don't mind, but she didn't. They looked at each other. A car passed between them. He didn't cross the road or anything. You alright then? he asked, after it had gone. Anne nodded, shrugged, I'm fine. I've got a house, Dad. He went on standing there, just looking at her. He didn't ask where. After a bit he said, Well, can't stand here all day. I'll be late at this rate. As if it was her fault. He wound the pedal round with his foot.

Alright?

Alright, Dad.

She raised a hand. He was poised to go.

Don't let your mother see you looking like that. Then he was speeding down the hill to the cruddy old chicken plant like always.

It was nice seeing her dad. Even if he was useless.

She did a lot of watching in the day. Often, after that, she'd wave and he'd take a hand gingerly off the handlebars and give her a little wave back. Sometimes Alright? would float back to her over his shoulder, thin on the air with the speed of his

57

passage as he shot by. Alright, Dad, she'd answer to herself, as he rounded the corner. It was comforting.

One day he stopped again, did his chicken-head look up and down the road and waddled his bike across to her. Bit of something extra, he said, and he gave her a tinfoil package before he mounted again and was gone.

That was a lovely day, opening the package in the sun on the bank, tomato ketchup and toast and she ate it right there and then. Afterwards she lay on her back and watched the leaves against the sky and the comings and goings of the birds, and a mouse with something enormous in its mouth ran down her arm and under a bramble. Perhaps it was her birthday or something. Who knew?

Sometimes she'd come back to the bank in the day and watch the rest of her family go to and fro up the hill past the wood. Mum in the car with Leanne and Connor, off to town. Michael and John on their bikes. Miss Madam off on a date. Anne kept quiet. She didn't want any of that lot seeing her. Only Connor saw her once and they waved at each other.

She wasn't always so idle. The coppicing she'd done to open up the clearing sprang and grew like magic. You couldn't keep it down. She had to dig round each stump and chop the roots out with an axe. It was back-breaking but she worked and worked to cut herself a patch. Just a small area at first, where there was least understorey, nothing sown yet, just ground clearance and protection against rabbits and deer. She fenced her plot, the size it would be when she'd finished, with a mixture of stakes and netting she'd found in a skip, strung with things to keep out the birds, anything she found on her wanders about the wood, dummies dropped out of babies' mouths in the car park, yards of tape from a broken cassette hung with ringpulls. It looked wicked and it worked. You had to be clever to survive.

When she was out and about, trundling down the paths, to the car park or the woodland café, Anne would keep her eyes open. She had taken to picking things up, litter mostly, which she did out of gratitude to the wood, as a sort of service, but then you never knew what might come in handy. She wasn't indiscriminate. She sorted it; it was like a job. The rubbish, she threw away in the car-park bins. The boxes or cartons that looked useful, she kept. She also kept the things that fell out of pushchairs, little teddies, books, plastic things that rattled or squeaked. Leanne had coloured plastic toys and soft toys. Lots of toys, Anne said to herself. Broken, some of them were. The ones that needed batteries that is, because Michael or John or Connor took the batteries out, lost the battery covers, and that was that usually. You needed toys if you were making a home. You couldn't have a home without things in it and Anne had nothing to begin with. Obviously she had to have things.

They were hard to come by, the really good things. You didn't find real things every day, so they were a rarity – Anne's treasures. She put up shelves round the walls to hold them and she spent much time, on rainy days, arranging. She had her favourites, the lilac teddy with a loop out of the top of his head and the plastic keys in rainbow colours on a clip-together ring. Sometimes she'd change it round, demote something from a prominent position because something else, more important, had been found, like the day she saw a spouty cup with juice still in it. It was red and the spout had been chewed so that there were little threads and peaks of plastic, like fur almost, all over it. On the side there was a picture of a panda smiling and stepping out. *Tommy Tippee*. Anne drank the juice, which tasted of dribble, and put the cup in the middle of the shelf above her bed. That was a find, that was. She felt really pleased after that.

When she ran out of shelf space she hung things on nails. The lilac teddy came off the shelf and hung above the door. He was her lucky charm. The plastic keys showed better on a nail, anyway, so they went to the side of the door. That was a joke: plastic keys for her door. You didn't just hang things anywhere, you hung them where they made sense. She sorted them by category: the useful, the decorative, the playthings and, smallest group of all, the objects of superstition. The most plentiful things were the teethers and comforters that fell out of babies' hands or mouths. They had a category of their own, on account of their superior number. She had two lines of them, plastic totems, up the length of the stakes, from roof to floor. She looked forward to when the walls would be completely covered.

Now, out collecting, Anne redoubled her efforts. She didn't dawdle along, watching the birds. She walked stooped and concentrating. She poked, with a stick, by the sides of the tracks, in the brambles and rushy grass in case she'd missed something. Once she'd picked up a comforter before the mother and buggy were properly past. She put it straight into her mouth – that was instinct, because sometimes they tasted of sugar or of pap. Then the mother had turned round, realising it was gone, just as Anne, having taken it out again, was holding it up for inspection. Nice one. Blue stopper with ring, clear teat. Little yellow ducks round the outside. It would hang nice.

*Ex*cuse me.

The mother gave her a murder-look. So vicious it left Anne with her mouth open. She snatched the comforter out of

60

Anne's hand, jolting the buggy so her baby cried. Anne heard – Some people and It's not safe any more – before they disappeared. That's got my spit on it, she thought, because the mother had put the dummy in her own mouth to clean it, before cramming it into the crying baby. Serve you right.

You couldn't tell with the people in the wood, whether they would be nice or nasty. Sometimes people talked to her. Sometimes they looked like she wasn't there. They were rude. Anne knew that. She wasn't exactly invisible. Once, when she was busy like this, at her job again, putting rubbish in a carrier bag, a man came round the corner. He had a big black bin liner and grey hair tied in a ponytail. He was collecting, like her.

Morning.

The way he said it, like it was a gift. Puffing it out on the morning air and bending slightly in Anne's direction. His smile, too, was a kind of benediction. How nice, he said, to see someone else doing their civic duty. He indicated his own bag, full of litter. Doing something for the common good. He collected a couple of times a week usually, how often did Anne collect – he'd never seen her before?

Every day. Anne collected nearly every day.

There was an awkward pause. Anne made half a move to go, only she couldn't because he was in the way.

Every day? Every day? The man repeated her words. He laughed a little barking laugh. Something was wrong. The man seemed cross. He looked at Anne hard, like she'd done something naughty. It was a disgusting reflection on society that there was enough litter to make picking it up a daily task. He said it as if it was Anne's fault. She should think about it – it could be that Anne, with her overzealous approach, was encouraging litter dropping. If people could rely on her to

61

pick up after them, they might well drop more. One should be wary of encouraging delinquency.

Someone else's dog lolloped past then, nose to the ground, back again, stopped, hooped itself to defecate. Dogs, dogs, dogs. The man swivelled, to look for its owner, stepping aside as she came up puffing. Morning. A second benediction. You will be scooping, I trust? The woman looked confused. She hadn't understood. That was obvious. She gave a puzzled half-smile, made a sort of sound in the back of her throat and walked on.

It is on the pathway, he boomed after her. It's on the pathway, madam. But she was disappearing fast.

Anne shifted from foot to foot. The thing that occupied her whole mind, the only thing that really mattered to her was, What has he got in his bag. It made her uneasy, someone else collecting in the same wood, but she didn't dare ask. Civic duty. She was puzzled by that one.

As if in apology, and because she didn't know what else to say, she said hesitantly, I've left home, holding her own bag slightly behind her and out of sight. She didn't know if he would want to check it.

It worked. The man's face relaxed. He leant back on his heels, holding his hands and the bag, clasped in front of him. Superior again. He shook his head. Leaving home. Leaving home. We all *think* we leave home. But – he opened his free hand wide – home is Mother Earth. Home is where the heart is and we can't leave the planet, can we? Oh no. We don't leave home. None of us do that. He looked so pleased, bending forwards now, delighted really. Think about it.

He gave her a wink and went on his way, left her to this new job, her civic duty. He sang a song as he went. No words, just Pom Pom Pom, but loudly.

She saw him again, from time to time, and he would wink at her or make a saying. To labour and not to seek for any reward. God is in the little things. That rules me out then, Anne thought, but she knew that already. Mostly she had no idea what he was talking about. He bought her a drink once, in the woodland café. She wanted Pepsi Max but he bought her fizzy water. It said natural sparkling mineral water on the bottle. It was disgusting. She had to pour it out when he wasn't looking.

His name was Nigel. She found that out when he bought her the drink. He couldn't buy a lady a drink without knowing her name. Anne had stared at him. When she told him her name he held out his hand, saying his own and bowing slightly. He said, pleased to meet you, Anne, even though he'd met her several days before. Inside the café he'd patted her shoulder, telling the lady behind the counter in a loud voice so the other customers could hear, Anne will have a sparkling water if you please. Litter-picker extraordinaire. She needs refreshment.

He never thought to ask her what she actually wanted. He wasn't that sort of man.

Because of Nigel, she got to know the woman in the café too. She was called Sue and she was Nigel's friend. They talked together about what they called *the planet* and the way people went on in the wood, dropping litter, so thoughtless. Society was on the wrong track. There was no sense of community. Anne was not interested in their conversations. She looked at the posters on the walls while they talked, or doodled with her finger in the drops of spilt tea on the table-tops. But she was interested in free sandwiches. Or half-eaten jacket potatoes. They were worth waiting for.

Sometimes, Anne went to the café without Nigel, to have a sit in a proper chair for a change, to be in the steam and smell of it. Lovely it was. Whenever she went in Sue would call out to her, loud like Nigel. Hello, Anne. And, How's it going? Here's a lady that knows her duty. Keeping it clean for the rest of us.

Anne thought they had nice conversations.

Once, as she was leaving the café, she heard Sue talking to someone else. Friend of yours? the other woman was asking, as Anne went out. Sue said, Bless her. She tapped her head, like Michael and John and Connor. That's our resident mental case. Doolally. It's a weird and wonderful world. Talk to anyone, me. I don't make judgements. Life's too short.

Anne turned round on the threshold because it was like someone had smacked the breath out of her. She put her hand to the door frame.

Ta-ta, Sue called out. Mind how you go.

Anne had a pain in her chest.

D'you think she heard?

No, Sue said, wiping the counter. Not her, away with the fairies that one.

Setbacks were bigger when you were on your own. For a week Anne nursed her hurt. She sat at the foot of the pollard, spine to spine, and watched the flittings and flutterings that went on around her. Birds and leaves, birds and leaves. Always something moving. She watched the tree creepers up their spiral staircases, so quick and neat. That's fast food, she thought. They were really kitted out for the job, the curved beak like a craft needle for leather, the ungainly feet. She didn't know their name. What d'you think you look like? she asked them, furious for a moment. Like ticks on that tree you are, that's what. It wasn't a nice name, tree tick, but that's

64

what she called them. She felt exhausted by the competence, the focus, of the natural world. With her thumb, she pushed an ant into the crescent of her fingernail. It was frantic, wheeling its antennae and all its sensors bleeping inaudibly. Ants are intelligent. They look like something out of a computer, small and shiny and to do with invisible signalling, although they die once they are in a fingernail.

Back to square one, that's what she was, back to sitting against the tree waiting for something to make sense. Until something quick and soft came, close to the ground, fleeing. A hare or a rabbit? Its ears were flat against its back. Behind it, someone's dog bounded into the clearing, all muscle and on the scent. Fear, you could smell it. The little birds twitched their heads and flicked away in alarm. For a moment the clearing was empty.

Well, she said. The little birds came back. Flick, flick, two tomtits. Some of the brown ones that all look the same. Always alert they were. She supposed she wasn't hunted. At least. That had to be something.

Afterwards, when she thought back to this first summer in the woods, Anne couldn't believe how improvident she'd been, how she'd wandered up and down, when she should have been storing food. So much time spent just learning the place, looking at it, in love with the wood, collecting nonsense or just walking, discovering the deeps where the deer went to calf, or the beech stands where the bluebells had been and the trees stood round with naked limbs, like swimmers, and the other, little known places, where the land fell and rose again and the modest oaks wore moss and ferns and went on for what looked like forever. She would lie down, here or there, with no thought for winter, and under her nose the wood would produce wild raspberries and she'd make a day of it, grazing on the fruit and idling, watching while a doe and a fawn picked and hopped their queer ballet through the undergrowth. Stopping, eating, looking up, eating again. If you were still, they looked right at you, like the bucks once, carrying, as if it were nothing, their own wood with them, elegant, effortless, this hefting of trees, holding their heads up and running. She watched them jump a fence and cross a field. It looked like they never even touched the ground, just cloud shadow swept across the green on a windy day. Although when she went to look Anne saw the slots their hooves had left, neat and definite in the earth.

Of all the animals that made their homes in or under or between the trees, in holes, or on high, it was the deer that were the spirit of the wood for Anne. Their flickering presence a kind of magic, like the trees come alive. She followed them obsessively. She'd travel miles to where she thought they'd be, where she'd seen them last, or where the food was, to whatever was dropping or shooting. And they taught her, without knowing it, how to eat in season, and where to find it.

She'd forgotten the message of the rain before she'd built the shelter and she did silly things, like lying for hours with some shortbread crumbs Sue had given her, on the edge of the wood, where she'd once seen pheasants, hoping to waylay one and throw Michael's fleece over it. She did that for several days and never managed. They're stupid, pheasants, but they're not that stupid.

On the way back, cutting through the field beyond the cows, she saw Steve, swinging along, gun lofted on his shoulder.

Hey up.

Hey up, Anne said back, shy and pleased.

What was she up to these days Steve wanted to know. Seen

any more foxes then?

Anne laughed. She hadn't seen foxes, nor cats neither. Then she explained about the pheasants and it was Steve's turn to laugh.

You'll want something a bit bloody quicker than a old jumper.

Unless it was a dead pheasant she was after.

They walked along together a bit and after a while a pheasant got up, cock cock cock cock cock. And bang, Steve shot it dead. Anne hadn't seen him run before.

Stick that in your hmm jumper and don't tell anyone. That's a bit bloody naughty that is, but I reckon old Smarty can spare a bird or two. Go on, get going and don't say a word.

Anne looked at him.

It's a fox, Steve.

She was so grateful, a whole pheasant just like that.

Steve laughed, softly this time.

It's a hmm bloody fox.

Anne plucked the pheasant, which was still warm, keeping the beautiful feathers, even the smallest of the down, shaking them from her fingers inside the bag she was using and giving a little cry if any of them floated away by mistake. Then she cut off the head and the feet and threw them out for the fox, and drew the bird like her dad had shown her on a chicken. She raked her fire to open out the coals, took water from the pool and boiled the pheasant with its liver, sitting and watching all the time with greedy eyes, inhaling the steam till her head spun and her belly growled with hunger. Then she ate the whole thing and drank the water.

Bloated. Eyes wide. Under the pollard in the sun, unable to

move for fear of overflow or burst. Later she crawled into the hut and she slept, for a long time.

When she woke up, it was morning. A fox was licking out the saucepan, which lay where she'd left it on the grass. She waved him away. He'd eaten every one of the bones. Hope they split you, Anne told him. He went slantwise, trotting nonchalant into the hazels. Vanished. She would have boiled the bones for stock. She should have taken them in with her when she'd gone to sleep. Another stupidity. The fox was always one step ahead. She picked up a stone and threw it after him.

Visiting Steve. Something she would like to do, but couldn't quite. Complicated reasons. She set off sometimes. She walked very purposeful up the field track like she was going somewhere. When she got to the end she looked up and down the road as if she was looking for someone, tapped her foot and shook her head, inconvenienced. Sometimes she extended the pretence with one or two comments, in case Steve was somewhere unnoticed and watching her, maybe, or maybe not. In case Steve, if he was watching or listening, thought she might be waiting for him. Then she'd turn and walk leisurely back up the track because maybe he'd be out after vermin a bit later today, checking the sun, if there was any, and wondering if she'd got the hour, which for her was rough anyway, rougher than usual.

She could have bagged up the rubbish she'd collected and taken it along. Just be a normal person going to the dump. Got some rubbish for the tip, or suchlike. But what if the tip cost? That was the question. She couldn't remember any money changing hands but then there was the jug. Although the jug was strictly not for tipping. The jug was in the trailers.

The jug was for sale. But the world out there was money money, Anne knew that. Up the track again, for the eighteenth time, in a summer wind and everything blowing about her.

At last she went. She didn't let on to herself that she was going all the way until she got there, right to the gates of the dump. *No more than 5 DIY waste items per week. No fly-tipping. No tyres.* She caught her breath at the chain-link fence, put her head down and charged pretty much, for the nearest shed. Beetling across the open ground between. Just looking. Just looking. Just like anyone else.

And it was so normal, like she was expected. He was barely even surprised when he saw her. Hey up, Anne, come for some bloody breakfast?

They went past a smaller shed with a radio on full blast, coming out of some rigged-up speakers. There were two others she hadn't met before, an old boy called Sid, in blue overalls, and a skinhead who worked the cranes. Going for some breakfast, Steve said to their bent heads. This is Anne. The table was covered with newspapers, boobs and bums by the looks of things. The men raised their heads, stared, nodded and went back to the boobs. Tea and fags and custard creams. The skinhead looked sick to the back teeth.

They crossed the yard to the bungalow with the pop music following them. Anne treasured to herself sheds full of junk, motionless cranes, the power lines zooming overhead. There was Mother, like before, Buster, the legless gnomes, the pylon.

Steve.

Not much conversation and the fire was on so it was hottish for making an effort. They ate the same breakfast and they listened in glazed companionship to Steve's digestion. The gas fire popped in sympathy.

Was she any good with her hands?

Anne, who was sitting with her hands fisted in her lap, raised them to table level, opened them out. The nails were painted in bizarre colours. She turned them over. Good with her hands? She looked at Steve. She was genius. I'm not boasting.

You can help me out if you want, every now and again. I can't pay you, mind, but you can have breakfast.

Which meant that on the way back the birds skidded about in a high-up sky. And along the main road, the cornfields ran with the wind, as if they were a sea, on which the trees, when Anne came to the edge of the wood, were sailing, bellied out and in full summer green. But Anne was up, right up above them all, above the trees, above the birds, up with the wind in infinity.

CHORUS OF TREES

A wood in the wind on a weekday. Emptyish. Just trees, turning their backs, with their leaves silvering so the light dances, wind-blown into the clearings. A pigeon drops out of an ash on the far side, snatched up and travelling now across the open field and handfuls of jackdaws flung about as if they were seed. Only the odd crow, who's too hard to make compromises, sitting it out, lookout, on a top-twig here or there, clinging on. Sees Anne coming up the track, like something on a spool, wound in, looking like the wind has got her too, full up and bouncing.

Well, it's summer. What did you expect? Most things are paired up now.

This wind is our voice, should you listen. Talking trees, pass it on.

Stand still, we might say. Face inwards. See us, canopy to canopy, managing the wind, each on our own. Just at the edge of each crown, knocking neighbours and lifting free, settling twig to twig again. A community of singles. Isn't that preferable? Each tree tuned like a handbell to its own tone, concentrating on a private resonance.

Now the ash rocks, and the wind passes, and in the bottom of a field maple a wren waits, her eyebrows pencilled white so she looks cross-eyed, staying low down as if on the seabed.

And even if the ash could tell Anne – just withstand, be

self-contained – Anne wouldn't hear. She has no choice but to follow her pulses, blindly. She has the heat of blood to contend with after all. At the top of the path, she puts out a hand, unthinking, as she enters the wood with the wind. She passes, touching bark, hearing nothing. And the tree bends again, single, however it's grouped, working without anyone's help. Channelling, water and minerals up, light and air in and down, sealing off disease, or leaf, or unwanted twig, more or less self-sufficient, pollinators aside. What's the difference?

I am what I am, it says to itself.

Disconnected, does it notice? Does it wonder why that one is so shy into leaf, why its leaves are pinkish, acid green or bronze? Does it ask how long the slow oak holds its leaves into winter, heaving like wet canvas, dangerous and heavy in the gales – or why the birds choose there, not here – or if the teacup nest is safe it balances on its knuckle-backs?

I just notice that the milking oak has hornets in its feet. Feel my hold loosen where the badgers squeeze a passage round my roots. Lift my crown in the wind. Pass it on to the next. Pass it on.

MAIDEN I

Steve originally said, Come Thursdays. But it was difficult for Anne to keep track, so in the end she went when she felt like it, or when she remembered, or felt particularly hungry.

She fixed things up for Steve, so he could sell them for a bit more. She chose what to do. He let her have one of the sheds to work in, let her use his tools. If she needed something special she told him, and he would get it for her for next time. She liked fossicking around among the junk. Never happier than upended in the boxes for reclamation, or the bins. She'd arrange things in the trailers so they looked more tempting, and it gave her ideas for her hut. She never took from Steve. They were his things. She didn't want to take his things. But he'd say to her, coming across her, beam up, What are you after now, Anne? And he'd give her shelves, nails, old tools he had no use for. Because he was a kind man. Possibly the only kind man, Anne thought.

You saw the whole of life at the tip, Mother said, and it was true. All different people came. So much to throw away, it was marvellous. Cleansing in every sense, you could see that. People went down the gangplank pleased with themselves. It was an achievement throwing out your junk. You were a better person when you'd done it, like you'd gone to church. That's a good job done, they'd say, dusting themselves off before getting back in the car. Or, We've had a really good clear-out.

They had virtue written all over their faces. Anne liked to stand at the top of the metal gangplank, next to the container – the size of a house the container was, you could live in it easily – and watch the people pull up and get out. She would guess what they were throwing from the car they drove. If it had a baby seat or not, things like that. She would watch the people do that strange tiptoeing walk they do when they think they are somewhere dirty, because the dump was an unsavoury place. It was threatening, almost, to the families in clean white trainers, who walked warily and held their junk at arm's length and dropped it quickly into the great gullets of the containers, barely risking a look to see it landed safe. As if the containers had appetites. Some of the men were more daring. Up the gangplanks with their unwanted gizmos, dead bits of electrical, old computers, sound systems. Heaved them up and over and as they clanged to rest, glanced timid over the side, just to prove they could.

When a container was full, Sid would come along and crash, clang, the gangplank was shut off and another one opened and another container gaped to be fed. And all the time a crane or a grabber operated by the skinhead, worked at bird height above the containers, swinging around, crushing things down, compacting the loads, occasionally at a shout from Steve, lifting this or that out with its claw, something gone in by mistake, something better perhaps, whisked out again and earmarked for resale. It was noisy at the dump, the metal machines, the clanging of gates, the engines, the pylon buzzing.

It was different for a change.

Anne would watch for hours, the arm's-length rejection of things that must once have been new, never a backward glance. The thing on its side at first and then how quickly it was buried – the loneliness of it all, the anonymity of broken things, the blind TVs, the filing cabinets with their mouths open, and the crushing from above. After the dump there was the landfill. Anne went to the landfill once or twice with Steve. Gulls screaming and picking everywhere and piles and piles, a whole mountain range of rubbish, being raked over by giant metal arms. No thank you.

But up on the gangplank, with the breeze blowing in her hair, and the mash of rubbish down below and the birds enjoying it up above, little puffs of white cloud and old Steve to and fro between the sheds, his side-to-side walk and the bulk of him and it was the best feeling there was. So that was where Anne spent her spare time, when she was taking a break from fixing something up, waiting for Steve to call up – Cuppa? So she could go down to the shed with the pop music in it and sit around with the others, with her cup on a boob that she never noticed and a blonde or a brunette wasting their newspaper smiles on her and pick the top off of a custard cream.

He wheezed when he walked, lung problems from the Forklinds. That's a hmm bloody good job, Anne. She liked it when he was pleased. Praise, that was a new pleasure and she wanted so much to please. She was a good little worker. Only, once or twice he asked questions and she couldn't answer, however much she wanted to. She was afraid of not pleasing him then. How come you're living in the hmm woods then? he asked her one day. She must have looked like a rabbit, eyes darting, head into her shoulders, looking for escape. She didn't say anything in the end. She picked at the top of the chest she was working on and Steve didn't push it. He just said, You're a bit bloody big to be a fairy, trying to make her laugh, which she did although it was mixed laughter, because she felt so awkward and because big was hurtful to her.

But he called her a good little worker, so maybe.

Other times he asked her, How's it going with the pheasants? Caught one yet?

She plucked up her courage and she brought him her snares. She'd been trying for rabbits. She hadn't caught a thing. And he took the snares in his big hands, turned them over. These ought to be just the job I reckon. What's the matter with the bloody bunnies these days? They don't know a good thing when they see one.

Tell you what, he told her, hop in the truck and we'll have a see. He'd help her get them set. He used to do a bit of bloody poaching in the old days. They'd have a crack at a pheasant and all. Have a bit of fun why not.

So Steve showed her. They parked the truck and Steve took his gun, because you never knew and he gave her a wink. Might see a tasty old fox. Anne smiled.

Steve said no point setting them where the fields were too busy so they walked, with the grass tall and wet up to their knees. Don't mind getting a bit damp do you? He had the gun up on his shoulder and Anne's snares hanging out of his pocket and as he went along he picked the heads of the grass with his finger and thumb.

She'd been setting the snares in the wrong place.

Set it on their usual track, see. Look for the droppings and the recent track. Set it up next to an obstruction so there's no going round. He was intent while he told her these things, half talking to himself a lot of the time, wheezing, looking around, surprisingly careful and skilled when he needed to be, parting the grasses with hands that had their own intelligence.

When she went back later to check, there was a rabbit in the first snare.

Steve could have got anything if he'd wanted. Steve could have got the birds out of the trees. Steve could have got a fish in a snare. He could have got a deer, a pheasant, a quiet woodcock. Steve was king in Anne's eyes after that rabbit.

She carried it carefully down to the dump because it was Steve's rabbit and he smiled when he saw her. He gave her the thumbs up. Let's have a bloody butcher's. Not bad, not bad. That's quite a nice young buck that is.

But Anne had had trouble killing it. It wasn't as easy as all that, killing rabbits. Rabbits wanted to live. They kicked and they scratched and you could make a mess of it if you weren't careful.

That's where you want to get him, Steve showed her on the back of the rabbit's neck. Hit him hard and down and we'd better get that cleaned up. He pointed to her hand, which she didn't know he'd noticed. You don't want that going bloody bad on you. He got down a little tin of first aid and he sorted out Anne's cuts with Dettol that made her eyes water. Give you a plaster on that one I reckon. Then he showed her how to paunch the rabbit and how to flay it. Lesson number one, he said at the end, wiping his hands down his tummy. How do you fancy rabbit for dinner? He had a lovely smile, Steve did.

After that it was easy. She knew how to do it, though she wasn't always successful. Sometimes she'd try different things herself, variations on her first snares, bait, different locations, anything she thought might increase her chances.

At teatime Steve would ask her how it was going. He'd give her advice, or he'd let her know, I've seen a hen pheasant with a nice little brood running about in the west field. Reckon you could have a go at the old cock. She'd show him the improved snares and he'd click his tongue. I tell you what, that's a nifty little piece of kit Anne. That's got a bloody good chance I reckon. Wouldn't mind giving that a go myself. And that was a compliment to make Anne hum inside.

She worked extra hard for him. She worked like a demon, not that it was difficult. She liked the dump. It fitted her almost as well as the wood. She liked its geography, the simple straight lines of the trailers and sheds, the blocks of the containers, the order of it. A little world in itself.

She'd go up the gangplank and look down on it all and take pleasure in her place in its odd order, the thing she was working on and her tools, her own shed and all the people she knew and who knew her coming and going.

Up there as usual, one day, enjoying herself, no indication that anything was different, expanding with the air and the perfect familiarity of it all, and, suddenly, there was Suzie.

She got out of a car and Anne opened her mouth and stared. Colour of blood the car was, with a man in a T-shirt and muscles like a bull. Small world, Anne's father had told her. Small bloody world.

Tip tap tip tap along the paths, Suzie went, between the trailers while the man went to and fro with the rubbish.

Anne panicked inside. Get out, Anne's head said to her, get out. But Suzie didn't hear. She just went on as if nothing had happened, tip-tapping down the paved path, picking up something to have a look. And now Anne's head filled up with Suzie's rubbish, with the bad words and the unkindness, and up on the gangplank, in plain view, she pulled at her great big fingers in distress. Better chuck her in too, Anne thought. Throw her over the side and see the cruncher mash her down and tip her out for the gulls, why not. That's all she's worth. Tip tap tip tap, Anne could hear it from the gangplank, with her pretty little heels and her pretty little nails and her hair all up and curled. I'm up here Suzie, she shouted in her head, it's your sister Anne up here on the gangplank. I'll push you in the rubbish where you belong. See how you like that. She's worth nothing she is. Can't do anything for herself. She wouldn't last two minutes.

And then Steve came round the corner, with his hair tousled and his shirt tight round his tummy and his shoulders dipping with his walk, like always, and he looked up and said, Hello Suzie, like he knew her already. Hello Suzie, and he smiled. And Anne had to watch while Suzie smiled back, with her head on one side like some stupid bird, while she wriggled and fluttered her hands to her hair and smoothed her skirt on her hips. Kick her up the arse and into one of those containers. Mash her down why don't you. Only Steve didn't look like he was going to do any kicking.

You couldn't hear everything they were saying whether you wanted to hear or not, not from up on the gangplank anyway, and Anne's feet were as if they had taken root.

But you could see. You could see that Steve was leant right forward and Suzie, you could see Suzie, still swaying about like a grass and doing a little laugh every now and again and the hands busy all the time, fluttering, fluttering, like the old days.

Then the man with the muscles was finished and calling her over, Come on, girl.

Hello, buddy, to Steve. Alright? Getting into his car and revving the engine. Suzie jerked her head over her shoulder at the car and the man and Steve looked up and nodded and didn't smile any more, and then, as Suzie walked back to the car, he just stood there, fixed and looked after her and didn't move.

So Anne came down the gangplank and didn't go to the tip for a bit, after that.

*

She didn't go to the tip but she couldn't help seeing, one day as she lay on the bank to watch her family, that Steve's truck went up the hill and came down again with Suzie in it.

Suzie was sat up in the front seat, dolled up and not touching the sides because it was dirty in the truck, Anne knew that. She won't last long, Anne thought sourly. She won't like the dump and old Buster if she doesn't like the truck. But the fact that she was there at all. That and the look on Steve's face. That was enough. That was more than enough.

Autumn came and Anne stood in a whirl of yellow, while the trees cried their leaves around her, as if it was the first time. She couldn't have left the wood at a time like this anyway, she told herself.

The first day the sky swapped its blue for a whipped grey and the wind got up, Anne noticed that it blew into the hut through the cracks in the palisade. She squatted inside with her chin in her hands, shivering and fighting panic. She wasn't going to make it if it was like this in the winter. It would be worse in winter. Then the wind got behind the fire and blew the smoke straight into the hut. She flapped at it with her jumper. It made no difference. Curling in, the smoke was, great choking billows of it making her eyes sting and pour. She got really wild. Since Suzie had come to the tip, things like this made her unreasonably and unmanageably angry. Sometimes they made her shout or cry. Sometimes she smashed things. Nothing, she thought, ever gave her a break. When night fell and the wind was still blowing, she lay in the dark and the trees clattered with it all night long and Anne swore like Suzie had taught her, every word she knew.

But in the morning the wind died down and Anne got up and went out, dogged once more, and plugged the cracks with wet mud and grass, from roof to floor. It was a long and exhausting job, day after day, cold-fingered and caked in mud herself. Then she put in a stake over every join, just for good measure, till her house was ridged like a shell all round. After that she rested. She sat inside for two days just feeling warm. She sat and she looked at her hands, that were big and that had built a house. So she'd survived rain and she'd survived hunger and cold and she wanted badly someone to tell it to. I made a house myself. I made it all nice with things and I made it warm. Keeps out the rain and the wind now. But there wasn't anyone to tell and it was commonplace to the birds, survival, house-building; they did it all the time. She thought of her elation when the hut had been roofed for the first time. Oh Steve. She put her head in her hands.

Fog, mud and drizzle. You had to fight to stop it getting inside you. Weather is catching. Anne raked leaves with her dad's rake. There were leaves everywhere, choking the ditches, clogging her pond. She dragged the pond clean with a board nailed onto a pole, pulled the leaves out onto the banks, clapped them up with two more boards that she wore on her hands, with straps made of folded plastic sacks, nailed to the back, with the nails bent over like staples. Good job Anne. Another good job.

She worked round the piles of leaves on the banks, barrowed them to the garden, where she heaped them up by the compost, edged them round with wood from the timber pile. Then she covered them to help them rot. A layer of plastic bags, weighted down with stones just to be sure. The rest she put straight into the soil. She trench-dug the plot as best she could, around the roots and suchlike. She put the leaves into the bottom and piled the earth back on top. She had no idea whether it would work or not but it used up the leaves and it was something to do.

At night Anne went to bed stumbling through the dark with exhaustion. Sometimes she fell asleep before she could get into the bag. Then she'd wake rigid with cold, and crawl in and shiver. And whenever she woke Steve was there, floating up out of her dead mind with his ball tummy and his old ways and Suzie like a tinny little lipstick beside him.

She'd got so familiar with her loss, she knew it like it was a place. She would prod it like a bruise first thing in the morning, as she lay on her back and looked at the ceiling of the hut and tried to get up. See if it still hurt. She visited it so often, doing her mindless tasks, making tools, scratching about in her garden, gathering wood for her store, that it lost its pleasurable ache and she began to question. Sometimes she couldn't even call to mind his face. She didn't know any more. Perhaps it wasn't just Steve. Only you had to have someone. Everyone had someone.

Paint my nails for me, Suzie, she said slowly in a voice that had cracked and rusted with no use. Paint my nails then, she shouted into the night's quiet, out loud, just because she could and because there was no one there, no one to slight her hands, to admire her house, to make her bloody breakfast.

One day, she fished for her old latchkey, in her pocket, where she'd kept it just in case. She threaded it onto a piece of string and tied it round her neck.

She sat on the floor of the hut, fingering the key and swallowing. Maybe she should go down to the dump, just to see some people. Nigel even, or down to the café, to sit and watch Sue. Anyone. Steady Anne.

Her eyes met the flat and shiny gaze of the lilac teddy above her door. There was always a project. She hadn't finished covering the walls yet, had she? And if she wanted something big to do, the dam needed seeing to. She had to keep that in constant trim. She needed things, a bed, a floor because the inside of her house turned into mud pudding in the rain. She needed something to store her food in, a stove for the winter when she couldn't sit over a fire outside, a proper door for goodness' sake. Anne put her hands over her eyes; it was never-ending making a house. Wash the pots for me Anne do the dishes mend Michael's bike fetch in the washing do your dad's tea bath the baby for me.

Nothing new there then, said Anne to herself. She took her hands away from her eyes. I'll keep going.

She took her barrow down to the fields at ploughing time and collected flints and cobbles that she wobbled home half a barrow at a time because of the weight. She started at the back of her house and worked towards the front, scraping out a section at a time, watering the floor, setting the stones in the wet mud and then sweeping the dry stuff back to fill up the cracks. It was nice when it was done.

When things became too much for her she would finger her key. She had her own house now, so she knew she could manage, but she could always go back if she felt like it. She might go back in fact; probably would go back, one day.

She did go back. She went back with the wheelbarrow, one autumn night. She wasn't going to go in. She didn't need to do that. She'd only come for the metal dustbin outside. She lifted the lid and wrinkled her nose at the contents. Her family didn't half smell. She shook the bin over the hedge, a chute of rubbish glinting briefly in the drizzle. Maybe they'd left her something she could eat. She half regretted not having checked through the bin first. But then she thought, Not likely, not those gannets. Anne crammed the lid on the empty bin and put the whole thing in the barrow. Her third visit. She shifted from foot to foot on the doorstep. She looked up at her window and touched the key like a talisman. At the gate she turned back. She thought of the telly sitting quiet in the dark, how it would wake up for her at the touch of a button, open its eye, show her its furious world. She took out the key and put it to the lock. Maybe one more bowl of cereal. The metal of the lock looked shiny even in so little light. There was pale new wood around it. She jiggled the key. No joy. She nearly got desperate. It was the thought of all those comforts, so close by. It was just stiff tonight, she said to herself. Must have been the rain. She took the key out and smoothed it with her finger and put it back inside her shirt. Another time then. Instead, Anne looked through the window at the kitchen, cupping her hand on the glass to see better, but it was dark except for a red light on the cooker. She wouldn't be surprised if they didn't burn the house down one of these days. Michael and John and Connor. Stupid twat, they used to call her, dizzy cow. But she never left the cooker on. Her feet made indents in the flower bed, big prints that her family would find in the morning. She turned away.

Down the hill with the bin in the barrow and not even the moon could be bothered with Anne tonight. Without its light she banged herself and stumbled. Once a car swept round a corner. That was scary. Anne saw the driver's face momentarily amazed and then he must have put his foot down because the car sped on its way, dumping Anne in deeper darkness than before.

The dustbin was Anne's stove. She punched out a ragged hole in the front and one in the lid for the smoke. She couldn't do a chimney but she cut an opening in the most sheltered wall of the house and pushed the bin in from outside, until the dome of the lid jammed, leaving the hole for the smoke on the wrong side and the hole for the fire in the room. Now she was warm and she was dry. She had water and more or less enough to eat. She settled into a season as slow as herself. She moved as little as she needed. Often she lay and observed inwardly the workings of her body, the rise and fall of its breath, its red tides, its silt and damps, spit and slime and hot streams.

The wood emptied. Just the regular dog walkers. Nigel occasionally, not much. He sat in the café mostly, Anne had seen him, sipping endless mugs, windbagging at Sue. Anne didn't go in when he was there, if she could help it. She shuffled through the rides thick with leaves, kicking them up to fall again. At the foot of the limes, and the larches, the ground was bright with yellow, lighter now than the sky most days. Grey days, while the wood waited. There was something fresh and quick about the air, and the dark came down earlier and round the rabbit fields at the edge of the wood the trees stood with their hands still full of leaves and watched the tinny lights of the town come on at tea.

Anne walked all day, hung about with bags. She listened to the leaves that whispered, plenty, above her head and she foraged, because the wood produced fruit in every corner. In every tangle, dip or dell, hips, haws, cobs, crabs, sloes and acorns. And in the feet of the trees and all the slips of space between dead wood and undergrowth, mushrooms pushed up, complete and solid, formed overnight with the speed that only autumn understands. She picked what she knew, the field mushrooms, the parasols, the penny buns, pinching them carefully at the root, smelling them before she put them in the bag.

Several times during each day she had to come back, to unload. In the clearing a moorhen had found its way to her pool. It looked precarious, roosting in the hawthorn, its red bill just like another berry. Anne put her bags down. Get out of it, she said, not to the moorhen, but to a fox nosing round her vegetable patch. They're all mine.

Then she'd head out again. Down the old ways and the trees with fire in their heads, blazing along the green rides, lighting the paths and the hollows, repeating by heart the long lesson of July and August and Indian September. Who needs the sun? Anne asked them, looking at their lights. You can do it for yourselves.

In the evenings she stayed up late, sorting, cooking, hanging things to smoke. Then she'd sleep till the wet autumn dawns woke her, with the air thick enough to taste, and she would be up and off, to the bramble thickets, or the hedgerows, competing with the birds for the berries. All the animals frantic. Quick, quick, winter's coming.

Winter was a knife, when it did come, a nail knocked into your fingernails and feet, a hammer. It happened to you, like it happened to the wood. The naked trees, the empty rides, just your footfall sounding in the dead white spaces.

Fog.

It was wetter mostly. All different types of rain, mizzle, drizzle and downpour, cold as metal always. Frost sometimes. The air thick at other times, white and opaque. To stay alive Anne roared like a stag, not afraid to make a noise now, not creeping invisible any more. Clumping on swollen feet, banging her hands, bellowing. A fight was how she saw it – an unequal battle, whoever thought that up. Flesh and blood against iron hammering the life out of you, gripping and wringing. It had a hard and pinching fist, winter did, and it never let go. She was ranged with the animals against it. Her noise was for them as she lumbered through the wood, because the cold bit at her throat when she breathed, because her toes and fingers were purple and burning, swollen with chilblains, itching like fire all night. Strange, Anne thought, how cold could feel so like its opposite.

There were compensations. The pink light of the fallen leaves, and the boles of the trees in the old stands of beech or oak. The winter moon so full of itself, swollen to the size of a world, and tangerine-coloured as it rose. She dug in holes and piles of leaves and found sleepy hedgehogs to tease out with sticks and she roasted them. She stayed in, burning everything she could find and huddling in her sleeping bag. She spent as much time as possible curled, waiting like everything else. She did like the squirrels, looking for their hidden hoards or sleeping.

Food, always food, scrimmaging about, scavenging, starving, always starving. Roots and berries, kale out of the fields, turnips if she could find them, roadkill, pheasants if she was lucky. Animals thin as pipe cleaners, sucking on bones, nibbling, whatever. The fox bolder than ever and handsome. But even he had hunger in his yellow eye. He'd come through the clearing, stinking, with his ears pricked. Got anything? Or she'd see him out in the fields, or when she was inspecting her traps. You eat one of these and I'll kill you, she'd say to him. The thought that he might have nabbed someone's chickens, or a duck was enough to make her crazy. How many did you kill this time? The whole henhouse I'll bet. What about me?

she asked him, through clenched teeth. What about me? She threw stones at him. Pest. Vermin. He just stared at her, turned himself round and trotted off. He couldn't care less. He was her rival. If he saw her coming back from one of her snares, dangling a rabbit or a prize woodcock, she felt proud. She'd shake it at him and jeer, imagining jealousy in that yellow eye. Look what I've got. Ya! Look what I've got. That really made her day.

Weather, always weather. By February she was sick with longing for green, walking through a wood that was slant with catkin rain, willing the sap to rise, the shoots to come. Still so empty. It seemed deserted, even by the animals. Where were the deer? Moved elsewhere, that's what, somewhere greener or more plentiful. She envied them their speed, their roaming nature. In her memory they were slight and summery, slipping through shade like a trick of the eye. She walked wider and wider, wearying herself in the search. If she could find them, she told herself, it would be alright. She'd survive if she could find the deer. Along the edges of the wood, the headlands full of skeleton grass, its seed heads frozen, rustling together with the thin memory of the sound of crickets. No droppings anywhere.

Had there ever been a winter as cold as this? There were days of illness, with her head swollen and burning like her feet. Flu maybe. Then two days of snow, with Anne dropping and feverish, and still she walked, partly because she was afraid to lie still in such cold. When finally she saw their tracks, neat slots in a field to the west of the wood, circling as if they'd been playing, trotting up along the fence line and then suddenly over and gone again, ghost deer, she cried with relief. Half mockery, half reward, she couldn't tell which.

When the snow melted and she was well again, Anne went to bed for longer and longer periods. How long does a winter last? For goodness' sake. Maybe when I wake up . . . Night after night, the pain in her hands and feet burning itself through sleep and into her consciousness. She dreamed that she opened her hands and spread the fingers with their fiery joints and stared. So this was it, winter had won. And this pain she felt, this was her withering at last, like the rest of the world. This was how it happened, fingers first, then wrist and elbow, shoulder, neck. She knew she was dying and she looked down at her hands expecting to see them shrunk to sticks, but the flesh on her outspread fingers was taut and inflamed. Something raged like fire or water under her skin. And now it was the terror of something that would burst out from herself, something that only the fragile barrier of her own skin held back. What if it broke? What if her skin couldn't hold? If it split and let it out, this force that burnt and boiled under her surfaces, that she could see straining and stretching. Was that a crease in her hand or the beginning of a tear? And, as she watched, her fingers did burst and out from knuckle and fist and finger end pushed little leaves. Greening all over, in an agony of birth, her hands put forth shoots. Baby leaflets, delicately creased and furled, unfolding in front of her gaze until she was covered. All around her she heard the rustling of herself, a million leaves moving. And birds came and sat in her fingers until her arms ached with the weight of holding them all up so gently.

She woke with her cheeks wet, weeping with relief, to find the wood still locked in its own death and the trees waiting.

She crawled to the doorway in her bag. How far advanced was the morning – eight, nine? She milked in the winter any time. She couldn't have survived without it. Breakfast of

93

something, but not much. Sitting just inside her door with the day's hunting ahead of her, she grumbled at the little birds that necessity had made into risk-takers. Old shyness forgotten in the search for food, they hopped over the end of her sleeping bag, flirting their tails, heads cocked, questioning. What makes you think I've got anything to spare? Go on. Get lost. Still, she shared what breakfast she had with them, shedding crumbs and complaining, and after everything was gone they went on fluttering back and forth, messing on her swaddled feet, bickering. Fox passed, gave Anne a sideways glance. Sodden and morose this morning. Even with his light and glancing tread, mud up to the hocks from the thaw. Anne clicked her tongue and reached behind her and threw him something extra that he took like a thief. No thanks, but recognition.

I won that time, Anne said to him from the warmth of her bag. I won. Then she sat nursing her hands to warm them, and rocked back and forth in her bag and steeled herself against getting up and going.

Rain, that morning, hard rain that made the boles of the trees and the wood of the hut black. Cold raining into your core. No point in hurrying until you saw whether it was going to ease up or not. When she did get up and she'd riddled her stove and got it set and found her cup, she set off. Dirty weather even without the rain. Grey and unrelenting. Heavy air and a grudging light. Why bother, Anne thought, banging her feet as she walked, if you can't do better? The air poking at you with freezing fingers between the trees. She looped the cup on a string round her waist and put her hands under her armpits out of kindness to the cows. Dusky Plum was her favourite. Dusky Plum let down her milk uncomplaining, even for a cold hand. If only I had something to give her,

Anne thought, as she made her way through the wood to the milking gate, taking her hands out every now and then, beating them together, moaning to herself and bellowing before jamming them under opposite arms again.

So she wasn't expecting anything as she came to the edge of the wood. Hey up stranger. Anne stood stock-still with her arms still crossed and her mouth fallen. Hear you a bloody mile away. There was Steve, leaning on his forearms, so his head hung forwards over the gate and his great big shoulders were up by his ears, in a tartan overshirt with a rip by the pocket and the moisture from the air beading his eyebrows, and his long, long lashes, more like a cow than ever, breathing out great plumes of steam. Anne could have cried to see him again. She couldn't tell whether she'd moved forward or stood still. She might have held out a hand, or put one to her open mouth, she didn't know. She didn't know whether or not she had smiled; only that, inside her and bigger, much bigger than herself, something live was burgeoning after all.

Been up a couple of times before but no sign. Thought I'd come and see that bloody hut of yours if you don't mind. Shall I come over?

They walked back single file because the path was too narrow, Anne leading with her mouth still open and her eyes unseeing on the ground. The noise. Why had she been making all that noise? Every now and then she glanced back, not because she thought he wasn't following, talk about hearing a mile away, wheezing and crashing about, but just to see him with her own eyes.

I'm still here. Hmm you haven't lost me hmm yet.

So that was how easily Steve came back into your life. There he just was, as if nothing had happened, which it probably hadn't, Anne couldn't remember, and she sat there shaking her head now and then, at her stupidity and at the miracle of him, sitting in her hut, with his knees up to his chest almost, and of his own accord. Bloody tidy little hut you've made yourself here Anne. Bloody good job. And Anne, feeling that her smile was too wide and that tears, or something, threatened, looked at her flint floor and made much of brushing out a crack with her finger and tried to remember what indifference looked like and how to wear it.

Steve rubbed his hands and wanted to look at everything. The stove was bloody brilliant for instance. But he bet it could get pretty parky in here. A bit bloody parky last week, I should think, and Anne made light of her despair, and she was still here anyway, wasn't she?

How are you keeping anyhow? How's Mother?

Fine, Mother was fine. She'd like to see you Anne. Thought you'd forgotten us.

And Anne couldn't bear her own petulance and looked at the floor ashamed and reddened and couldn't find the words. Abandon them? The thought horrified her, she would never do that. She looked at Steve and still didn't know how to say it.

Sorry? Half mumbled and tentative.

But Steve was only joking. They needed her back at the dump. The place was filling up with stuff that needed sorting out. Then Steve looked round the hut. What are you finding to eat Anne? You're not going bloody hungry are you? Come back for a bite of breakfast Anne, Mother'd like to see you.

She'd said yes without thinking and now, all the time they were walking back to the truck, there was one question going round and round on a loop in Anne's mind, in letters as high as the advertisements in town. Been back, has she been back, Suzie, has she been? What if Suzie was there when they got to the dump? Better not to know. Face it when it comes, she thought. Breakfast and Steve and somewhere to go – you couldn't fight that.

In the truck with the heater full blast and old Buster in his usual position, Anne began to thaw at last. She leant back against the seat and shut her eyes because of the pleasure and because of the pain flaring in her joints. Thawing hurts, when you've got cold enough. Over the bumps her head back, and for a moment the pain got the better of her. How long until spring Steve? As though she couldn't cope, her voice so small it surprised her. And she opened her eyes to see Steve give her one of his gentle looks.

Any minute now Anne. Any bloody minute.

He walked her into the bungalow, his big hands on her shoulders. Look who I've brought to see you Mother.

Like she was a real surprise.

And Mother smiled so you could see the bridge and said, Hey up stranger, long time no see, just like her son.

That was the best day yet, they fussed over her so. They were proud of how she'd done. She'd done really well, Steve said. She'd made a right tidy little place, a stove and a bed, and he clapped Anne on the shoulder. She was a survivor that's what. I tell you what Mother, she could teach some of them new recruits a bloody thing or two. We could have done with her in the Special Forces, and he laughed the old laugh and his tummy shook.

Mother sat by her gas fire and listened to it all and asked Steve questions as if Anne wasn't there, like, How'd she make it Steve? And Steve told her what he'd seen and asked Anne himself, Where'd you get the timber then? Did you cut it yourself or what? Anne told them everything and they nodded their heads and clicked their approval with tongues and teeth and raised their eyebrows at each other in a good way, shaking their heads at her cleverness. She was a right bloody little genius. She was a good little fixer.

After breakfast they made her sit in the other chair next to the fire. Mother sat opposite nodding every now and then. You've done well you have, she said, every time Anne caught her eye. Anne drifted into sleep and they let her. They must have seen the dumb look in her eye, her inability to keep up the pretence of coping. She slept and woke and slept and woke and every now and then Steve would get up and go out, to take deliveries or whatever, and Anne would open a dazed eye to see the great bulk of him tiptoe in again and try to sit without waking her, before she fell back into warmth and unconsciousness once more.

And they let her be like that, she didn't know for how long. They sat in silence and waited for her to surface. Eventually she woke. She looked from one to the other. I'm sorry Steve. Sorry Mother. I'm not used to the heat. She thought she must have dropped off. Maybe she should be getting back. But when she said it she could hardly keep her face from twisting and a stone of dread fell into her chest and lay there heavy.

No bother Anne. No bother at all, Steve said. And, It does you good a good sleep. You need a rest. I know, I've been there, haven't I, Mother? Lived in a ditch for three months, I know what it's like. You sit there. You can go when you're ready, can't she? And Mother nodded, repeating snatches of Steve's conversation in support, nodding and shaking her head as the observation demanded. Good sleep. Ditch. When you're ready. No bother at all.

How about a cuppa? Cup of tea and a biscuit. And then Steve'd make her some sarnies to take back. How about it Mother? Mother nodded, looking at Anne. Sandwiches can be a nice comfort to you, she told Anne. Know you've got something then, don't you?

So they had the tea and Anne tried not to think about the dark of her hut and the damp coming up through the forest floor and the hard cold biting into her. She didn't know if she could do it again. She said nothing, but she looked from Steve to Mother, as she drank. She wanted desperately to please them with her hardihood, but she didn't think she could manage. How could she manage on her own in the cold, after this? She gave a game little smile, but her eyes said, Help me. Help me.

But Steve was going to fix her up. He wasn't having her cold at night. He wasn't having her cold in the day neither, come to that. She wasn't going to be cold and she wasn't going hungry any more. Not if he could help it. They had plenty to spare, didn't they, Mother?

And Mother, who had been following his comments with close attention, picking out the odd word now and then, got herself in a muddle with nodding and shaking. Oh no, she said, catching up with herself and shaking confidently now, not cold. Can't have that, being cold. She'd catch a chill, Steve, and she'd never get shot of it. And Steve stood looking down at Anne, his indoor shirt stretched tight at the button-holes and nodded too. Mother was right. She didn't want to go getting herself poorly.

Did she have a coat? Steve wanted to know.

No, she didn't.

Did she have any proper boots? Steve looked down at her feet.

No again.

Right then, see what we can do. And Anne heard him rummaging in the back room, where she'd never been – the bedroom perhaps. He was talking to himself while he looked. That would be about right. Where were those bloody boots? And other things muttered too low to hear. He came back with his arms full. First a military jacket. SBS regulation hand-out that was. Got you through all weathers. Dug themselves into a ditch in the Forklinds and lived out for three months. Never felt a thing. Warm as bloody toast that was. Put it on and have a see. He held it out to Anne. Anne got shyly out of her chair and Steve put her into the jacket, showing her how to do it right up. Just the job, what d'you reckon, Mother? She looks a right bloody little trooper. It had deep pockets, look, to keep your hands warm, although he had some gloves somewhere that he'd find in a minute. She should give the boots a try. Her feet looked much of a size with his. Pad them out a bit maybe but at least they'd keep out the weather.

She arrived back in time to see the barn owl launch himself on his night shift, his great white wings beating against the dusk. Off down the side of the wood now, she heard him go, beating his bounds, marking out his map of screams. As if she hadn't slept enough already, she crawled straight into her sleeping bag, to eat half of the packet of sarnies in the dark. The other half she hung in a plastic bag on a nail so it dangled inches above her ear. Too many robbers about in this wood. That thieving old fox for one. He wouldn't be above stealing sandwiches no matter how many chickens he'd eaten.

It was easy after that. Steve's coat gave her strength, and his boots. She felt protected wherever she went. She'd survive. Three months in a ditch and he never felt a thing. It was as if he'd suffered for her.

And then the first mild days, out of the blue as it were. Imagine the high of that, of the cold yielding after all. The sky softening and opening out again. The day the air smelt possible for the first time. One or two birds noticed it the same as Anne. Their songs, which through the winter had been hard and chipped, because nothing could be spared, not even song, melting suddenly. From somewhere unseen, liquid rushes of sequential notes bubbling over each other. Spring songs. They stopped Anne in her tracks. Her legs gave way and she sat down hard. Hear that? she said to a robin cocking its head at her from a hazel. She couldn't name the bird, when she found it. It was high up in one of the limes, a black and ordinary-looking silhouette, beak wide against the sky. Nothing special to be given such a job, to sing the spring back for the wood. She watched it quivering up in the top of the tree, with song or with wind, Anne didn't know. Calling to one of its kind somewhere else. Then she shut her eyes to see the trees dressed again. Sound blossoms among the bare twigs. Any minute, she said to the robin, in Steve's words. Any bloody minute.

No matter, after that, if there was a week of frost, which there was, or more iron days of drizzle. Anne had found her rhythm again. Own days and dump days, only this time she no longer felt awkward about going to the dump just for refuge. Steve had given her a bumper pack of plastic lighters. He wasn't having that stove going out on her. Every colour of the rainbow they were and their name was Cricket, like summer. She kept them for special but because they were pretty she unpacked them and stood them in a rainbow row on her best shelf.

Steve helped her all the time. He taught her to walk straight away when she got up in the morning. Don't sit in over the stove. Get going. Get the blood going. Doesn't matter where you go to. And don't press on till you get tired. Just till you feel warm enough to do without the jacket, then come back. So that was what she did, if it was dry, walked until she was warm, because exercise gets your spirits up. You can face the day after that. If she couldn't face the day, she went to the dump. In Steve's jacket and boots she belonged there now. She felt no uncertainty any more. I mean he didn't give Suzie his boots or his jacket, did he?

Whenever she rolled in, pink from the walk, Steve wasn't the least surprised to see her. Hey up. Jacket still doing its stuff? And he'd give her a smile and lumber off. Then Anne would get into what he called a project and she'd work at it for several days at a stretch, mending something, stripping down a dresser once, using Nitromors. The skinhead put his head round the door at her. His name was Carl. He had a red crest of hair now. You want to be careful using that stuff. He nodded at the tin. Lefal that is. Do your head in. He was friendlier now. He wanted to work in theatre. He'd come and tell Anne, when it was cold and he was on a fag break. One day he'd probably go to college. Do design or something. Work in theatre, only he said featre. Then he'd go out again and Anne would watch his skinny cockatoo frame, back to the cranes, hitch his trousers, duck his head so as not to knock the crest and swing up into the cab.

Back to work, painting, switching the old handles over on something that was destined for the wood pile, unscrewing hinges to keep for another project. She kept all the bits and bobs in old ice-cream tubs Mother gave her. Hinges, nails, assorted screws, handles, brackets, you name it. You could start up a DIY shop in there, Steve said. When she'd finished, she always made her way down the path to the bungalow.

Sit by the fire a bit. Warm up before you walk home, and have something hot while you're about it.

One day, working like this, but slowly because it was a real hard one, minus five Steve had told her when she arrived, she had to give it up before she was finished. Her fingers wouldn't work any more and she was missing with the hammer. So she left it and went up to the bungalow. Too cold, Steve, she said, when he opened the door.

That's alright Anne, you go on in.

There was a little girl in spindle-berry colours trundling around the room, her hair up in a fountain on the top of her head, like Leanne's used to be. Steve's little girl. Rosie, she was called, but he just called her Littl'un.

Hello Mother.

Mother was in one of her moods. She jerked her head at Rosie. You won't get no peace and quiet here if that's what you're wanting, she told Anne. Anne said nothing. She sat in her normal chair at the table, opposite Steve. Rosie stood at the end of the table, her chin at tabletop height. She pointed her hand at Anne. What's that Daddy? What's that one?

That's Anne.

What's that?

That's Anne, sweetheart. You going to say hello? Rosie lowered her hand and stared. Is that one Nanne? Pointing again. Yes, I told you. Say hello then.

Mother swivelled her head. It's rude to point. You should tell her Steve. It's rude to point. Didn't your mother tell you?

Let her alone Mother. She's only little.

Rosie lost interest in Anne and went back to her game. She was playing with a porcelain pig off Mother's mantelpiece, trotting it about on the end of the table and muttering to herself under her breath.

You mind that, Mother called at her. That's valuable that is. Steve was leaning on his forearms, watching. She's alright,

Mother. She's careful, aren't you, Littl'un? Then, to Anne, she's very forward for her age. Very forward, isn't she, Mother? Mother grunted and looked away again. Gets it from her mother, Steve said. She doesn't get it from us. I was never great at school, was I, Mother?

It's choosing wives you were no good at. Great lummock.

There was no getting round Mother. She was out of sorts, you could see that a mile off.

Anne was sorry for Steve. She'd never seen Mother this bad.

'Lo Nanne. Rosie looked at Anne looking at Steve.

Is it two Nans, Daddy, is it two?

That made Steve laugh. No, sweetheart. One's enough. That's your nan. This is Anne. Rosie's direct and uncomprehending stare. Go on. You can say Anne, can't you?

Rosie went back to the pig without committing herself.

Steve went out to take a delivery. Mother wasn't talking. She sat by the fire with her mouth turned down. Mind she doesn't break that ornament, she told Anne again, when Steve was gone.

Anne made a newspaper home for the pig and the pig went to bed. Rosie put her finger to her lips and whispered, Mustn't wake him up. Anne nodded.

MORNING TIME, Rosie put the whole of her body into shouting, back arched, tummy forward. Mother and Anne both jumped. Bedtime again immediately. This time Rosie was cross. No more juice, she told pig. That's my last warning. Steve came back in. MORNING TIME.

Oi! Steve said. Keep the noise down. You've got a big mouth for a little girl.

Rosie looked at Anne. Morning time I said.

Pig came out and trotted across the table. Anne told Rosie, You better give him some breakfast. He's a hungry pig.

What can he have for breakfast?

What does he want? Anne asked.

Rosie bent to the pig. What do you want for your breakfast? Apple juice and a cakey.

Steve sat watching. Seen Anne playing with Littl'un, Mother? Tell you what, she's got a right bloody touch with kids. You made a friend there, Anne, I reckon.

Mother looked round, still with her mardy face on. She has got a touch. She's a good girl that's what, not like that piece of work.

How did Steve stay so even-tempered?

Fancy a bit of dinner?

Rosie said, I'm busy.

I'll make you a sarnie and you can have it while you're playing, how's that – a Dad's special?

Hoops, Dad. I want hoops. Without looking up from her game.

Say please.

Steve got up and made four plates of spaghetti hoops. Pig trod in the tomato sauce. Mother started up again in earnest. Rosie cried. Anne took the pig and wiped it carefully on her own jumper and put it to bed. It's alright Mother. It's not broken.

Rosie whispered to Anne through her tears. Morning time. You're that good with kids, you got family, Anne?

Anne startled and looked down. Steve hadn't asked about her background for a long time. Steve and Mother were both looking at her now, as if they'd seen her in a new light. She hid the redness rising in her face in pig's wants. No she didn't. She didn't have no family. She said it without looking up. Not getting involved with that lot again, she thought. Not having Suzie brought into it again, not now anyway.

Mother and Steve looked at each other. Steve's mate Barry arrived and the bungalow got crowded. Stopping for tea Barry?

Anne thought she'd better go. What are you doing, Rosie wanted to know. Are you putting your coat on now?

Barry sat down in Anne's chair. Smarty's sold half his land for development. Had Steve heard?

You're joking.

I am not.

Silence, while the men looked at each other across the table. Steve rubbed his hand over his head. Bang goes our shooting then.

That's it, Barry said. We've got till the end of March apparently.

Well, bloody hell. Bloody Smarty. Who'd have thought it.

He got a good price for it apparently.

Steve sat rubbing his chin. I'll bloody bet he did.

Even Mother was interested now. The place is changing, she told Steve. The place is changing.

Thought I'd see if you fancied some lamping, Barry said.

Why not, Steve nodded at him. Why not. Sandra will be up to collect the Littl'un after work, sevenish sound OK? He looked across at Anne. You fancy coming along Anne? We'll get you some rabbits for the pot.

Rabbits, that was plural. Her face said yes without her opening her mouth. Steve laughed. That's set then.

Thank you, Steve. Thanks, Barry. Anne folded her arms across her chest and held tight, to keep the pleasure in. Steve gave her his alarm clock, so she'd know when to be at the gate. We'll meet you at quarter past, how's that?

Can I come with you? Rosie was looking up at Anne. Can I come at your house, can I?

Anne looked at Steve.

Not today, sweetheart.

Dad, can I come at big Nanne's house? Then without waiting for a reply she told Anne, her finger raised in admonishment, Wait a minute 'fore I put my boots on.

Anne didn't know what to say.

Steve got up from the table. That's alright Anne, you get going. He picked Rosie up. What do you think Mummy will say if I tell her you've gone off to the woods with Anne for the night? You can come with me some other time, alright?

As Anne went out, Mother was crowing with laughter in her chair, her top teeth flying forwards every time she opened her mouth. You see what that piece of work says about you taking her down the woods. I'd like to see her face when she hears.

Anne banged the door behind her.

Give it a rest Mother, Steve said from behind the closed door.

They were already there when she got to the gate, leaning on their arms, black bulks in the dark. Barry was smoking. She could see the red end of his cigarette moving around like a firefly. Hey up, in a soft voice. Had they been waiting long? No, love, only a couple of minutes. Very cold. Frost underfoot already and a black star-pricked sky. No moon, which helped. Across the field to the truck where Buster was whining. Anne in the cramped back seat and Barry driving. Get the old heater going, Steve said, rubbing his big hands. Bloody brass monkeys. They bumped about the field, the headlights catching the glint of eyes.

Something over there Barry, and Barry turned the truck and the lamp picked out the silly little rabbits, hopping and nibbling. Bang. Bang. And their back legs kicked and windmilled and they lay still. Round and round the fields. To Anne, getting out of the truck to pick up, it was a feast. It was nights of eating, rabbit stew with turnips from the fields. It was luxury for no effort. She couldn't believe it. She was practically singing.

Sling the rabbits into the back of the truck and off again, the lamp sending its shaft across the inky spaces. Once, as it swung round, she saw him – reddish, sharpish. He had his head up, ears pricked, and he was beautiful, but it was only a second. He flashed round as soon as seen, his big tail swinging wide. He knew what they were about. He was no fool, the fox. And bang.

Steve was an expert shot. She didn't think he ever missed and only this time did she let out a cry, because, although she knew, she hoped so much that it wasn't her fox.

Steve and Barry looked round. What's up Anne? It's alright Anne, just a bloody fox.

But she couldn't explain, so she got out and went to pick him up.

Holding the body still warm in her hands and the live stink of him, his lips curled back to show his teeth. She stood with her back to the truck. She didn't turn round immediately. She just stood with her shoulders bent over and the fox lying across her open hands. She couldn't explain how hard he'd worked at staying alive that winter. How he'd used his wits to the last drop, how he was clever and fast and kept her company through the desperate days, the wood's great predators, herself and him. She couldn't explain how she'd envied him, how he was better at survival than she was.

He was just a bloody fox after all.

So she slung him over, among the rabbits and got back into the truck.

Alright Anne? Steve looked concerned.

OK Steve.

And she stared out into the blackness and crossed her fingers, for nothing. Goodbye fox, she said in her head, over and over, and the tears made hot tracks, which turned cold under her chin. Goodbye fox.

MAIDEN II

You make your house and you roof it, and you warm it with a stove and it keeps you safe and it keeps you dry, but the place where you live is not your house. Where you really live is inside the framework of your life. That's what keeps you going, stops you going round the bend. You have to build yourself a routine, as well as a house. You have to have a structure to your days. Anne had own days and dump days. And she fitted her own days, with their duties, round the dump, which was always the centre. She had milking time and hunting time, gardening and fixing up and collecting, and she shifted them round as need be, ordering herself within them in a pattern that only she and the season understood. It pleased her, like a kaleidoscope.

A dump day, and Anne went down to the sheds, to fossick for projects. There was a chest of drawers, drunk-looking, on three legs, quite a nice cabinet, with the bottoms of the drawers gone, could be made good quite easy. Lately, with spring arrived, she'd hoick the piece onto the hard standing, in the sun, if sun there was, because it was nicer to work outside. Also that way if she was there, Rosie'd see her and come down. They had nice chats and Rosie would pick out the nails with her little fiddly fingers, or find the handles in the boxes. And often, when Anne was finished, she'd make something for Rosie, like a little house for a teddy or for the spider they'd found in the cupboard that Anne was working on that day. Until Rosie's demands got too much and then Anne would stop. He wants a car big Nanne. That's not a car. He wants a car what drives.

But there was no sun today and no Rosie, so Anne fixed herself up in the workshop, where the music was on all day, and the men came to have a cuppa at teatime. She'd been going a while, but she couldn't concentrate. She'd got like the animals now, one ear pricked all the time and an extra sense for when things weren't right. No Steve. Anne came out of the shed and stood in the middle of the dump. Sid, the old man, was taking deliveries but he never spoke to Anne so she wasn't asking him. Carl was far away, under his crest, in the crane, fag clenched between his teeth, dreaming of drama school while the grabber swung out and back. Light drizzle, otherwise quiet. The pylon, obviously, and a few starlings hopping about, doing everything together, flicking themselves into the sky all at once, like a handful of pepper thrown. Perhaps he was in the bungalow.

Up the garden path. She had meant to fix that gnome. Fall into the birdbath one of these days if it wasn't careful. She could have sworn it was getting worse. Knock on the door and open it like normal, and Steve met her in the little passage. All wrong, Anne could see that at once. He just stared at her for a moment, like he didn't recognise her, and his hair looked worse than hers and his clothes were as if he'd slept in them, or not slept in them more like. Really at a loss he was.

What's up Steve?

They looked at each other in silence and Steve's face did something unusual, a sort of twitch. Mother's gone. Passed away. He stood back to let Anne into the old room. No fire on. Empty. Just plates and cups about anywhere. Steve sat down again, in his chair, still looking at Anne, as if she could have fixed it for him, put it all back together again, like she did the furniture. His eyes were soft with tears.

First Anne sat down opposite him and just looked her sympathy. Sorry Steve. It was almost a whisper. Then, later, she said, She was old, wasn't she? And, When did she die? And Steve told her. It had been very sudden. Sunday night she was taken bad and they had the doctor out but she wasn't going to hospital. You know what Mother was, Steve said. And Anne nodded. She knew. Died Tuesday.

Then Anne made them both tea and toast. She did the washing up and tidied and made one of Mother's breakfasts.

You're a good girl Anne. Mother always said that.

They ate the breakfast. Between mouthfuls Steve looked nervously at Mother's chair. You wouldn't think moaning was company, would you?

Anne nodded. She knew. You can take your time Steve. After a while she said in a small voice that rose at the end, as though it was a question and not a statement, I could help.

Course you could Anne, without taking his eyes off Mother's chair. You do. You do help.

Anne spent the day in the bungalow, being company and making him food and sorting things. Sometimes they just sat looking at each other in silence. Sometimes Steve would have a cry. Then Anne would make another cup of tea and Steve would blow his nose with a noise like a trumpet and there would be quiet again.

Funeral's the day after tomorrow. Fancy coming along? Mother would like it.

It was hard not to look pleased, in a way. Of course she would come. Of course she would. She would be honoured, Steve. Then she looked, for the first time, at the empty chair and the porcelain animals on the mantelpiece, at pig, who had survived, and the cold fire, and then she cried too. Steve put his big hand over hers on the table and stroked her wrist with his thumb and they sat in tears and in silence again.

Barry came by, popped his head round the door. He thought he'd come and see if there was anything Steve wanted. I see you're being well looked after. He nodded at Anne.

Oh yes, Steve said, Anne's done great. She's done a good job alright.

Coming out then? Barry wanted to know. Come on, mate, come and have a quick one. It'll do you good. You haven't been out of here for three days. You're starting to smell. You'll grow mould if you sit here much longer. Won't he, Anne? You coming and all? – that was to Anne.

But Anne didn't want to go to the pub. So she looked down. No thanks Barry. You take Steve. I'll be off home now.

The funeral service was something else. The little coffin – you never saw what was inside it – so shiny and brass-handled, going into the ground. The ordinary ground, with worms and millipedes and little snails and things. How was Mother lying? Anne wondered. And what was she wearing – her nightie, or her day clothes? The lilac bonnet? Her old stick legs and her feet, that were so swollen by the gas fire, sticking out naked at the end and her scratty hair lying on the shiny floor of the coffin no doubt, spread out thin and soft underground. And Anne had a pain in her chest wanting to protect Mother from the cold of it, the grit of it. She couldn't bear the lonely bed in the dark, the little body. She swept away the leaf mould outside her hut when she got back and looked at the ground. Then she lay with her cheek on the earth and thought about Mother alone under there and Steve alone on his bed in the bungalow and it seemed incomprehensible to her.

Then there were the words that you used for burying a person. Words of a richness, a grandeur that struck Anne with awe. She wished she could remember more. Resurrection and ashes. But she had the taste of all those consonants, the thickness, the mouthful of it, for days afterwards. She moved slowly about the wood as though she were a cupful that risked spilling. She felt a new respect. Would they all get that when they died, the walkers, the joggers, the children down the paths on bicycles? The weight of those words and the demands of the grave, so heavy to Anne – they were worn marvellously light, by the people that she stared at with new eyes, in the woodland rides or sitting, sipping coffee, at the café.

There had been quite a few at the funeral. People she didn't know, aunts and uncles of Steve's, family, Barry, Rosie and her mum Sandra. And even so, Steve had excused himself to take her home. Going to run Anne back, Barry. Can you see to everything? He'd said an awkward goodbye to Sandra and then kissed her on the cheek. Thanks for coming, love. And Rosie had started up.

Don't bother Daddy now, sweetheart. That was what Sandra had said. Daddy's tired. You can see him another day. You come home with me in Uncle Barry's car.

They'd driven back towards the wood but when they came abreast of the track Steve said, Come for a cuppa Anne? I don't fancy being on my own just yet.

So they'd gone back to the bungalow and sat quiet and Steve had put on the fire again and it was really nice.

Thanks for coming Anne. You're a good girl.

No bother Steve, Anne said. I liked it.

We gave her a good send-off anyway. And Anne nodded

and they sat quiet again. Later Steve rubbed his hands over his face until his eyebrows tangled and said, I've got to get my life together Anne. I've got to get sorted.

And later still, Anne looked out and saw the dark fallen and stirred herself reluctantly to go and Steve looked up at her with pleading eyes and said, Fancy a night in a bed Anne?

So she slept in Steve's bed, which smelt of Steve, so that she didn't sleep after all but lay there in the miraculous dark, lying in the dip his body had made and looking at the nothing he must look at every night and listening to him snoring softly in Mother's chair next door.

The next morning Barry looked in on his way to work. You're here early, he said to Anne when he saw her and he gave Steve a look like, I told you. Seven o'clock then, he said to Steve. Go on, you've got nothing to lose. I'll be there and all.

Anne thought this time she'd go too. Because Steve needed her and she was looking after him now. She smiled at Barry, waiting for him to say, Coming along and all then, Anne? But Barry looked away and said, Righto, in a shifty sort of voice and pulled the door to behind him.

She worked all day, not sure whether to say anything to Steve about the pub. She went up, when Carl and Sid went off, and made Steve something to eat and tidied up. No sign of Barry yet and there wasn't anything else to do.

Pulling the door to behind her, undecided, Anne stood for a moment on the path outside the bungalow. In the scrubby lilacs along the chain-link fence a thrush flooded the road with its song and now, and again now, a car hissed past too quick to listen. Softening sky, the pylon and the crane, distant relations, angular and hard-edged against the summer evening. A single, crossing crow, going home. Something was uneasy-making. Anne didn't know what. But the air was sweet after the fustiness of the bungalow and gulping at it as if it was water, she thought maybe Steve didn't want to go to the pub again. Maybe he'd rather take a walk, check the snares, he enjoyed that. They could walk the fields this side of the wood, with the birds making their settling noises and the light sinking and the air freshening with night and that would be better than a pub. Walking raises the spirits, Steve had told her that himself, and she hesitated, half turned to go inside again.

But she was shy. It was different when Steve asked her. She'd never suggested anything to him before. And what if he said no?

Down the path, instead, past the containers, their mouths open to the evening. Heading for the line of sheds. Feeling muddled. Work. Work took your mind off things and then she'd be near if Steve needed her, if he wanted her to go to the pub after all, for instance. And that must be Barry's car pulling up now. Anne's heart beat fast and she busied herself with her tools. She heard Barry go up the path and knock for Steve. She heard them both come out of the bungalow, talking, watched them, out of the corner of her eye, down the path towards Steve's truck, with Buster rolling anxious and uneven behind them. She saw Barry hold his keys up and wave Steve towards his car. He had his head turned over his shoulder. He was saying, Come on, mate, we'll take mine. That way you can have a few without worrying. Do you good, Anne heard, and then, I'm picking Suzie up at hers first. Reckon I'm in with a chance there. Anne shocked at Suzie's name. So that was it. Barry was fine. She didn't care about Barry. She let out a quiet breath. She didn't have a problem with Suzie and Barry, not at all.

Slam, slam, and the engine starting up and the car headed out of the gates. Buster came limping and whining into the shed. Anne didn't mind. No way was she going to the pub with Suzie. That was a near miss.

She got a custard cream for Buster and one for herself and she went back to work on the chest of drawers. Buster lay down on her coat and watched her out of his only eye and Anne sang a couple of songs and when she'd run out of songs she kept up a commentary on what she was doing. Give this a bit of a sand-down, she told Buster, in Steve's language. Give the old legs a couple of screws for stability. So he would feel comforted at being left behind. You and me Buster. You and me.

Then, when she'd about done, she wiped her tools and put them all in their proper places and swept the shed of shavings. No hurry. Not that she was waiting for Steve to come back, just that she liked being there, that's all, and if a job's worth doing . . . as Steve would say. She watched the early dark settle over the dump, the swallows going on feeding, scooping low across the yard, long into the bats' first shift. Anne sat on her haunches in the workshop, one hand on old Buster's head, and smelt the smells of dust and grease and metal, that were special to the shed, as they sharpened with the cool of the coming night.

She'd borrow a mug and milk one of the cows on the way home. Bring it back tomorrow. And as she readied herself to go, Barry's car swept back into the yard and Steve got out. Buster heaved himself to his feet, tail wagging, and left Anne in the dark workshop. She could see Steve's sadness in the way he stood, his shoulders forward and down, his tummy out. He bent to shut the passenger door. Anne could see Barry, inside the car, lean over and give Steve a wave. Cheers then. Cheers,

Barry. Lights on, engine firing and a burst of music with it and Anne watched the tail lights out of the dump and turn left for town.

Steve walked back up the path to the bungalow. Anne stood at the door of the shed and watched him, her mind fizzing like the pylon.

The dark space between them seemed to her something stretched to its limit. A piece of elastic ready to snap back, its tension impossible.

Surely he would turn round?

Steve fumbled his key at the door, dipping his shoulders to go in. He was so sad.

You don't have to be alone Steve.

For a long time Anne stood on the path. Several times she raised her hand at the door to knock. Then she didn't.

There was always tomorrow.

The walk home was long for some reason. When she got to the cows' field she sat with her forehead against Dusky Plum's flank. Smooth and warm and smelling of pats. It should have been a comfort.

And later, in the hut she sat in front of the stove and held her left hand in her right and stroked her wrist with her thumb and remembered, while something horrible was rising up in her mind and would not be squashed back down.

How to describe the fluttery feeling that Anne had all the time now. The mixture of dawdling and rushing that went on in her mind and her body, of daze and panic. Sitting by the pond smelling herself. Did she smell bad? Washing a lot and then looking at herself in the stillness of her pool. What did she look like? It was as if she'd never thought about it before. Was a round flat face good or bad? And sometimes it would seem to her that her strings of hair were a mockery and even the animals looked better than that and she'd slap her palm down through the surface of the water to break its mirror and watch her face wobble back to flat again.

What did she want – did she even know?

Worst at night of course. In the fusty dark of the hut, with the door open now and the night glimmering at her, through the doorway, with its dark shining and its promises and all its mysteries wheedling at her outside. What if? Anne let it say to her. What if?

Steve, in his own dark, elsewhere, breathing upwards into that little room. Anne held her left hand in her right and stroked her wrist with her thumb and added one to one and made infinity. Once or twice she turned over on her side and tried to force herself to sleep. Then she sat up and said out loud, For goodness' sake, and, What are you thinking of?

Night after night like this. Lying on her back, listening to the owls about the wood. Nightingale season too. That didn't help. Such a dullish bird, invisible brown, hiding in the blackthorn thickets, waiting till night-time mostly, not me – I'm nothing. Take no notice.

But what a pouring out when no one's listening. Like taking a stopper out of a tipped bottle and all that sweetness and variety, singing out the unspeakable into the thorn's long spurs, in the double dark, in the thicket, in the night.

I'm a good girl, Anne said to herself, after a session by the pool, swinging at last, late, down the track to the dump. Steve likes me, doesn't he? Cow parsley high in the hedges and the elder slopping its white saucers at her. All the birds were run off their feet raising families. Ski jump ski jump ski jump, a great tit was saying over and over. Anne picked a grass stalk, unthinking, as she passed. I know he likes me. He came to find me in the winter, didn't he? He gave me his coat. He took me back after the funeral. He wanted me to stay the night, didn't he? And then Anne gave her hands a squeeze and caught her breath. She looked upwards at a swept sky. She could stay the night again, one night.

Rosie likes me. I'm company, aren't I?

Then with half an eye open, squinting out sideways as though she didn't dare, Anne peeped at a future. Shut it again quick. No. That was ridiculous, that was. So why, as she reached the gate to the road, did she make an odd little unnecessary jump?

Barry was there when she got to the dump. Was she imagining it, or was Barry less friendly than he used to be? He was taking Steve out again, he rolled down the window to tell her, as he left. Anne nodded, Good. But he'd said it almost like it was a warning. Then, as if he regretted his unkindness, he said, We've got to get him set up again, you and I, haven't we? He needs a wife, that's what. Then he gave her a sort of look and a cheery wave as though he hadn't meant anything after all, and drove away.

That was the trouble with things these days. Most of the time you were swinging around like something on the end of the crane. Up, down, side to side. You didn't know where you were most of the time. Carl, the skinhead, came in, fag in the side of his mouth like a nest-building bird. He gave her one of his creased-up smiles. Don't break your heart over it. Life's too short, whoever he is. Anne stared. His trousers were right down over the bum he didn't have, so you could see his underpants. He hitched at them with one hand, scaled-up kettle in the other, waving it to and fro at Anne. Cuppa?

Steve came in, looking distracted, gave Anne a big smile. Hey up, sleepyhead. Thought you'd never get here.

See.

He really smiles when he sees me. He must like me.

But when they had their tea Steve slipped into distraction again. They'd never said much before, Anne told herself, but then Steve had never been so absent. He'd been quiet but he'd been there. Now he was always somewhere else. She watched him with troubled eyes.

When he'd gone Anne went to swill out the cups and Carl paused in the doorway. You know Barry's trying to get him and the wife together. For the kid. You know. Just in case you thought – only he said fought, and then nothing more.

Anne turned half round and couldn't help a tightness in her voice.

Oh yeah. I know.

In her head – *What?*

When Carl had gone back to the crane, the whole of her shouting inside – *What?*

She sat in the workshop among the ruins and toyed with her tools while her mind, like Steve's, was elsewhere. She tried to make it into a happy story. It needn't change anything, need it? But, then, what if it did? And it would. And why couldn't it be – no point going on. Why, Steve? You like me, don't you? And then Mother's voice would come to her, Anne's a good girl, not like that piece of work.

Piece of work, she said out loud, without thinking, her eyes out of focus, and Sid, who was passing the open door clicked his tongue and sneered away at the sky. Tramp.

Until Mother died, Anne had never seen Steve look tidy.

Before Carl had said anything she'd told herself that Steve had tidied himself for the funeral, because there were quite a few people, after all, and she could understand wanting to be tidy for that. But then it got to be all the time. Of course there were still normal days, when he wore his checked workshirt and Barry wasn't around too much, when it was quiet and just like it had always been. Steve pottering about and the deliveries coming and going, tea break in the shed, just the four of them, and eggs and frankfurters in the bungalow, Rosie from time to time. Lovely days, when she thought about them afterwards. But at the time they were spoilt for Anne by the worry. If he looked at his watch in the afternoon, her stomach would lurch. She watched him constantly out of the corner of her eye. She dreaded him going back up the path too early. She couldn't relax. Was he going inside to change? Was he going out again?

He'd come out with his hair brushed down wet and his checked work shirt changed for a polo neck and a jacket. He looked so uncomfortable. There was something in his walk down to the truck that mixed apology with stupid uncertainty. It was stupid, Anne thought. He looked stupid. Like he was trying to please all the time. She couldn't bear the humiliation of it for him. He even walked differently.

Often he'd give her a game little smile before getting into the truck. Bye Annie, he'd say. Be good. See you tomorrow then. Or sometimes he said, Off on the razzle dazzle, but he didn't look like it. He looked like he was going for an interview more like. And Anne would watch him go and give him a little wave maybe and once, because everyone else had gone home and the dump was empty, she shouted after him, as the truck turned into the road, You can be yourself, you know. Yourself is fine. And tears ran into the corners of her mouth as he went through the gear changes oblivious. Shouting again, at the vanishing truck, You've left Buster behind again, in case you've forgotten, Steve.

Then Sandra came. Anne was in the workshop, edgy like every day now, watching. It was the nearest she'd seen Steve to moving quick. He was out of the driver's door and round to her side, helping her out, hoisting Rosie up into a side-carry, one hand on Sandra's back all the time. Alright, love? Up the path to the bungalow. Anne couldn't get any work done, watching for her to come out again.

She did come out, several times over the days and weeks, but always she went back in. Up and down the path, making a swishing noise when she moved. You couldn't help thinking of things rubbing together when she walked and her clothes were fluffy and stretched over roundness. Sandra was shiny. Shiny and soft and round. Soft bottom and soft boobs like the girls in the newspapers and a soft face with round shiny eyes. Blonde hair like a kind of candyfloss, in a nice cut. She was a nice person, that's what everyone said. The men liked her anyway. Sid didn't seem to like anyone but he liked Sandra. Carl the skinhead liked her. Sandra brought them extra biscuits when she'd been shopping, never came past without a joke or a comment. Go blind if you sit there all day looking at them things, she'd say putting the biscuits down on some busting mound or other. Look at the size of them, ought to carry a government health warning, and she'd stick her own boobs forward for them. When she turned round and walked out, Sid's eyes looked like they might pop out into his tea.

Sandra was kind. She brought Anne an extra Thermos of tea down to the workshop and a plate of sandwiches she'd made herself. To keep her going. That way it saves you having to come up to the bungalow to get them, Sandra said, smiling her shiny smile. There we go, sweetheart, chicken and mayo and a choccy bar. How's that? She did it every day. Cheese and chutney, ham and pickle, smoked turkey.

Once or twice Anne took the plate back up the path when she'd finished and Sandra came to the door. Bless! Sandra's roundnesses filled the whole doorway. Like she was a cork. What a gorgeous day, she said, breathing in so she expanded even more. Lucky you to be going back to the wood, not stuck inside like us housewives. Anne couldn't help craning to see round her. Was Steve in there? she asked herself. Was he inside too?

You didn't need to bother with the dirties, I would have picked them up for you on my way back. Got nothing else to do, have I? Another swamping smile and Sandra took the plate and Thermos off Anne on the doorstep. Mind how you go then. See you tomorrow.

Anne turned miserably away past the cockeyed gnomes. She couldn't tell because she hadn't been in but she thought it looked different.

She sat alone in the workshop eating the piles of sandwiches Sandra made for her, throwing crumbs for the bickering starlings and telling herself it was a sunny day. It would be different in the winter, wouldn't it? What did Anne want with being inside on a day like this anyway? But all the same, she watched the window of the bungalow in case Steve's bulk should cross it. When it did, she imagined how it was for the three of them, sitting round the old table, eating, minding Rosie's manners. She thought of Steve's forearms and his shoulders, how he chomped his food, head forward, absorbed, and she watched for him coming out again after dinner time. Then, the minute the door opened, she was busy.

Sometimes Steve came and sat with her in the workshop, if Sandra was out and nothing much was happening. In the old days they would have sat in the bungalow. He looked at Anne as if he was going to say something and then thought better of it, or just couldn't find the words. He looked bothered. So they sat in silence, and Steve massaged his head till his hair stood up, and ran the palms of his hands over his face, till his eyebrows tangled. Or he looked at the bungalow and then back at Anne, who was sometimes working, sometimes just sitting near him. She's got a kind heart, Sandra, he said. Anne looked at him and nodded. She's a very kind-hearted person, Steve said again. He sounded puzzled.

Sometimes Steve just stopped at the workshop, stood in the doorway to watch Anne working. How's it going? Or, Hey up, softly. We don't see so much of you these days Anne, and Anne looked down at her hands, cradling her tools, confused. She didn't know what to say except a mumbled, No.

Was it her fault? She couldn't get into the bungalow with Sandra on the doorstep, could she? She couldn't just barge in. But she didn't want to say anything about Sandra to Steve. Are you sorted now, Steve? she wanted to ask him. Is your life together? Because, really, she thought it had been better before.

Piece of work.

The other person Anne didn't see any more was Rosie. Once or twice, early on, Rosie appeared in the workshop, like she used to before Sandra came and never went. Anne had looked up to see her trotting down the path, with her fountain of hair wobbling on top of her head. 'Lo, big Nanne. Can I do that, can I? What are you doing that for? Anne had been mending a wardrobe. One of the doors was off its hinges. They'd got happily started together. Rosie made a bed for the screws to keep them safe. You say when you need them and I'll give them at you. You don't take them Nanne. Anne had a mouthful of screws to be going on with. Alright Rosie, out of the corner of her mouth so as not to drop any. I won't.

The screws' bed was an old rag. Rosie pushed them under with their tops showing, tucked them up. They had names. John and Barry and Ryan and Tod. Naughty boys. Every now and then one of them came out and got smacked with the hammer. I told you.

Sandra came down the path, swish swish swish. Come on, Rosie, leave Anne be. The last thing she wants is you muddling around when she needs to get on. And a smile of course.

No, Anne said much too quickly, I like it. We always played, before, didn't we, Rosie? She's no bother.

Rosie banged John or Tod. We always played, she said, squatting on the workshop floor, copying Anne's intonation.

Sandra sank down to Rosie's level. She put her hand over the hammer that Rosie was still clutching. Put that down, love. That's not for you. You're going to give yourself a nasty bang with that. There was something in her voice that was not so kind, Anne thought.

Rosie set up the beginnings of a wail. I'm doing it hammering, Mum. Nanne said I can do it. I'm doing it.

Rosie, come on now. Leave Anne in peace. What about helping me with the shopping? Sandra made a pretend sad face. I'll be all on my own.

Rosie didn't look at her mother. She was rearranging the screws' bedcover. You're a big girl now, she told Sandra, still without looking. You won't cry and I'll be back soon when I finished hammering with Nanne.

Mummy buy you some sweeties if you come now.

Rosie stood up, kicking the screws as she went. Sandra took her hand, in case she changed her mind probably. They walked out into the sunshine.

Anne picked up her hammer.

John and Ryan and Tod were left scattered anyhow about the floor.

Pride would have helped, if she'd had any. Through the late spring and into summer, which opened its flowers and offered its luxuriance with Anne almost unnoticing. Pride would have stopped her going to the dump day after day, rubbing her own nose in it, to be smacked in the face again. Pride would have stopped her from sitting dumb through tea, with hurt eyes, or through dinner time, mechanically chewing at the sickening sandwiches and watching the bungalow. It would have stopped her from hearing, which she did, when Sandra said, Get a bit of sun for a change. As though the sun hadn't shone unbroken for a week at least. Viva España. And then, Well – we thought, why not?

These days Sandra talked to the men as though Anne was invisible.

To be so big and so unnoticed. So Anne sat in the shed a witness, just a dumb witness, even to her own life.

What's here for us? Sandra asked Carl and Sid. You get a lot more for your money out there, believe me. It was a no-brainer. Rosie would be bilingual, she said. Steve could do building, sort them out. They'd have an olive press, maybe do export or something.

Anne went straight up on the gangplank after that. The

dread of what Sandra meant had hold of her. *What's here?* she repeated, looking down the long lines between the containers, at the geometry of the pylon and the crane, this precious little world. *What's here for us?*

The dump's here, that's what.

I'll have it, Anne said. I'll have it if you don't want it. Steve was happy with it before. It was enough for him and Mother.

They all joked about it, as though it meant nothing to them, the possible loss of their jobs, the change. That was the effect Sandra had. Every time she came down with the biscuits or filled up the tea caddy, she'd put one hand on her hip, hold the other one stupidly above her head. *O lay.* And Sid's eyes popped and so did his trousers.

At tea, while Anne sat like a rabbit in the headlights, they ribbed Steve. You'll be getting your bikini out then, Steve, giving it a bit of the old castanets. That was Barry. And Sid just licked his lips and sniggered and looked at Sandra again. Steve said, slowly like always, that he wasn't much for heat himself, but the shooting was good. Shoot anywhere out there. Then he paused for a while. Then he looked at Anne, just in time to see her run over again, eyes wide, immobile against the onrush of disaster.

They might as well give it a go. Sold Sandra's place in town and got a good price for it. Another pause. Give the Littl'un something better than she's got here.

Summer holidays and the wood blossomed with people. Anne sat dazed in the café and watched them as they walked slowly here and there, in family groups to the picnic tables. Have a sit-down, they said to each other, blowing at the heat. It's further than you think. And banging their car doors, nut brown with health, the ramblers stepped out at a brisker pace armed with their maps and cutters, conscientiously keeping the footpaths open. She saw them elsewhere in the wood, pushing purposefully through what summer had grown over, snipping back.

Anne put her thumb over one of the cuts after they'd gone, rubbed the weeping sap. Does it hurt? she asked the hazel's green coins.

But they are nothing, these cuts.

We grow differently, the trees shrug their leaves in the breeze, however you cut us. We think nothing of you, you nibblers, strippers, choppers. We are good at retrenching. A fistful of stems for every trunk lost – coppice; another for every limb – pollard. We produce epicormics and suckers. We grow more. We last longer. We are adaptable in form.

It must be easy being a tree, Anne said, and she rested her head against the bark of the next. She walked up the rides, to take the edge off her own pain, through long lozenges of green light. Tell me how to survive.

We sit on our hands mainly. But Anne couldn't hear. We are above and below. We hold you in these quiet rides, where the brambles loop over and the clematis hangs down from the canopy in ropes, and the ferns hold up their fronds in fans, like a hand of cards. We balance you, while you don't think of us. So you don't need to worry. Just know, when you walk down here, that you walk on our interlaced hands.

But trees were no comfort this time.

The last few days before Steve was leaving, and Anne was in free fall. You can't shut your eyes when the ground's coming at you. You can't sleep, much, or tell sleep from waking, whichever it is. She stared at the eye of her pool, as unblinking as her own, by day and by night. Got out of bed dizzy and went and sat by it, knees to chest, hoping to be soothed. But it didn't work. She walked vertiginous. Any minute now you'll smash.

Summer. So the sun got up every day, laced the clearing with shade and died in pink and gold across the woodland rides, whether Anne noticed or not. Trees made minute adjustments to the angle of their leaves, deepened their green to summer's spinach. Pairs of birds turned into flocks. Swallows came and dipped in her pool and she never saw them. Early morning now, for instance, and the sun angled unnoticed again across the water and the randy cuckoo called. Anne was blind like every day. Deaf, so she didn't hear, as she would normally have done, the blackbird scold in alarm at approaching footfall. Sitting so motionless that a shrew ran finicky over her foot thinking it just another of the pool stones.

So Steve was almost standing on her before Anne heard him and looked up into the old face.

Surprise.

Anne stopped falling and the wind, as it passed her where she hung in mid-air, roared in her ears, and far away she heard his voice which made her think of moss.

You were miles away there, girl. He was in his old check shirt, carrying a square hamper. Brought you something so you don't forget us.

Seeing him, real, after so much time in her head. It was too much to adjust to. Illogical hopes flared and died. She hadn't managed anything, not even a grunt of recognition, hadn't changed her position, didn't think to stand, to hold out a hand, couldn't understand what he was saying. She just sat and stared while her mind caught up with her. *So you don't forget us.* Anne went back to falling once more. She couldn't return his smile. As if.

Is it that bad? he asked her, putting the hamper down beside her. Aye? It was hard for him to sit on the ground but he eased himself down knees bent, arms looped over his knees. Is it?

And at last Anne's mouth unstuck itself and she managed, Sorry, and, I thought, before tailing off into silence.

If she'd thought about it, as she did afterwards, the last thing she would have wanted was to be surly with him. He didn't have to explain anything. He didn't have to apologise. He was just trying to get his life together, and he had to go. I have to do what's best for the family like, he said. Trying to coax her round. She was behaving like Mother. It's a good life out there and Sandra was never much for the dump. You know that.

Anne knew. They looked at the water in silence. She would have said, by way of explanation, I'm down there Steve. I'm under all that water, on the bottom, looking up at a world that keeps shaking out of focus. But she didn't think of it. So instead she struggled up to the surface for his sake. Ten or so pretty little birds swung in acrobatics round the twigs above the pool, their tails out like teaspoons. Bum barrels, Steve called them. Syrup syrup syrup. Steve was happy not saying much. They heard the blackbird somewhere and the cuckoo still in the distance.

Tell you what – Steve looked up through the leaves – it's right peaceful here. There are worse places. Then he paused and looked again. There are worse places. And Anne nodded. You'll be alright girl.

At the pool there was a constant flutter of little birds hopping and paddling. A wood pigeon dropped into the clearing, tummy out like Steve, sipped and messed at the water's edge and breasted up again to cock and preen in one of the ashes. Have him for supper, Steve said, aye? Pity I didn't bring my gun. And Anne smiled. They'd have him for shooting in the wood, she said.

He'd shoot them and all. Shoot the lot of them.

Families of birds everywhere flying and singing.

Come on then. Have a look inside. Steve got up on his haunches to pick up the hamper and put it on Anne's lap. Facing her, one knee on the ground, his arm resting over the other, and their eyes were on a level. Anne either made no attempt, or was unable, to hide what hers contained, and Steve never looked away. Like that for a long time, threaded to each other on a look.

How old are you Anne?

So it was Anne who looked down. I was fifteen once, she said in confusion.

I thought so. He said it very quietly, still looking at her. He might have been talking to himself. Then, after a while, Go on then. Louder, Have a look. Don't open it. Just look through the grille there.

Anne found herself looking into the fury of a black bead eye. A cockerel, his comb and his dignity crushed under a wicker lid. And two hens, Steve added.

White Sussex, nothing fancy, but they were good layers, and in time she'd have a flock, some for eggs and some for meat.

Happy now?

Anne couldn't find the words.

Keep you going in the winter anyway, Steve said. Only eat the old ones, not the new layers. Unless you've got too many. It's always best to carry a surplus of layers though, in case of mishap.

Only they'd better get a shuffle on, if they were going to get a run made for them. She couldn't keep them in the open. Bloody old fox would get them.

He had a day spare.

If something like that happened you had to fix everything in your mind, for later. Exactly how the precious day went. How they tramped to and fro, from the truck to the hut, carrying the materials for the run. You had to remember Steve with the big roll of chicken wire, balanced on his shoulder because he was so strong, swaying ahead, wheezing, his trousers low slung. How he used a big steel post rammer, with handles either side, thumping it down in a rhythm, not a mallet like she had. How the hair grew so thick and soft on his forearms, which you could see when you were working close. How they sat with their legs out in the pool at dinner time, halfway through. You had to remember how Steve's shoulders sloped relaxed, and his ball tummy, which was hard with muscle not soft, and the beads of sweat tracking down his face. His neck, where his shirt was open, slicked. While the sun's finger that reached down into the clearing all day, pointed out, You have so many hours left, you have so many hours less. Till at last, sloping almost to lying in the woodland rides, it said, Time's up, and Steve swinging the door to the run on its newly fixed hinges, said, That's a bloody good job I reckon. Go on then Anne. Let them out. And the chickens were half tipped, half shaken, discomfited, mardy as Mother, to cluck up and down the run. Anne and Steve leant on their tools to watch. The chickens ran up and back, stiff-legged, hysterical. You couldn't not laugh.

They'll sort themselves soon enough, Steve said. The hens talked to each other, turning over the leaves, making little noises of excitement when they found something edible or with legs.

Well, time to go I reckon. Softly.

She never said a word. Just looked at him. Staring eyes she must have had. She couldn't manage. She wouldn't cope without him, would she? She couldn't make it if he went. What about the winter? She had no words, only the one syllable of his name. So she never opened her mouth.

Steve.

She never said anything at all.

It wasn't as though she hadn't thought about it, how Steve would say goodbye, only that life was so much more matter-of-fact than how you planned it. She never said the things she'd thought, and nor did he. She never made him change his mind.

Just once, gruffly, Come here, and she had to reconstruct it later, it was gone so quick, the once and only time she felt her face in the fuzz of his neck, smelt his thick Steve smell.

He had held her away from him. You'll be alright girl. You're a survivor you are. Then looking at her face, he had shaken his head slowly.

And Anne had nodded at him through a world cockeyed and swimming. She wasn't stopping him.

Look after yourself, mind.

And Barry was going to keep an eye. Tell Barry if you need anything girl, and stay here so when I come back visiting I know where to find you. He looked serious. Alright? Come and wave us off if you feel like it. Have a cuppa and see Rosie. She'd like to say goodbye. Three days' time, alright?

Nod. And hold onto yourself with a stone in your throat till he was actually gone, just the black bulk of him giving a last wave at the hedge by the track. Listen for the truck cough and start off back, before turning to the empty wood.

She went over and over it, after, taking apart all the words that he'd said, shredding them of all meaning, spent and dry, like matchsticks on the floor of her hut. Three more days till they actually went. She told herself that his arms were strong and holding, although she couldn't really remember.

Crying day and night, in time with the rain, because it rained that night and both the following days. Fat summer rain, sounding through the leaves and on the roof of the hut. Drop drop drop and the birds singing through water, like bubbles. Anne lay, and listened to Steve and Mother and Rosie, croodling to each other in their pen, and tried not to count the dawn and the dusk and the hoot-filled night. Dawn again. She must have dozed because she was woken by Steve crowing into the falling wet. The whole wood running with water. So no one would have expected her to go and say a formal goodbye, although she would like to have seen Rosie. No one would have expected her to walk across ground that sucked like a sponge, with her hair plastered over her face and her ragbag clothes clinging. No one expected her to lie in a ditch and watch the gates of the dump for hours, until the truck came crawling under its snail-shell of luggage and turned away for the coast at last.

And no one, looking back, would have expected to see Anne, standing upright now in the ditch. Black, sodden, looking after the vanishing truck.

Still standing, a long time after, with the road empty except for the rain. The water streaming off her.

Just the cut stump, with its memories of luxuriance, leaking sap at a sodden sky.

*

Ache now. And up the track, feet clodded. Cold. Rain-blinded. Up to the wood.

Dumb.

Stark.

Stood in the hut. Dust, drips. Stripped. Sodden.

Naked.

Took Steve's coat off its hook and wrapped the arms around her neck and got into bed and lay on it empty. Face in the collar.

The cloth in the dark. So thin. So flat. So nothing. Just a coat after all.

Even the smell of him gone.

CHORUS OF TREES

Nothing remains. We accept that. Standing and watching the flying sky, leaving behind the bad summer, the cold spring, the muggy winter. Now, summer slips over the horizon and goes elsewhere, and autumn takes the wood with a rocking wind.

The colours are irrelevant. They are for others. They mean nothing to the trees, the reds and golds. They are just the memory of burning days.

Letting the lovely leaves slip through cold fingers. Twigs too stiff to stop them; not cut out for holding. Sift them, sift them. All that stored sunlight. Hoping to shed them on your own roots at least. Keep them in some form or other. On a still day is best, just falling your own leaves on your own feet.

More often a breeze or a snatching wind, this time of year, whirling and squandering. Clatter the blind branches. Watch the trees make light of the wind, literally, flash and flicker in the stripped stands. Dangerous, you can see that. It's a flashing sky in between. A glare and the sun like a mad eye.

See us toss the wind about, like a ball, between us, till it twists one without warning.

Crack and snap, and that's years work gone. And the wind, damage done, barrelling away down the rides.

We are barely abreast of it. Sap-sunk. Waiting.

Everything suffers. Vixen shifting about the wood,

balancing her hunger to see where she feels it least. Carry it high, in the head is best, rage in her eye.

Survival is a question of cork, if you are a tree. Conservation and reduction, and the efficiency of cork, replicating itself across twig ends, sealing off the leaves, loved and cast off, blocking decay, damage, retrenching against what can't be prevented or reversed. The scars seen and unseen. So many. So much to survive.

Most things have no cure. This is a fallow season. Look inwards down the rings, through the thickening wood that keeps the secrets of other times circled and safe.

A living record.

Here is Anne, for instance, moving slowly through the winter, with Steve gone. Smoke rising out of her chimney thin and grey like the ghost of a sapling. This ring has her breaking a hole in the edge of her pool, with the clean end of her hoe, filling a pan for boiling. Looking up with an animal eye at a pigeon above her, sitting sunk in its feathers. She watches it and a single feather, shaken loose when the pigeon puffed itself up for warmth, rocks through the still air like a boat, as if it were nothing precious. No one notices, except Anne.

On the floor of the wood, the small technology of down, unremarked among a mush of leaves. That's nature for you.

Let it go, the branches clatter. Let it go. The trees stand in the cold and face inwards, towards memory. And the balsams that someone planted once dream the richness of a sticky fragrance given to the breeze, and the ashes dream their complicated quivers of leaves, and in the cherry stands, they dream of being in a condition to waste blossom on the ground. Fragility and scent, blowing about their heads. Let it go. Let it go.

BOLLING I

Autumn, winter. Waiting. Spring, summer, autumn again.

More autumns. Slow, mud-clagged to mid-calf sometimes, legs feathered with fallen leaves, stumbling about the jobs of survival. Because Anne was a survivor, Steve had said so. Forage, repair, cultivate. Sometimes a disabling pang that brought you to your knees, which could have been the pain of spring, after so long, or could have been Steve. He was taking a long time. If he was coming, that is.

Dry and wet, waiting. Sudden blossom and fall and long cauterising winters.

Then not waiting. One day, for no particular reason, waiting no longer. Just the wood's slow revolution. Cut and sprung again, chopped or fallen, then push and bud and leaf. Up again and onward. Anne forgot her anchoring hope and let herself be rolled too. You could feel the ground turning underneath your feet, if you stood still long enough. You could tell you were moving because the skies raced backwards. Sometimes the clouds left the birds standing. Mist, lifting to bone in winter, or flecked mackerel. Swept skies, after a night of storm. Grey and a glimmer of gold towards evening, or just the fog that seeped out of your brain in the morning and never left till you closed it in again at night. The plough swinging about the sky in the dark. And the wind.

I'm counting on you, Anne still said to herself, although she knew she'd given up – was it long ago, or was it just the other day? For a while, on the wood pile there was a heap of notched sticks but she'd stopped notching and she'd burnt the pile, so she had no idea how long. She'd seen the dump under new management, a dirty-looking man with a ponytail and a missing front tooth; not going to ask him if she could help. It wouldn't be the same. She'd forgotten Barry, who was no good anyway. She'd watched Carl, skinny cockatoo, take his life plan down the road to the town, where she'd lost him. Sid too, but separately, had gone to the town, taken his nicotine smile to the girls who were made of flesh, not newsprint, where Anne hoped he had finally burst.

Over time, Anne changed. You do change with exposure. The skin coarsens and grows dark. She lost her soft moon face. Her fat limbs hung loose and sinewed. Her fingers became jointed and knobbled like roots. Hard as wood she was now. Much of the time, when it was mild enough and she wasn't collecting, or fixing her hut, or down at the café, she sat against the pollard ash because there was something familiar to her about its apologetic slump, the centuries of mutilation it had survived. She looked at its leaves, so fresh in spring, its delicate, arrow points. She'd been vain of her hair once. Now she held its thin strands, roped in her hands. You've got pretty leaves, she murmured. How come you get such pretty leaves? In her mind and when she talked to it in her thoughts, the pollard was always female. She sat on its feet, fitted her head between the boils and bumps on its trunk, suffered the bristle of its epicormic growth. What are you doing, ash tree? her fingers asked its mossy bulges.

Nothing any more. Just sitting it out.

And, Me neither, she would answer. Sitting it out. Me too.

*

At some point, along with her body, Anne lost time.

January, February, March. Wednesday. One week, Friday, August, Octember. A fortnight o'clock. Breakfast, six, seven, tea, morning, noon, nine-time. It is important to Anne that she doesn't forget. She doesn't know why. She rolls the different words round her mouth while she does whatever she does, to remind herself and so as not to lose everything. She doesn't like orienteering her way through life without a map but she doesn't have much choice. She holds on to before and after. With a flash of recognition and usually once only, she can do dark and sap-sunk winter and waking spring and the lazy idyll of summer. Sometimes she finds a word like Easter or Christmas in her mouth, for no reason and at probably inappropriate times. Valentines, she says to herself while skinning a rabbit. Mothering Sunday. She has to keep her wits about her. You couldn't find your way around the simplest life without time. Dawn, dusk. Night and Pancake Day.

Look at her now though, now she's learnt a stillness of sorts, and acceptance. She has a rabbit-skin waistcoat that she wears under Steve's jacket when it's cold, belted over an assortment of ill-shaped items. Patchwork lady. Ragbag. But she's strong. She moves differently, with a slow and rolling gait, lifting her feet clear of sensed obstructions, or mud. Her hands, like Steve's, have their own intelligence. She is quiet, steady. She knows the creatures about her, their tastes, their habits. She lies watching her hens, for instance, listening to them talking to each other. Chickens make a lot of different noises. She puts her face close to the netting and she talks back. She has no idea what she is saying.

Look at her tools, propped inside the door, tidy, alive with constant use. The matt satin shaft of her hoe, the clean prongs of her fork. And the dip of her bed, or her floor, by the door, or the stove, where passage has shaped it; the tarry inside of the hut, warm and Anne smelling.

Outside, Anne raises her head, tells the weather, the season, the time. She smells rain and coming frost, fog and drought. She hears the fox on mossy paws in the dusk. She sees the woodcock that thinks itself invisible on the woodland floor.

If she could give herself up finally to the roll of the years, to the round and round and round. If she could live self-sufficient, in a circle.

But there is no match for her in the wood. Nothing looks back at her and says, I am yours. We fit, you and me. Her blood is full of different urges, and she is driven by her blood. Monthly, she is reminded of her thwarted function. Coping with the disaster of it, a week's humiliation, the rags, the wretchedness. And who invented a woman's body? For goodness' sake. What was that about?

She can't get away from it. She can only be human. So she must go on, down the line of her life, and now, if she is rudderless in terms of time, she compensates with place. Her place, which is the wood. Not just its geography, she knows that well by now – the web of interconnecting paths and rides, the private tangles of the unwalked parts, the café, the car park, the visitor centre and picnic glades, the surrounding fields and their hedgerows or fences – but her place in the context of the wood and the onion layers of its world. She's a survivor. She watches and she tries to understand.

She holds the fresh kill in her hands, weighing its loss; how is it, she thinks, that it weighs heavier with life gone than it did before? Wondering about herself, her doggedness in the matter of survival.

She looks at her kill, just the bulk of the bird, flopped

anyhow, wings up over its head like a woman's dress, heavy with death. Will she too be heavier with the yeast of her life gone?

On a stone by the pool, she lays out the little bags and pipes, the red and blue and buff of heart and stomach and spleen. She isolates each organ and looks at it with reference to herself. Does she contain these lurid colours? Lying on her bed afterwards, she pictures the pouches full of half-digested food, juice and effluent and blood, coiled and colourful inside her. How clever and how complicated, she thinks.

She watches her generations of chicks hatch, wobble on reed legs about the run. Steve after Steve after Steve. She has stopped naming the hens. Mother is an old lady, mardy and flea-bitten. Anne has eaten so many Steves. Done her best to fatten them, then wrung their necks. At first she ran round the pen after them. Mayhem. The whole flock in a flap, impossible to catch. Then she learnt that if you go in when they've roosted you can get them easy. They're quiet on their perches, so long as you don't mess about. If you get the wrong one, you leave it for a bit. You don't want the whole lot going wild on you. She has eaten Rosie.

You can see the life in animals and birds. It is a light in the eye that goes out with the twisting of the neck or with the snap of the spinal cord. There is a period when this is Anne's chief preoccupation, this moment when the light is extinguished, when the bright eye veils itself with death. Then she loses interest. She turns her attention to plants, to the trees that arch above her. Waiting for leaf burst, how do they know? Now! she shouts at an oak one slow spring. Now! Hazel and thorn first, always. She looks at the thickening buds. Where is your life? She peels the bark to the quick wood, rubs her finger in the colourless sap, licks it. If you collected enough sap, would it be green? Is it the sap that is the life? Or something else, some green current deeper inside, that signals rather than courses through the stems and trunks around her, large and small alike? She doesn't know. Nothing tells her. But she doesn't give up. She just tries harder.

Everything in the wood has a meaning, she tells herself. You just have to set yourself to understanding. This is the task she undertakes, the task that will orientate her, even in the absence of time. She decodes everything, the noises the animals make around her, one noise for mating, another for the marking of territories, for fear, or warning. This is pleasing. Every noise the animals make, she decides, is made for a reason. They change their coats, or their feathers, for a reason. They hunt to eat, or to keep in practice for eating, so as not to lose the efficiency of a skill.

The plants, too, oblige more often than not. They put out colours to attract the bee or the female, to entice or to warn – touch me, don't touch; eat me, don't eat. Everything meant something if you looked at it right. But however matter-of-fact Anne has become, however much she assumes, in her role as decoder of the natural world, that scrutiny will make all things offer up their meaning in the end, there are some secrets that the wood still keeps. She has noticed how the bark of the trees changes colour in the spring, according to type. The oaks go pink, the limes and sycamores green, before leaf-burst. This means that the tree is full of sap again, that the leaves are coming. Even so the arrival of the first leaves is always unpredictable. Every year the spring plays grandmother's footsteps with her, despite her vigilance. Twig, twig, bud. Bud, fat bud. Leaf. There is, Anne thinks, a step missing.

The wood is changing, slowly. Anne doesn't know why.

But there is much to learn there, too. Besides trees and scrub and the plants of the woodland floor, the wood is growing signs. Anne reads all the signs dutifully as they spring up on the walking tracks and around the ponds and ditches of the public parts. They, too, she assumes, are part of understanding. They are the only evidence she has of how other human beings view the wood and its plants and creatures.

Ponds are very important habitats, she reads on a board in front of one of the wood's natural basins. *Not only do they support their own aquatic communities of animals and plants but they are also a focus for other woodland wildlife such as deer, bats and birds.* Anne looks at the flies on the surface of the water. She can't get close enough to see the aquatic community because there are rails all the way round. She doesn't know what they are protecting – her, or the silt-choked shallows.

In the evening she looks at her own pond. An important habitat, she thinks.

The pond skater, she repeats out loud, battling with the sign and its meaning, on another occasion; *is a mini marauding predator. It detects vibrations through the water of drowning insects and then without breaking the surface tension skates over the surface to devour the hapless beast.* She can't help it; she says out loud – But it was drowning, it would have died anyway. She is puzzled by this sign. What's the big deal?

Equally puzzling are the signs now at all the intersections of the rides. They are solid and varnished, with red and green lettering cut into them, inside circles or triangles like road signs. *Parking. No parking. Warning horse trail ahead.* Then, within four feet, on the other side, *No horse riding please. Cycle trail*, she reads. *No cycling. Warning cycle trail ahead.* Only occasionally does she see anyone on a horse or a bicycle, but she pictures them conscientiously, and in droves elsewhere in the wood mounting, dismounting, preparing themselves for the sight of rider or cyclist, before mounting once more. What a rigmarole.

The people, she decides, who are in charge of the signs must be the men she has seen from time to time, carrying clipboards and consulting each other among the trees. They have soft white faces like their own intestines. They wear padded clothes and shoes that make them tiptoe. In their pockets there are mobile phones which trill like a separate population of birds and which they answer with an air of the highest purpose. Anne is fascinated by these men. If she has the good luck to stumble on any, she positions herself in the shade and watches them greedily. But they are rare. They come very seldom and she doesn't ever see them in the same place more than once or twice. They talk and they write things down and they punch numbers into their phones and issue instructions to people in other places. Where? Anne wonders.

She comes across a group of them once, on a quiet track, not one of the main rides. One of them is clearly more important than the rest. He is angry about something. Has enough has been done to address the mud issue? The others look anxious and contrite. The mud issue is their fault. They crease their soft and gut-white faces. They consult their clipboards. Well, they hope so. They think this time they have. They glance at each other and nod in mutual reassurance. Yes, this time he will see a big difference.

In her clearing that evening Anne worries about this new obligation. Has she failed in her duty of care, she wonders, to mud or to no mud? She doesn't know which. Some time later, crossing the place of their meeting, she sees young people in khaki clothes, boys, and girls that look like boys, with fresh faces and their hair scraped back. The wood thumps with music from the radio of their parked truck. They are having a good time and addressing the mud issue. For a long time to come they are here, joking each other along, laying down a permeable membrane, dumping stone on top, pounding it down on the breathing roots of the trees, raking grey granite chippings, the same as a road, over all.

She doesn't like the new road. She has lived in the wood long enough to be able to feel the slow suffocation of the trees, to worry about their roots groaning under this new weight. She feels the old feelings of claustrophobia and unhappiness. She spends several whole days just sitting still and breathing. She watches her pool by night and by day. She looks at her house with the ash tree rising out of it. She thinks of her garden, scratched out of the clearing at her back. Are these incursions any different from the road? Is she wrong in what she is doing? If it is just a question of degree, then will she too get there in the end? Because, on the whole, she would like to think she has improved the wood where she lives. It is lighter now where she has coppiced the hazels and field maples. There is grass in the glade where there used to be ferns and sparse nettles. Is this good or bad? Who is to say whether grass is more deserving than ferns? The nettles don't seem to mind either way.

And the animals that she kills, the alien plants that she raises in her garden, the trees that she cuts or crops or burns in her stove – what do all of these make of her arrival in the wood? For several days she doesn't know how to live. She swings between wild extremes. There are times when she feels power coursing through her veins because she can do these things. Live, die. Grow, wither. She is the ruler of her glade, the only one who decides. Look, she blinks on one of her hubris days, her left eye is the sun and her right the moon. Day, night, day, night, she says, blinking them in turn.

After a while Anne forgets the road and carries on in her old way. Once or twice, when she has seen Nigel at the end of a ride, with his lumpy tracksuit and his hair, windbagging on at some walker, she has turned and gone the other way, because she can't face him. But that's not always. And she's been to the café too, not to scavenge, because she is so much more self-sufficient now, but just to sit in the luxury of the chairs, under electric light, taking in the world.

She likes to return to the glade and catch the whiff of herself on the evening air. Everything has a smell of its own. Foxes, rabbits, badgers. Their lairs and burrows are all identifiable, their tracks, their excrement, all tell of themselves. Anne is pleased to have something that marks the glade as her own. It makes her feel she belongs. She remembers, long ago, the night of the dustbin, the chute of rubbish in the rain and the first time her family smelt wrong.

Territory is important, in the world of the wood. Anne knows that. You need to know what is what, and whose. Because there are many people in the wood now, especially in the evenings. There are the walkers, riders, joggers, cyclists, whose arrivals and departures are like a pulse, beating along the tracks and pathways, the veins of the wood, by day. There are people by night, who move differently, in furtive and predatory rushes, singly or in little knots, their eyes round with seeing, their breathing audible. And at any time, there is a man called Ranger, who drives everywhere he can, even where there aren't paths. He has rolled-up sleeves and clean khaki clothes and he leans out of his truck one day, arriving in the clearing for the first time.

Anne hears the engine scream its approach and comes scuttling round from the back. She is terrified. It is as if the wood had been torn. The truck is monstrous here, breathing the smell of diesel and flexing light off its metal sides.

I been looking for you. They told me you were living in the wood. Litter collection you do, isn't it? Regular litter depot you got here, if you ask me. Litter central.

Anne can't find her voice.

He asks questions she doesn't know the answer to.

How long you been here? You got pretty well settled in. He talks out of the side of his mouth and there is a mixture of mockery and officialdom in his voice.

Anne looks sideways and at the ground. She is trying to reel in her mind. She holds one hand backwards in a protective gesture, palm flat and open towards her hut, the pen, the little garden full of vegetables, this world she has made from the wild.

He jerks his thumb in the direction of the hut. Get it down by tomorrow, and get going.

Shaking, she drags odd bits of brash across the scars the truck has left, barricading herself against his return, as if that were possible. She makes a helpless blockade of twigs and rotten wood, listening to the revving engine dim as it finds one of the wood's roads until she's left to the clearing's rustle and her heartbeat. The birds that had fled at Ranger's arrival come back. A grey wagtail hops and dips on a stone in the stream. A chaffinch sings its territory in the middle canopy.

Anne sits at the foot of the pollard twisting her big hands. The corners of her mouth pull down as if they were subject to gravity. What does he mean? She lifts her hand as if to remove a stake from the roof, mouthing his instruction. As if it were possible. She looks at the products of her long labours. What if he pulls up her roots from here? In her stomach she feels sick and dizzy as though she were falling into something black and deep. She sits there a long time, looking straight ahead, her arms neatly by her sides, the hands now flat on the ground, now raised and twisting each other with the joints cracking. Later, she retches once into her lap, a dry noise like the night bark of a fox. Blank. She doesn't trust herself to stand. She thinks of crawling across the glade to her shelter, if this is to be her last night, but stays where she is. She doesn't know why. At some point she must have lost consciousness or slept because she wakes to the fallen dark and the sound of the owls hunting.

From somewhere just above her head, as though it had been perched on one of the branches waiting for her to wake, Ranger's threat settles again in her mind. She is shivering. She tries to look sensibly into the future but she finds there is only now.

When Ranger returns Anne is numb, where he left her. She has a look in her eyes, like a rabbit in the headlights. Alright, Ranger says, leaning his clean elbow out of the truck window. The way he says it indicates that something big is following, some huge and mechanical action as though Anne and her house were to be torn by force from their ground, as though a giant digger were to bite, scoop, rumble off with them in its metal mouth, spit them out, roots up, on some tip or wasteland to die. Anne doesn't move. She waits, staring.

But Ranger says nothing. It is clear even to him that she can't go. It is clear too that he is angry, with himself as well as her, because he is not a heartless man. He hasn't the stomach for the job. He shouts at her, You keep out of the way. He doesn't want the general public getting a fright. Keep your garbage in here and nowhere else, is that clear? He waves his hand round to indicate the bags and bottles that Anne has collected, the careful things she has kept against one day. I don't need bag ladies in my wood. Then he takes his anger out on the truck, throwing it into too tight a turn, making the engine scream. For a kind man he can be pretty unkind. In the sobbing relief of her humiliation and reprieve Anne slumps against the tree, nursing to herself the hands she twisted all night. *Garbage*, she says to herself, *garbage*? And, *my wood*?

She looks up into the branches of the ash, contorted with cut and regrowth, listens to the soothing, seen-it-all-before rustle. He had driven straight over her barricade, mashed it into the ground. We were here before you, she whispers to herself. Whose wood then, and whose garbage?

But Anne creeps about the wood after this, often at night. She begins to resemble the night people in the way she moves and breathes, looking over her shoulder in case she should have strayed too far, fearful of Ranger. She's never been so far at night before and in this new, inverted world she sees among the trees people she used to know. One of her teachers once. That was a surprise.

She sees the cars in the car park. One light means I'm on my own, two for two and you can watch. The car park is busy at night. She is amazed. Once she sees Suzie. On a night off from Barry, she supposes. Suzie's with the Parcel Force man and he is bucking her like a pony. Anne just watches. It isn't the first time Anne has seen Suzie. She was young when she started, before Anne left, even, behind the shed one evening. Anne didn't know the man. You tell anyone and I'll smack you so you won't see or tell anything ever again. Understand?

Every now and again Ranger comes in his truck. At first he just looks at her and drives away. Later he starts to ask questions, just a few at first. You make that with my timber? I could get you just for that. That's viable-habitat timber, that is. He never gets out of the truck. That waterproof, is it? I bet you felt it last week. What do you eat? You want to be careful you don't poison yourself with one of those mushrooms. Don't want to come and find you out stiff. That's about all I need, a dead body in the wood.

In the winter, one day, he brings her some venison. He leans over the seat beside him, throws it at her. Might as well have it. It got hit on the road. Don't want you dying on me.

That was a good day.

The next time Ranger comes, he has a picture with him. He beckons her over. It is a coracle, a kind of boat. She's good with her hands, could she make him one? For the visitor centre. She might as well do something to pay the rent.

Anne takes trouble over it, as an insurance policy. When he comes to take it away, she hands it over with reluctance. It is better than she'd expected. He, too, is impressed.

He is friendlier after that. He brings her things she needs, vegetable seeds, a needle and cotton, food. Sometimes he brings her packets of biscuits. Those are red-letter days. Anne eats the packets at one sitting. She can't help it. She gorges herself and then sits at the foot of the pollard, burping softly in a sugar haze. She remembers custard creams at the dump. Where is Steve now?

Dark falls and Anne tries to settle her unease. Maybe it will be alright?

She watches as the barn owl, that had been perched outside his hole, sweeps sudden on his evening flight, wings too wide for the wood's small spaces, heading out to the grassland and the field ditches, then she goes in. He is late.

In the hut Anne has made reed mats from the rushy grasses that grow down all the rides. They are plaited together in complicated patterns with the seed heads facing out all round the edge like tassels. She made them because the flint floor got so cold in winter. Looking at them by the light of the stove, she thinks they might please Ranger. She carries them out to show him on his next visit.

Those are quite a tidy effort, they are. He'd like her to make some for the shop. They are promoting local and traditional crafts.

Shop?

Nowadays he asks her things he needs to know. How many head of deer does she think there are? She knows there are thirty-six and a doe about to calve. Did she see the take-and-bake boys firing the stolen car – how many and how old? How many were there in the Woodpecker car park last night? He doesn't mind about the spectators, they are just perverts, but if he can get the number plates of the porno stars he can do them for it. That could make it quite embarrassing for some people. Some of them have quite good jobs, I'll bet.

And Anne tells him.

Anne regards these exchanges with Ranger, like she regards the mat- or coracle-making, as a form of rent, paying for her unwanted presence in his wood. She doesn't like doing it. When she tells him these things, she never looks at him. She looks at the ground between them and talks in an automatic voice. If she had been able to meet his gaze, he would have seen that what was in her eyes, when he came back into the clearing to see her off, had never left. Even when he is gone and she is by herself again, Anne is not at ease in the way she used to be. She sits in her hut, plaiting for him, and she feels she will never get free of the threat he represents. Under, over, under, over, under, over and back; turning the grasses, deft and unseeing, she plaits his hold over her into mat after mat.

Sometimes, halfway through, she will stop suddenly and look at nothing and shiver, mesmerised like the rabbits she sees on the road at night. How come the animals haven't noticed the change?

When she is not plaiting, Anne worries. She worries about what is allowed and what is not, about whether she can lay claim to any of the things she used to think of as hers, or whether all of it is his. She is up with her bag, almost at dawn. She collects frantically, against what – she doesn't know. She combs the wood for things that will come in handy, protect her against cold, change, displacement, disaster. Sometimes the things she picks up are useful, sometimes they are not. She has quite a collection of single gloves, of hats, scarves, a trainer, a broken umbrella. Once she found a mustard-coloured jumper, nearly new, that must have slipped from someone's waist as they got into the car. It had been driven over; there were tyre marks right across the front but it was otherwise undamaged. She put it on straight away. She wears as many of the things as she can. That way there is less risk of them being taken from her. Ownership is a cloud in her head that won't go away. She is sure of it only when she is in physical possession.

Anne worries about what might happen if she is not careful, behind her back, when she is asleep, and she worries about food. She worries about the grey-stoned paths that are snaking their way through more and more of the wood, and about the people who belong on them. Who says how a wood should be? – the animals and the trees, or the people who fill it up? At the back of Anne's mind, so she can feel it all the time, lies something huge and frozen; something that is worse than winter, a dark expanse, against which she gathers and stores and preserves. She works demonically in her garden, producing more than she can eat, giving the excess to Ranger when he visits. They look nice, he says, eyeing the carrots, or the beans or the fat, bullet cabbages. Quite fancy some of them. And Anne lumbers over, pulls them up and offers them to him, without looking. Afterwards she worries that she gave him too much, counting how many are left, cursing herself for her stupidity. Clumsy tart. Bitch. Sod.

It doesn't occur to her to curse him.

At night Anne suffers from bad dreams that leave her dizzy and sweating. Sometimes she wakes up with her eyes dry and wide, stretched against a darkness as opaque as her future. Sometimes it is her own cry that wakes her. It is often the same dream. She dreams she has no house. Something has happened to it that she struggles in the dream to remember or to understand. She is making her way through the wood to the clearing, fighting with brambles and undergrowth, wearying herself with clambering over and under fallen timber. She panics that she has taken a wrong turn. She doubles back and tries again. She thinks someone has taken it away, that it has been moved or pulled down. But when suddenly she breaks into the clearing, she remembers. She knows that there is someone else in it; Ranger has taken it over. There are cars parked and it is his house now. He sits big and friendly, with his sleeves rolled up, in her doorway. His little boy plays up and down a grey expanse of grit, where her garden used to be. They wave at her.

Or, she dreams she is sleeping under her barrow, her knees

jammed under her chin, her head locked downwards to fit under the metal rim of what little shelter it offers. The barrow is not in the wood, it is out on the road and her sleep is fraught with the worry of the cars she can hear swerving to avoid her in the dark. She strains her ears for the sound of a bicycle. The bicycle will rescue her, she thinks. She hears the swish of its tyres approaching and with a thumping heart she opens her mouth to call out but, however hard she tries, the muscles in her neck taut and her chest bursting, she is unable to do more than whisper. She wakes braced against impact.

Stumbling out to calm herself, Anne stands swaying in her doorway. There is a young vixen out there, rootling among her possessions. The fox stops, head towards Anne. Anne can see the liquid glint of her eyes, weighing her up, as surprised as she is. Then she's off, loping into the trees, lugging her tail behind her, like a piece of baggage. Anne thinks she can't go on like this. She has become so unsettled. In the morning she stands over Ranger's tyre tracks, the route he has made for himself into her clearing. The ruts are deep and permanent.

BOLLING II

Anne's mum and dad paid rent. She can remember that. The money was kept in a tin on the top shelf in the kitchen and once a month someone from the council came to collect. To make it easier for you, Mrs Tarbot. We know it can be difficult getting out with all these young ones to worry about. But that wasn't the reason, everyone knew. It was to make sure they got their money, that's why they called, standing on the doorstep with their mouths pulled back in a dead sort of smile. My goodness she'd got her hands full and wasn't everyone growing fast. They looked at Anne when they said that. Mrs Tarbot must have done something to deserve all those children and they'd laugh, heh, heh, heh, a dead sort of laugh and all the little Tarbots would just stare and not laugh back. They weren't fooled. Often the tin had been raided for something or other and the money was short. It was humiliating, the whole thing. That was when Anne was young, before her dad got his job at the poultry plant. It was better after that. The money went straight to the council by direct debit.

Direct debit was abracadabra. Direct debit would get rid of Ranger.

It was winter, Anne's worst time, so she was in no hurry to get up. She lay under Steve's coat, in bed, sifting things slowly through her head, things that had been and things as they were and things that needed resolving.

Everyone had worked at the poultry plant. How obvious was that? She couldn't remember whether her dad had looked like a chicken before he started the job, or whether looking like a chicken was something that came after, with exposure. But it was unforgettable, the end of his first week at the plant; the first time he brought back one of those polystyrene trays and the pale mound of its contents, that glistened even after the cling wrap had been removed. The celebration they'd had, a golden dawn that heralded a new era, and that smelt of frying chicken.

It was just as obvious now, so obvious that she sat up in bed, her eyes wide, and smacked her forehead with the flat of her palm. The abattoir. It was what she had always planned after all. She couldn't think how or when she had forgotten. She lay back panting with exertion. How lovely the soft and permanent dusk of her hut seemed then, its thick and ashy air. She rolled her head to take it in. *Her* hut, *her* bed. She was sure of that suddenly and she touched the side of the bed with one hand, *her* stove, *her* food hanging in the smoke that filled the room. *Her* collectibles crowding the shelves, racked like a library along the back wall, at angles of slide and balance. The totems of dummies and teethers beading the stakes, the individual books, bottles, soft toys, sweet wrappers that had caught her eye, baby mittens, socks, bonnets that hung over all the walls, on binder twine, or wire, or plaited sedge.

Anne raised her other arm upright, waved it slowly and in an arc of inclusion, My place, she whispered to herself, not his; and round her arm, as she moved, the dusty darkness swirled and closed, like soup. All day Anne basked in her solution. It was enough just to have had the idea. The execution of it was something for later. So she lay, at ease for the first time in she couldn't tell how long, and let her idea filter through her and absorb.

Afterwards and in the days that followed, Anne tried to think how it would be. It was difficult. She wasn't good at imagining and she had to steel herself against encountering other people, against talking and working with people every day, after so long, against the smallness and business of the world outside. While she adjusted to the idea, she practised. She walked through the wood towards the edge in the direction of the abattoir and she smiled and said, Hello, over and over again, as she went, to nothing, to the jays that flirted their tails at her and screamed across the rides, to the small birds that blinked at her and jinked their heads in the high-up branches, to the fallen leaves underfoot and the winter boles of the trees. Hello. Hello. Hello. I'd like a job.

Every day she went a little further until finally, one day, she found herself on the edge of the wood, facing Smarty's fields and beyond them a new housing estate that was still under construction and that she hadn't seen before. She stared at the half-finished houses with their eye sockets and their gawping mouths, and they stared back. She was horrified. So many and so soon to be finished. Then they would be filled, she supposed, with people and the people would all want jobs and where would they find those? In the abattoir, that's where. Everyone went to the abattoir sooner or later. It looked like there wasn't a minute to lose. She stood a moment and then turned to go back into the wood. She could go tomorrow for instance. But then, You got to, Anne, she said to herself facing round again. You got no choice. It's now or never, and she plunged forward, across the sodden field. Direct debit.

Hello. I'd like a job.

She said it in what she hoped was a casual way, leaning on the fence of the layerage pens and smiling her practised smile. Then, as an afterthought, Why are you not wearing white?

The man stared at her. You're having a laugh, aren't you?

Anne felt the old confusions. Was he friendly or not? She couldn't tell. He was looking at her jumper. She tried a little laugh, in case having a laugh was the right thing to be doing, but he didn't join her and the little laugh strangled itself in her throat. The man rolled his eyes and went back to hauling the partitions of the pens. Anne waited for the answer to her question. After a while she tried again: I'd like a job. Please.

He looked up, irritated, jerked his thumb in the direction of the buildings. Well, fuck off to the office then. No good asking me, is there? He faced her with his hands on his hips. His fore-arms were covered in coloured tattoos. *Sheffield Chapter, Roxy, Hell.* He shook his head. You gotta be having a laugh, you have.

The buildings were shiny and brand new. They had signs on the doors that said, *Gut Room, Offal Room, Packing.* It was nice. Anne walked between them, in her ragbag assortment of clothes, a funny tiptoeing walk, not her usual lope. Where the entrance road forked there was a little signpost, like on a real road, *Fridges to the Right, Office Left* and an arrow. Anne went left. She stopped outside, smoothed down her tyre-marked jersey, readied herself. The office had a high counter made of shiny veneer with a buzzer on it. *Please ring for attention.* Anne rang and waited. No one came. In a room behind, she could hear a radio and people discussing something that was more important than Anne, a grievance that bordered on outrage. After a while a girl emerged from the back, still talking over her shoulder. She had nails like Suzie.

Here goes.

She'd already told her, the girl was saying, to someone Anne couldn't see. She'd already told her, she didn't want anything to do with it and if they couldn't sort themselves out then frankly they could get stuffed.

Hello. I'd like a job.

Afterwards it occurred to Anne that perhaps she hadn't timed it very well, her enquiry. She should have waited for the girl to turn round before she started speaking, but the man in the layerage pens had knocked her confidence. Blurting it out, at someone's back, how stupid was that.

When the girl had turned round Anne tried again, bared her teeth in a brave smile, repeated her request as brightly as she could.

The girl's eyes popped. Louise! she called without taking them off Anne, Louise! Someone here wants a job.

Louise had a bad smell under her nose. That's how it looked to Anne. Anne would need to see *Personnel*. They didn't have many women working there, what did she want exactly? Anne didn't know *Personnel* and she didn't know what kind of jobs there were. She began to feel panicky. It was so much worse than she'd imagined. She didn't know what to ask for, what to say. She cleared her throat and then said nothing at all.

But Louise didn't have much time. It wasn't her day for being kind.

Behind Anne the safety hinge on the office door wheezed and a boy shouldered in with his hands in his pockets. Louise's attention shifted. He had his mouth inside the zip top of his fleece. Come about a job, he said without removing his mouth. Louise picked up some papers from a shelf under the counter. She had a bored sing-song voice and looked neither at Anne, nor at the boy, but between them, at a picture of a poppy meadow on the back wall. There were no vacancies in packing, or evisceration, slaughtering was men only, or fridges. No vacancies in the office and some part-time slots only in the layerage pens. She handed the boy one of the papers and paused, then she passed one over to Anne too, as an afterthought. She might as well have one, shrugging her shoulders, still smelling the bad smell. Fill in the forms and come back next Tuesday for an appointment with *Personnel.*

Outside, the wind smacked Anne in the face, for nothing. Come back on Tuesday? When was Tuesday for goodness' sake? Anne looked at the form in her hand. *Name, Address, DOB. NI number.* It wasn't even written in English. *You are required to provide a doctor's certificate.* The boy hadn't looked at his, just pushed it into a pocket along with his hands, and walked off. She could see him ahead of her, shoulders up, fleece over his nose now against the wind, which, unable to get at his face, was pointing out what thin legs he had. Anne would have liked to ask him what he was going to do. Was he going to try, despite Tuesday, despite the foreign form? But he was too far ahead. Good luck, she thought to him sadly, as she set out behind him at a slower pace.

No one would have been able to tell, had they looked at Anne, as she left, the dead weight of disappointment that she hefted under all those strange and ill-assorted garments, belted in under the ragbag layers, crushing the breath out of her so she had to move even more slowly than usual. Anyone who happened to see her would have thought that she looked almost normal, for a weirdo. You get some strange ones, they might have said to themselves, or, It takes all sorts. They would have looked at her and carried on, into the offal room for instance, or packing, checking their watch to see how long till tea, noting that the rain that was forecast had held off after all.

Anne shuffled down the abattoir's toy roads, back to the entrance. Two hours it had taken her to walk here and that was with hope urging her along. By the layerage pens she stopped for a rest. The man with the tattoos was still working, his brown overalls strained across a back as wide as a bullock's. I didn't get it, she said to him in her head, so I'm definitely not having a laugh now. No way. Then she added, to herself and in passing, it isn't like Christmas, not at all.

By the entrance, turning in as she turned out, Anne saw Suzie. It didn't surprise her. It was a small world, she knew that already. Suzie was pushing a buggy and sucking on a cigarette. She looked grey. Oh Suzie, Suzie. Anne was suddenly excited, flapping her big hands, forgetting. She didn't see that Suzie's eyes were as hard as her nails. She didn't see the past, or Suzie's scrabbling future. She saw belonging. That's all.

That your baby, Suzie? Is it? Is it a boy or a girl? Is it Barry's baby?

Suzie stepped back at first, when Anne approached. She had her mouth open like a fish. Next minute she was leaning right forward over the handles of the buggy, eyes screwed hard at Anne.

Who the fuck of all the crazy cows – is that you, Anne? You mind your own business, yeah. And keep your trap shut. What's it to you whose kids I fucking have?

Suzie had a way of spitting out her consonants as if they were pips. And what do you think you look like? She moved her head from side to side to see if anyone was watching.

Even as it all went wrong, as she saw Suzie's realisation give way to revulsion, Anne couldn't help herself. The words tumbled out of her mouth before she could stop them.

I'll help you Suzie. I'm good at looking after. You still got nice hair Suzie and your nails painted.

Suzie wasn't having any of it. She was disgusted; Anne could see that. Anne stepped back from the buggy, holding her hands together now, her head on one side and down. I'm living in the woods Suzie, she faltered, apologetic. Where you living?

But Suzie didn't want anyone to see that she knew Anne; that was clear too. She banged the buggy round, hissed at Anne, Yeah an you look like it. I don't know you, get it? I got to get a job here see and I'm on a list for a council house so I don't need you coming and spoiling it. You stay away from me from now on. Twat. And she clip-clopped away pushing the baby, which stared at Anne with eyes like marbles, its fat cheeks working at a comforter.

In another life Suzie would have been pleased. Anne would have said, Come in the woods with me, Suzie, bring that baby, and Suzie would have said, Thank you, Anne, I will, and they would have gone home together. Taking it in turns to push the buggy, but Anne pushing most because she was so strong and Suzie wasn't.

On the outside, crawling in the cold along the limits of the abattoir, Anne took out the forms, looked at them and then threw them over the fence into the last of the layerage pens. Some surprised bullocks bucked in panic. She shouted over her shoulder, to no one now, You'll fit right in there, Suzie. It's just right for you, you'll see.

When she'd been walking about an hour, Anne stopped in

a mud-clogged field. Slowly and out loud, she said, Auntie Anne. It was dark when she reached the hut.

No direct debit after all. So Ranger was there to stay. Anne felt his presence like the electric pressure of thunder. Sometimes when she heard him drive into the clearing she would lie down in the dark, wherever she was, on the floor, anywhere, and wait for him to go. Once or twice – the cheek of it – he leant in the doorway, undeterred by her silence, and asked what she was doing on the floor. Were his hurdles ready and he'd fancy some of those veggies this week. So next time he came Anne shouted out, from where she was lying, Not ready yet – in the hope of stopping him coming in. It didn't work. She never looked round but she saw the square of light that the doorway threw on the back wall of the hut eclipsed by his bulk. She wanted to get up off the floor, do some work for a change, that's what she wanted. Or was she ill? Anne didn't answer.

For a while Anne went, every morning, to the old bank by the road, where she lay, whatever the weather, and watched her father go to work. It soothed her to see him, like a long rhythm, and it gave her something to hold on to. Dad, she said to herself, like learning a language, mum, auntie. She was lonely now. Suzie had a baby. A baby was something of your own. No one could say a baby wasn't yours, if you had one.

In the clearing Anne lay on the ground, face on a level with the floor of the pen. Another Steve, cocking it, separate, flexing his wings and flapping chest forward. He took no notice of the mother and her brood. In her hand Anne held an egg. It was amazing an egg was. She held its warmth in, testing it against her cheek absent-mindedly while she watched. What if she hatched it herself? But it wouldn't be the same – it would only be a chicken after all. It was spring. The chaffinches had come back to the wood. Between the trees the tit flocks were turned extrovert. Sky-skating, watch me, watch me. Swank at speed, tumbling in pairs.

Everything was coupling, reproducing, all around her. The birds clattering on top of each other and against gravity in the trees overhead. On the ground animals exploded into activity, foxes, buck rabbits, badgers bungling it in the twilight. Anne sat with her back against the pollard, looking at the slim trunks of the next generations. How many of these are yours? she asked it. Things everywhere pushing into leaf and flower, the oaks' diffident tassels, the showy chestnuts, tarting themselves to the bees. Honeysuckle, old man's beard, clasping the boles of trees, the dog rose's loose and punishing embrace. I love you, everywhere. Only Anne alone and unproductive. She thought about Leanne, about Rosie. How long had she been away? How old was Leanne? Already a little girl by this time, probably. She wouldn't recognise Anne either.

She half thought she'd go home; pay a call like a visitor, polite on the doorstep. Hello, it's Anne – your daughter? – I was passing so I thought I'd pop in. Only Suzie's reaction at the abattoir still haunted her.

Then she did go, but not as a visitor. She went at dusk and stood by the old tree that used to have their swing hung from its lowest branch, a monkey swing that you sat astride and twizzled on. The lights were on. She saw her dad shuffle past the window with a plate of something, his bedtime snack most likely. She saw the old front garden and the little gate. She saw the side of the shed, where she used to see Suzie with her men, and she saw John at it now, the dirty beggar. Pushing his luck with Ally Thompson, she thought it was. She could see him grabbing at things he shouldn't, breathing and wheedling. Then the dark got up proper and there was nothing but the old cheesewire moon, grinning its glinty grin, cutting her.

She sat under the swing tree most of the night, silent, till she was numb. There was no one out there, none of her night-time familiars, except a fox that she didn't know, which came skulking round the bins.

Oi! her father would have shouted if he'd seen. Oi! Get out of it. What d'you think you're doing, fox? Nothing. I'm not doing anything. Well, do nothing somewhere else. The old phrases coming back to Anne. She looked up at her window. Who had her room now? Leanne probably. Another little girl to lean her elbows on the sill and stare and grow as big as the moon too quick. Where have I gone? Anne asked herself under the tree. Where have I gone?

In the morning Next Door's cat came back, knackered. It rubbed itself against and round Anne's legs, tail up, showing its anus. Purring. Gett losst, it said.

Stiff and misshapen, Anne lumped down the hill. A couple of cars honked her, in a hurry. She was cross enough to flap one of her great arms at them, swatting as if she was walking through midges.

She ducked back into the wood, down one of its green throats. Everything looked so fresh and the birds were celebrating. Was it only the trees, and the moon, who were allowed to get young again? All dressed up, as if it was the first time. Anne had nothing new to wear. She stopped after a bit and opened the hazel's little concertina leaves. She spread one over her thumb, a perfect party dress. All the way back to her hut she picked leaves, one hand pulling out the front of her jumper to hold them. When she got back she lay down and threw the leaves up in handfuls so they fluttered over her. Now I'm decked, she said.

Nights spent watching the moon swell. Now it was radiant, heaving itself up the sky, its fullness swathed for modesty, reaching its arms out round its belly.

And then days when she felt really bad. She lay on the bed she'd made herself, and just watched the light move its blade around her room. When it got too bright she spread her fingers out to canopy her face, and wished she had fruit or flowers. Then she'd go to sleep and dream herself a man to match her, or a baby with glass eyes and a comforter. How long? she asked herself for the first time. How long?

Ranger came more often, swerving into the clearing with unnecessary vigour. He stood over her and made a variety of noises with his tongue and the back of his throat. This is not working out, he said, on a number of occasions. This is not working out at all. Anne lay on her back and stared him out.

Mr Stallard was coming down soon. This wood was designated rural infrastructure now. Mr Stallard had a lot of ideas for it, for its enhancement. She wanted to think about that.

Anne had no idea who Mr Stallard was.

One morning, when the sun was warm, she got up because she was hungry. She took the last of the woodland apples from last year, to eat by the pool. Shrivelled things they were and still sour. She laughed. What a face, reflected in the water. Think if she had any sloes to eat. But even eating she did differently now. Before, when she found apples, she never messed around; she would eat the whole thing, crunching it up like a horse, core, stalk and all. Now she nibbled round it, feeling superstitious about the pips. She picked them out with a fingernail, holding them in her palm until she'd finished. Then she swallowed them whole, like her mum used to take tablets.

That way, she thought, at least where she shat, would spring up a grove; blossom in springtime, apples in autumn, all with the flavour and stamp of herself, trees with her rhythm this time. They'd carry the boom of her blood flow under their bark. That was one solution. When she walked the wood that day she thought of the seed cradled, hot and dark, readying itself to be eased out again into the world – when? – and supported on her excreta. She comforted herself with the mystery of it. It was a motherhood of sorts after all. She should be happy-ish with that.

But a grove is slow. When she got tired of imagining its invisible growth, Anne went back to sitting like a boulder by her pool, where she watched her aquatic community and hungered for small things, or else she clumped through the woods. Most of the time, walking or sitting, she watched other things live. So, it was natural, when the boy came, for her to watch him too.

FAUNA

Sitting with her knees to her chin in the ferns that fringed her pool, Anne heard him before she saw him. He was jumping along the brook behind her chanting something as he went, but she didn't look round. Say what you wanna say be what you wanna be Addams Familee. Addams Familee. Nothing in the wood so far had noticed her watching, so she sat still and he jumped, intent on his rhythm, right past her and up to the pool. Out of the shade and into the sun of the clearing. Addams Familee. Anne swallowed. Something she had forgotten pushed up through the mould of her mind, blossomed. A boy. She couldn't stop herself staring. She thought he was nimble, slippery, a trout of a thing. He made the hairs stand up on the back of her neck.

He was squatting at the edge of the pool. He must have seen the water shrimps. She saw his lips move, whispering something to himself. Wicked. And he stirred at the pool with a finger, flicked at the water boatmen. He was a fidget, never still. What's he at? He wouldn't catch anything like that. They were quicker than thoughts, the pond creatures; so quick that sometimes you thought you'd only imagined them, the fat little brown fish or the flatheads. You had to pretend you weren't looking, sit like a stone or they'd be gone. She could teach him. Hop, hop, like a bird now, balance and peer, making noises of encouragement to the shrimps in each new place.

Anne wondered whether to tell him, Oi! Get out of it. He wasn't being that careful. He shouldn't have been there. She didn't want people finding her clearing. But the watching got the better of her. This was rare. She watched his different parts and then she watched him whole. She saw how delight animated his hands into little flicks and flutters. He had nice hands, for instance, live like Suzie's only not precious, not hard, and he took no notice of them. He used them, like she used hers, Anne thought. Little pink nails like shells.

He had a nice head too. Fuzzed gold and bullet-round like one of her cabbages. She saw how the pulse of his concentration beat in his temple, how his pink lizard tongue darted in and out when he did something difficult, how his lashes were like the deer's, when she'd seen them resting in the sun with their fawns. She marvelled at his feet, which flashed with red lights when he jumped from stone to stone. When he took off his shoes to paddle, they were dead without him. She watched the breeze come across the water to ruffle his hair and she watched what the sun did on his head and the flat tops of his knees when he hunkered between them.

Every now and then he seemed to look at her, but he never said anything. He was too busy for that. He did things that he shouldn't have done. It wasn't his pool. He puddled out little harbours at the water's edge. He scooped out handfuls of mud and threw them at the water shrimps. She didn't know why she let him do it.

Later he stood back, took a rock and, raising it behind his head with both hands, hurled it down into the water. He wheeled his arms and made noises of explosion. Take that, suckers. Then he glanced sideways and quick at Anne and bent over the surface of the water again.

Excuse me, what's these things? These wigglers? He was

greedy for the water shrimps. Can you catch them?

But Anne was still trying to understand the sudden violence of the rock-throwing. The new stone on the smooth bottom of her pool lodged itself in her head. She couldn't get her thoughts round it, so she said nothing. Just went on sitting with her knees under her chin.

Are you deaf or something? He straightened up and looked at her. He had his hands on his hips like a man. He made big eyes at her, put his hands either side of his face, the fingers starred, I been told bad things happen to little boys who talk to strange men in the woods. What are you . . . a man or a lady? I need to know.

Anne thought the way he talked wasn't how he looked. His attention made her awkward. Instinctively her eyes slid sideways and away. But she wanted to talk to him. Talking would keep him there longer. She knew that. She swallowed again. She wanted to talk to him so much it was like a stone in her throat. Lady, was all she could manage for the moment. He didn't have to be rude.

He went back to the water shrimps and she went back to watching, drinking him up with a giant thirst.

So, is your beard real or did you get it from a joke shop?

He was turning over the stones, looking for things underneath. Was he talking to her? Anne put a hand to her face. Was her beard real? It wasn't a beard. She had studied it in the surface of the pool. It was a reddish down – just down like you found on the stems of the ferns, not a beard at all.

She found her voice at last.

Don't you go to school?

He didn't think much to school. They only done Chinese New Year and Diwali. What's the point of that? And spellings. They did spellings every Monday.

Anne couldn't remember when Monday was.

It didn't seem to matter. He went back to his stone-throwing and his harbour-making, wading backwards and forwards, till the pond was all swirled up in a mud soup. Anne thought of what to say. She thought, Please don't muddy the water. Please take the rock out of the pool and put it back. She thought, I live here, did you know that? Would you like to see my hut? I have many things. I could catch you some water shrimps. But her tongue was dead in her mouth, bloated like a drowned thing.

Then he sat on the ground to put his shoes on. They woke up and flashed. He could wake anything up, Anne thought. He stood up, flicked back the one long bit of hair he had at the front; then, as she knew he would, he went.

When he'd gone she sat where she was, in front of the pool, and the wood was nothing but a wood. The trees shot up and away from her, like the first time. They were only trees after all. The bats dipped and flicked about her head in silence and all the things that were busy at night went about their business. Above her head, white in the moonlight, the barn owl coughed up his black babies, dropped them at her feet, sad little stillborns of sticks and jawbones, papoosed in fur. Through the leaves and grass around her a shrew fussed and rustled.

Anne had nothing to do except breathe, whether she liked it or not. Did it matter that she'd been found a second time? Would other people come? She thought of the silt he'd stirred up, suspended in the pool, still settling to a changed place. She felt the water bothered round the rock, uncomfortable. She drew no conclusions. But over and over again, like a video recording, she replayed his golden jump into the clearing.

At midday he came back. He was wearing a false moustache so large that it reached his jaw on either side. He was walking very delicately with his head held slightly back so as not to move the glue. He stopped in front of her, put his hand on his hip. Was he laughing at her?

We are ladies.

He said it in a falsetto. Anne just stared. He peeled the moustache off, shaking his head.

You are one fucking geek.

He had bad language then, like Suzie.

What was her name anyway? he wanted to know. Had she sat there all night?

Her name was Anne.

He put the moustache on a stone. Keep an eye on that. He was going to hunt for shrimps. He had brought a jam jar with him, a series of holes punched into its lid. He never asked, he just waded in, and all the silt that had spent the night settling, got up and stirred around again.

Knock, knock . . . he called to her from the middle of the pool. You say, who's there?

Who's there?

Anne. She remembered this now, from before.

Anne who?

Anne ant.

She knew to laugh but she laughed too much. It was embarrassing the noise she made, the size of her pleasure. She was laughing because he'd coupled her with something so very tiny.

What was his name? She tried not to sound greedy. He considered her sidelong. *Peter Parker*. Then he crouched down, his arms up and bent at the elbow, his fingers pointing curiously.

She didn't know how to respond but she absorbed the information gravely, murmured the name over to herself. Peter Parker. Thank you.

Watching him again, only out of the corner of her eye this time, Anne thought that he fitted the wood better than she did. The sun treated his hair the same as it treated the leaves. He was fresh. He was made without awkwardnesses. Nothing missed, nothing skimped, a miracle of exactness. He fitted himself like a glove. Wow, Anne thought, as she forced her gaze away. And already, the little things that she actually disliked about him, tickled and caught in her neck, as though she had swallowed thistledown.

He put his head in through her door uninvited. He made faces and coughed and backed away waving his hand in front of his nose. That is rank, he told her. You want to clean your house. Don't you wash? He could sell her some soap if she wanted. He could get some out of his mum's cupboard. She wouldn't notice. Anne could have it for like fifty pee.

Are you a caveman?

He was chattier this time. She was well weird. Did she live there? He wanted to see everything, her house, her garden. He wanted to know how she cooked her food, where she went to the toilet. Did she get letters, and who looked after her if she got ill – did she go to the Doctor's?

Are you a bag lady?

She hadn't half got some stuff.

Anne wasn't used to conversation. She couldn't always think of the answer to one question before he was on to the next. She was dull, dazzled. It was as if a bee had got stuck inside her head.

They were standing at her back door. He had inspected

everything, admiring, running his small hand over the stockade like a professional. You're like Robinson Crusoe, you are. Don't you get lonely?

He looked at her, perhaps for the first time, perhaps not. Either way, it was the moment she couldn't forget, afterwards. He looked at her right out of himself and his eyes opened through her like a sky. There was a weasel once, had sat up on its hind legs, its white front showing, and hooked its gaze into hers out of its separate world. It was so small, so fiercely itself, though the connection that opened between them seemed to say otherwise. Impossible. She had to look away.

As if to cover Anne's silence, the boy laughed, shook his head at her. He checked in a professional way for overhead wires, obviously she couldn't have a telly. Hadn't she even got any music? She should think about getting a soundbox. He had one. They ran on batteries so they would work in the wood. He was getting a new one soon. He could let her have the old one for like fifty quid. Anne said nothing. OK, thirty. Thirty was fair.

After all, he was so stupid. She didn't have any money, did she? And Anne raised her hands empty. He irritated her.

Ranger arrived. As if things needed complicating. Anne heard the truck pull up on the other side of the clearing, heard the woodpecker sound of his handbrake and the door slam.

There wasn't time to adjust, to think anything out. What did he want? He already had a boy. He didn't need another. She put her hand out to push the boy into the hut, hesitated, turned. Then she thought it would be better if she distracted Ranger with something else. She left Peter Parker and set off across the clearing, calling out as she went, arms wheeling. I can make those hurdles for you by this afternoon, I can. Stall him, that's what. Maybe he hadn't seen. Give her time to work it out. She was moving uncharacteristically fast.

From opposite sides of the clearing the boy and the Ranger watched her in surprise.

Who have we got here? Ranger wanted to know, when Anne got up to him. He jerked his head in the direction of the boy. You never had a visitor before.

Anne stood in front of him, shielding the boy, hoping. Make him mind his own business.

Peter Parker. He's called Peter Parker. You got a boy, haven't you?

Ranger had his hands on his hips. I've got a boy alright. He smiled out of the side of his mouth, nodded. Oh yes. Peter Parker, is it? I got one of them at home.

The boy looked uneasy but Anne didn't notice. She was flooded with relief. She smiled from one to the other. Too good to be true. For a moment she almost liked Ranger.

Well, Peter Parker, does your mum know you're here?

He seemed smaller now, with Ranger asking questions, smaller and keener to please. His mum knew where he was, of course she did. She didn't mind anyway, if he went out. He was allowed down the bomb hole on his bike only his bike had a puncture yesterday so he left it and thought he'd have a little look around and his sister's boyfriend was meant to fix it but he hadn't yet.

Anne caught the note of anxiety in his voice. She made a little helpless gesture with her hands. That was alright, wasn't it? He was safe here. Anne was good at looking after.

But Ranger thought his mum would want him back for his tea. He kept his hands on his hips, his legs slightly apart. Mums worried, that was their job. They even worried about super-heroes. Anne wouldn't know, she wasn't a mother, was she?

And tea – oh obviously he was going to be back for tea. He'd be well back for tea, Peter Parker said.

You'd better hop in the truck, then, or you won't make it, unless you were planning to fly.

But Peter Parker held his small hands up and flicked back his hair. No way. No way was he going anywhere with a stranger. He wasn't daft. He wasn't going in no truck, even a flash one like that. Is that your own? Bet that cost a lot.

Ranger laughed. It most certainly was his truck but Peter Parker could dream on because it was unnickable. It had the latest immobilisers. Or are you a bit young to be nicking cars yet?

Get lost. Peter Parker had his face pressed to his cupped hands against the driver's window. I don't nick anything. How fast does it go? Does it go over all terrains?

You could go over the Atlas Mountains in that, if you knew where the Atlas Mountains were, that is. Now get going if you're not taking a lift. As it happened, Ranger said, he was effectively the woodland policeman, so it was perfectly safe, but it was quite right to refuse. Go on, get running. You don't want to be seen in broad daylight in a shirt like that anyway.

Peter Parker looked down at his shirt, lifted his hands in a gesture of supplication. Milan Baros, my main man. Who do you support then?

Who did he think? Newcastle obviously. Now get lost.

The boy raised a hand, Cheers then, and started running. From the other side of the clearing he called back – Bunch of divers – and then he was off again, trotting between the trees, jumping the ferns, the sun spotting his back.

Ranger turned back to Anne, who hadn't moved. Where did she find him? Scamp. He'd be back for the hurdles in the evening, when he'd had his own tea.

So Anne was left alone among her slow uprights, with the print of their conversation still on the air. Too many horizontals, jagging about – that was how they talked. Something tricky and deft, like a ball bounced to and fro, a silly game of catch and where did that get you? Anne thought, cross because she couldn't do it. Just the breeze now and the little birds that flicked by of their own accord, faster than a throw, more effortless. They sang, coo co co roo ro ro; it's a stranger. That was fast too, how they trilled it out. Faster than you could move your slug tongue, mister. Anne stood and listened to them draw their maps of sound. They sang more in the evening, same as the morning; singing against the dark, as though the dark erased everything that their songs affirmed, their place, their identity, the condition of that part of the wood. That was something to say. That was important. I am chaffinch, robin, mistle thrush. This is my nest. This is my tree. This is me. Now. Watch me watch me. Too bad. Got it. Lost lost lost. Look out! They were unseen, inexplicably varied, the songs, and always upwards, like bubbles through the wood's green water.

So all was more or less as it had been. More or less. She began to feel the tiredness of her night's sleeplessness steal over her. Forget about it, that's what. Put it right out of your head. Start again.

When the Ranger came back for his hurdles, he found her on her back in the hut, snoring.

She didn't forget, of course, but she didn't bother either. Just that it took her mind off Ranger and it was nice, going about the wood as usual, to think that Peter Parker was probably there somewhere, on his bike down the bomb hole with his friends, and that he might turn up again, with a joke for her, or some new fancy, a beard, who knows, the moustache maybe, and irradiate the clearing with his lightness of hair and step – because he could do that, lighten things. The wood felt different to Anne in the days that followed, just because of him.

Not that she looked for him, because she didn't, but she looked out, in case she were to see him, flicking past, fidgeting. His movement was what she liked best about him, after his colouring. She thought a lot about that, about how he moved, how he fitted the wood, hopping and darting unconscious, not lumbering and careful like her.

Tidy up, that's what. Change. Anne took trouble now, because an interest like that gave you something to work for. She felt she had a purpose again. She got her garden in trim. Things were coming up fast now and she kept it right up to the mark, weed-free, mulched, the rows of sturdy little plants pricked out and watered, in case he came. She had conversations with him in her head as she worked. Have a carrot, Peter Parker. Would he be impressed by that? Did you grow it yourself? I certainly did. Have a wild strawberry, a raspberry, a currant. She could give him a picnic, if he ever came back again.

Rankness though, that was something that bothered her. She stood in the doorway smelling the smell that had always so pleased her. Was it a bad thing, a smell? In the end, on a fine day, she took off the top layer of her clothes, pounded them with water mint on one of the stones in her pool and laid them out to dry in the sun. They dried stiff and smelling of leaves and water. In the dark of her hut she changed them for the ones she'd left on, like sloughing a skin. She felt like the trees, new-dressed. Why hadn't she thought of it before? After that she washed her clothes all the time.

She finished Ranger's hurdles, and he fetched them,

grumbling at her and raising his eyebrows – took your time, didn't you? what did you do, grow the trees yourself? – although she'd worked with extra care and they were well made, because of Peter Parker. Three more by next Thursday, he said as he threw them into the back of the truck. Got to justify your existence now. I don't know what Mr Stallard would say if he knew. I'm soft in the head, that's what.

He went round past the veggies and peered over. They're coming on, they are. And, talking of soft in the head, seen that little mate of yours?

Anne started.

Which one?

As though she didn't know.

Spider-Man. He's been a right pest this week. Buzzing round my truck on their bikes every time I pull up. Ranger put on a squeaky voice, opening the door and swinging into the driver's seat. Give us a ride then. Give us a ride, mister. You tell him, if he comes round here again – Ranger had his elbow out of the window now like always, and Anne bent awkwardly to meet his gaze – you tell him I'm the Forest Ranger, not a one-man amusement park.

Anne nodded.

I'll take some eggs if you've got any.

She found the bomb hole by accident. Coming back from digging up some wild gooseberry seedlings at the far end of the wood, she heard shouts in a place where no one used to go and she followed, out of curiosity and because they were children's voices and she thought – maybe – you never knew. The noise was coming from the dell, off the track that led away to the new housing – not the cow field, but two away, on Smarty's old land, where Steve and Barry had taken her rabbit shooting.

The wood was fenced now, on that side, with posts and wire netting, but they'd bent the fencing over to climb in, lifting their bikes probably. When Anne had known it, before, it had been quiet, steep-sided, ash and sycamore saplings, straight-boled down to the bottom. Now the sides were mud tracks, cans and bottles in the bottom among the wood sorrel, sweet wrappers like gaudy blossom at the foot of the trees, caught in the crook of a dock or a nettle.

A puffy boy with orange hair was eating crisps at the top, wiping his fingers on his trousers, spouting crumbs out of a full mouth every time he shouted. Three seconds is the time to beat. Three seconds, you guys.

Four or five others were standing round or pushing bikes back up the hill. Peter Parker was at the top, standing on one leg, scratching his calf, shaking the hair back from his eyes in that way Anne remembered. She sucked her breath in.

Be a tree. Stand still among the other trunks and no one sees you.

They took it in turns, haul up, bomb down, shouting. At the top they pushed around, straddling their bikes, lifting up the front wheels, boasting. Did you see my jump? I did this massive jump. I like flicked it over. They talked over the top of each other. I was heading straight for that tree and I didn't notice. I just had to slam my brakes and turn it. You should try going as fast as I did. That was wicked. But some of them looked scared going down, putting on the brakes, knuckles gripped, eyes round, juddering over the roots. The puffy boy was timing them, on his wristwatch, between mouthfuls. When he'd finished he let the empty packet drift from his fingers without glancing down. Another giant blossom.

Five seconds. Gay.

No way. I was faster than that. Come on, that was fast.

Another boy, halfway up the slope, looked over his shoulder, Yeah, you put your brakes on. You've got to bomb it, man.

Peter Parker's bike was muddiest. He just floated down, standing on the pedals, jumped the bike when he hit the roots. At the bottom he swung it round in a skid to stop, looked up for his time. It was amazing how the sun found him out, even in the shade, lit him up gold.

Woh, two seconds! They clapped right hands with him at head height. Yess. Give me five.

He was the king. He looked like he didn't even care.

Anne found herself drawn to the bomb hole after that. She went often, when she should have been doing other things, not just to admire Peter Parker, but to listen to the foreign country of childhood that he lived in. The jostling for position, the occasional punishments, as if the herd of bucks she saw at different times in the wood had suddenly learnt her language, or she theirs. They fought once, two of them she didn't know, kicking each other first and then rolling in the dirt at the top of the dell, not for long. Then the smaller one limped off, tear-stained and filthy, flicking V-signs, pulling his bike beside him and wiping his eyes on his sleeve. Fucker. Brendan fucking Higham. He went a little way, limping still, and then turned and shouted back through his tears and flicked some more, balled his fist in the crook of his small arm. Fucking mother fucker. She saw him hoick his bike over the fencing and climb over after it. It was hard not to feel sorry. She watched him grow small on the track back to the estate.

Meanwhile, the other boys had gone quiet, gathered round the winner in an anxious knot. Uhoh trouble now. Sniff, look down, scuff the ground, flex their hands on the brakes or lift the front wheel, look up. They moved mostly because they couldn't stand still, Anne noticed, but they weren't conscious of what they did. They looked up, constantly referring to the one boy in the middle while making little unconscious movements with their bodies. From time to time, they spat, small gobs of white froth that held themselves proud of the dirt.

He asked for it.

Loser.

But they didn't sound like they were sure. A little boy leaning forward to get in on it said, Just say it weren't you.

Oh yeah, that was genius, that was. Like they'd believe that, Callum dickbrain.

But the little boy was cocky. He shrugged. It was just an idea.

One day they brought cigarettes. It was the puffy boy who produced them out of the big pockets on the side of his trousers. Who's up for it? Ten pee a fag. One or two of them shook their heads. No way. They didn't call Peter Parker, Peter. They called him Simon. That was confusing at first, although Anne still called him Peter in her head.

Simon, you having one?

Not bothered.

The puffy boy leant forward wheezing, the cigarette held between two fingers.

Peter Parker looked at it. I'm not paying you for it. He flicked out a hand and had the cigarette before the boy had time to withdraw it.

Alright, Simon doesn't have to pay, since he still has the fastest time.

No way. That was no fair.

There might have been another fight, only the cigarettes

were too new. It took solidarity to smoke a cigarette, that much was obvious. And they all had one in the end, sitting on the ground by their bikes, glancing at each other and bragging, quietly, for once, so you could hear the woodland sounds and the occasional horn on the road to the estate, a motorbike, an aeroplane. Then the puffy boy was sick.

That brought them back to themselves. Everyone looked. Someone pushed someone else into it. Rank. They held their noses. Ugh, man. I can see a Dorito.

Where?

Puffy raised his head. I never had no Doritos.

Yes you did. There. That's Doritos. Isn't that Doritos?

They all looked again, leaning on each other's shoulders while the Doritos were pointed out with a stick.

Gross.

Totally. One of them retched loudly in pretence and the boy he was leaning on whipped round. Get lost. Inordinate laughter. Retard. Then they all pretended to be sick on each other. Then they biked again. They went home early.

It must have been that day they saw Anne. Probably she had got careless. She couldn't remember moving but her leg might have cramped and she might have made a sound. She couldn't remember. But she did notice them looking in her direction once. She saw them huddle against her. She saw Peter Parker glance over, heard them talk in low voices, but then they went back to what they were doing. So maybe it hadn't been that day after all. Or maybe they didn't mind being watched. She couldn't tell.

Sometimes they weren't there. Once she sat down, at the top of the dell, and looked over. She picked up a crisp packet and fingered it, shook the few damp crumbs that were left, along with the ants that had found them, into her mouth, and watched the dell be empty. But she didn't linger in case they came and found her sitting there.

Then there were days when she felt uneasy. She saw things, or she thought she did. She heard laughter sometimes and running. Or was she imagining it? She looked round when she was working in the garden. What was that now? A fat pigeon startled from its roost, falling away through the wood. Anyone there? Once when she'd gone down the path to her latrine and was squatting and straining in the undergrowth she heard scuffling, a series of snorts that were not animal. She didn't like to shout out. She didn't want to draw attention to herself. But it was only for a while. It wasn't all the time. So she forgot.

She'd been out collecting early. It must have been midday because the sun was squinting straight down through the canopy and the wood was filling up with dinner-time walkers. She had two bags of rubbish banging against her legs, fullish, and it was getting warm. She heard them as she came along Steve's path – that's what she called it, the path past the milking field. Shouts. Her animal sense pricked her into panic. Freeze, in the spotted sunlight, on the old track with the new sounds all wrong. It must just be kids on the bike path. No one came this far over. There had never been anyone this side before. That's what she tried to think but her heart was banging in her chest and, now she was going again, she had never walked so fast. Rounding the last bend tripping and stumbling in her haste, till she broke into the end of the clearing almost at a run. Her place all laid out before her, the pool that should have been so still, and the hut beyond. They were everywhere, or so it seemed at first, like ants crawling under and over. How many of them, in the pool, kicking up the water, their backs to her, taunting someone beyond. It was a game of catch. A dark boy leaping out onto one of the stones, doing a rude little dance.

Mrs Shit-in-the-Woods. Hands up by his ears, palms open, jiggling. Mrs Shit-in-the-Woods. Catch me, Mrs Shit-in-the-Woods. Throwing himself sideways and twisting away, as a boy with fair hair lunged for him and missed. Peter Parker?

She didn't know she was doing it, although halfway across the clearing she heard her voice, as though it was someone else's, the strange noise that hurt and anger make.

At the door of her hut, she remembered later, the puffy boy, his hair foxy in the sun and flat to his head, and his look of amazement giving way to fear. Then they were running, all of them, though they didn't know which way to go, some of them doubling back to find the path again, past Anne with their eyes wide. Shit man fucking get out of here. She hated their filthy little mouths. Which of them screamed? She couldn't remember but she swung out with her bags full of bottles and cans, caught at least one of them. Whack. Round the side of the head and one on the back as he ran. Their high little screams and one or two laughing from the safety of the path.

She'd frightened them.

Anne was taking in the damage they had done to her garden, the mess of the pool, muddied and the stones dislodged, so she didn't see Ranger, bumping over the ruts in his truck, how he nearly ran two of the boys over. Peter Parker, jumping to the driver's side, banged his small fist on the bonnet.

Jesus fuckinell man you nearly had me.

And Ranger flicking out his arm, to its full extent, grabbed him by the scruff of his neck, but not too hard because he had a boy of his own.

Oi! Don't you go banging your hands on no one's truck, you understand.

There were things turned over and broken in Anne's hut. Where she lived. Where she'd made it nice. Not even Ranger went in her hut when she wasn't there, or she didn't think he did. She was standing inside now, so she never saw how the boys lost their vinegar all of a sudden, with Ranger cross, how four of them slunk off, and the rest stood dumb, while Peter Parker and another, darker boy, stammered and wriggled.

We weren't doing nothing.

It was that mad lady, she tried to kill us.

She was like raging out of control. She was out of order. Peter Parker looked up, gathering momentum with his story, nearly himself again. Don't go down there I'm telling you. She'll have you and all.

But Ranger wasn't having none of it. He'd had just about enough of Peter Parker and his little lot. If you've done nothing, then you've nothing to be afraid of, have you? So get in and we'll go and get this sorted.

And the boys didn't want to go and several of them talked at once. It wasn't my idea. I never. We was just like going along. I never knew. I wouldn't of.

Ranger got out of the truck. He was taller than he looked inside it. He was big and he was all dressed in khaki like he was in the army and his truck had this badge on the side like a coat of arms and it said *Forest Ranger* like he was official. He had his hands on his hips and he was mad.

Silenced.

Right, you and you, in the truck now, pointing at Peter Parker and the dark boy. The rest of you, F off home and don't come back. Get it?

Gone.

But Peter Parker wasn't finished yet. He had a high voice and he talked quick. This is public anyway, he said. This wood. It's public, you can go where you like in this, if it's public. You can't do us for that.

Cocky little so-and-so, aren't you? Ranger looked over his shoulder as he started up the truck. Just because it's public access doesn't mean it's open to every little hooligan that wants to come and make a nuisance of himself. This is triple S I, if you don't mind.

They bumped into the clearing in silence. Anne was looking wild, the bags of rubbish lying where they'd dropped, spilling their contents out of shocked mouths. She didn't say anything as the Ranger pushed the boys ahead of him. She didn't say anything because her mind was running round and round in her head like her chickens unsettled in their pen. When she put her hand up to touch the down on her face, in a gesture of bafflement and loss, her hand was shaking.

There were things in her clearing that didn't belong there. Violence for a start, her own as well as theirs. There were footprints where there shouldn't have been. There were things interrupted, things broken and disturbed. Anne opened her other hand in a gesture towards the pool and the garden, to herself almost, and let it fall.

Everything alright, Anne? Although it obviously wasn't. Ranger still had his hands on the boys' shoulders. Found these two troublemakers making a run for it.

He was looking round as he spoke, taking it all in, the mess and jumble of what they'd left.

You little buggers. He said it almost under his breath, to himself, sucking his breath in through his teeth. You made a right job of it, didn't you?

And Anne held her shaking hand to her face and said, as if to persuade herself of its truth, Been in my hut. They been in my garden, on my plants. They've broke my plants. To think she'd put her garden in order in case Peter Parker came back. She felt a fool as well. And when he had come, he hadn't noticed. Its order had been invisible to him. He knew nothing, and she looked at him for a moment and felt scorn.

Peter Parker didn't like being looked at. It's only plants, he said, his eyes on his feet. You can grow another one. They was only small.

He knew nothing. See. That was a precious month's growth. That was early rain and stored sun that might not come again. That was her food, real food like you got in a house, not wild stuff that you scrabbled and chanced for. *Grow another one.* And where did he think she'd get seeds from? she asked him. That was last year's seed saved and kept dry through the winter. That meant less to eat this summer and less to store for next year. He knew nothing.

Ranger walked round while she spoke, looked at the damage for himself and came back round the side. He was surprisingly angry. What a bloody mess. Don't you lot never think? He looked from one to the other. Hey? They wanted their heads banging together, that's what. Tell you what, he said, if you were mine I'd give you a bloody good hiding. No respect. And an apology was in order. Go on. What you going to say then?

Sorry. Barely audible.

Yih, Peter Parker said, sorry.

And that wasn't all. They had a choice. They could go back

and he'd talk to their parents and let them know they weren't coming down the wood again, right? Or they'd say nothing for now and they could both come back and make themselves useful to Anne, sort out some of this mess.

What about the others, Peter Parker wanted to know, how come they didn't have to do nothing? That was no way fair.

Who told you life was fair, hey? Ranger still looked pretty grim. And who brought that crowd down here anyway? Who was it knew where Anne lived? Are you going to tell me they'd all been down for tea and biscuits?

Busted.

Make your mind up then, what's it to be? Are you coming back to help, or am I talking to Mum and Dad?

Come back.

Yih, come back and help, again barely audible.

Right then, she'd have two boys, nice and early tomorrow morning. Tomorrow was Sunday so no school. Ranger would bring them down himself. You just have a think about what you want them to do, Anne, and we'll get some of this put back.

After that, he was hers. Ranger gave him to her, pretty much. One boy for you, he said, as he and Peter Parker got out the next morning. Anne was in the middle of the pool when they drove up, at work already. It was her life. She had no choice.

Put him to work, mind. And no slacking, you. He'll see himself home. He's got a watch. And if I find you've gone home before dinner time I'll come and fetch you back after school tomorrow.

Peter Parker was bent over, poking the laces of his trainer inside. No way would he be able to get him tomorrow. Tomorrow was track training at the senior school and Mr

Tomkins was a stress bag. He wanted a hundred per cent, even out of the juniors. He straightened up again. That's commitment.

I'll give you commitment. Now get in that water and get busy.

He was dapper, like a bird, smoothing his T-shirt down at the front. Alright. I heard you. You're as bad as Mr Tomkins nearly. He looked up. Anyway, me and Anne are friends, aren't we?

It was so barefaced. It took your breath away. Anne and Ranger looked at each other and opened their mouths and looked at him again, cocky, destructive, sunlit as usual. You couldn't believe it, how he could stand there, after all, as if nothing had happened and be like that.

Funny idea of friendship you've got, Ranger said. I'd like to see how you treat your enemies.

Right cocky little so-and-so he was. And he wasn't even really conscious of it either. Flicking his hair back, smiling. He was just his small self, stepping towards the water, rubbing his hands at the edge of the pool, like he must have seen some grown-up or other do.

Right, Anne, what's it to be? Give it to me, he said, I'm a man, and he struck a pose, his hands now on his hips.

He was preposterous. Ranger got back into the truck shaking his head. Good luck then, he said to Anne. I'll be back later. And Anne held a wet armful of stones against herself and tried to make head or tail of it all.

He was different on his own, like he had been the first times he came. He was nicer without his friends.

What had happened to the other boy? Anne wanted to know. She talked in the rhythm of her work, a little breathless as she went up and down, wading slowly, scanning for the next stone and then her free arm fishing, her back straining and the other arm crooked round the ones she had reclaimed. Then up again and on, eyes always down.

The other boy had cried to his mum when he got home. He was scared.

Anne unloaded and stood up to rest her back. What of?

Peter Parker was sitting on a rock at the pool side. He made a stupid face. Hello? What did she think he was scared of? Then he held his arms out from his sides and did a quick impersonation of Anne, swinging rubbish bags, bellowing. If I didn't know you a bit I'd of been scared.

Anne stared at him. Well, you ran away too.

I was worried they'd get lost in the wood.

He didn't even believe it himself. Anne could see that. She gave a little snorting laugh and bent back to the water.

Bucky, the other boy was called. He was scared of trouble, Bucky was, Peter Parker said. He's not coming down the wood no more. None of them was coming down the wood, not even to the bomb hole. They was going down the new rec instead.

Anne was wading about in the middle of the pool again, having a last look for stones. Peter Parker stayed on the edge throwing pebbles and bits of stick into the water. She didn't know how to put someone to work and anyway he wouldn't have been any good at it. You could see that a mile off. He had no patience. It was difficult making a proper edge. That was the point. You had to think what you were doing. You had to make it tight. He wouldn't have had the first clue. So she let him alone.

After a bit, he climbed up one of the sycamores that overhung the pool. It was as if he weighed nothing. He was so agile, swinging his legs up to where his arms were clasped, hanging upside down one minute and astride the branch the next. Anne looked up at him and said nothing. He walked along the branch out over the pool. You be careful, she thought. You be careful you don't slip because I won't be able to catch you, and she caught her breath at the thought of it, his wheeling fall.

He lay down full-length along the branch, like a cat. There's one over there, he told Anne. You missed one over there and there's a massive one in the middle. I can't believe you missed that. You want your eyes testing.

Anne waded over and picked out the one she'd missed. The one in the middle was the one he'd thrown the first time. The pool had got used to that one. She was leaving that. It was a reminder, kind of, and a warning. I'm leaving that one. And my eyes are perfect.

He laughed at her. She went to work on replacing the stones and Peter Parker lay on his branch and spat into the water.

Oi. Anne whipped round, angry. That's my drinking water. You just don't get it, do you? Then she said slowly and clearly to him, as if it would make any difference, as if he would understand what it meant, I'm trying to live here.

Silence, for a while.

Are you nearly finished doing them stones? I'm getting fed up.

Anne didn't bother to answer.

Then a little later. How deep is it? Shall I drop?

Do what you like.

Go on then. Dare me. I'll do it. What do you bet me I can do it?

Anne had had enough of him. She got up and headed off

for her hut. Have a break, that's what. Sit in the shade for a bit and get some peace and quiet. Peter Parker climbed down from the tree. He didn't drop.

He came in after her.

Why don't you get lost off home? she asked him.

I can't. It's not dinner time yet. That man'll come and get me tomorrow. What are you eating then? I'm starving.

She was eating a sort of stew of fat hen and fern buds, from last night, that she was spooning up cold, sucking up the plant legs when they dangled down her chin.

He peered in her pot. No way. That's leaves you're eating. That is rank. No way would I ever eat that. He was disgusted. It was as if she was an animal or something. Don't you ever eat meat or normal stuff?

Of course she did. She ate rabbits, when she caught them and chicken from time to time, woodcock.

What?

Woodcock. Didn't he know what woodcock were? And duck, presumably he'd heard of duck and pheasant, loads of things.

So where did she get these wood whatevers? And how did she catch them? He was really interested now. Do you hunt like with a spear and stuff? He jumped in front of her in the way he imagined a hunter would, moving his head exaggeratedly from side to side, an imaginary spear raised, shoulders up. I could do that. I could hunt. Come on, let's go hunting now. That would be wicked. I want to see how you do it.

Not now. Anne wasn't hunting now. She was finishing the pool and sorting out the mess here first.

Peter Parker was almost in despair. Oh stones! Not more stones. You done the stones. Please, he kept saying, please take me. Come on. Then, when Anne was unmoved, can you take me tomorrow? He said tomorrer. Come on, you need meat. You'll get sick if you just eat leaves. Anne went on spooning her green mess and sucking the juice out of her beard. Where's your spears then? At least show me the spears.

She didn't have spears. He looked crestfallen. She used snares and things. Anyway wasn't he doing something tomorrow, wasn't it training he'd said, tomorrow?

Well, then the day after. Next time I come. Take me next time, yeah?

Maybe.

She hadn't been to the café in ages. The weather had changed, colder and grey, and the wood was rocking with summer wind. When she got to the car park, the crows and jackdaws were sitting it out in the tops of the trees, all of them, beaks like weathervanes, pointing, so the wind couldn't ruffle them from behind. That was a difference, Anne thought. She would always put her back into the wind. That was a drawback to being a bird, bouncing about like that on a branch, with your eyes watering, watching for the least change in direction. She sat in one of the outside chairs to read the notice boards and watch the walkers. She always read the noticeboards, even if she knew them by heart, to keep in practice and because she liked the words. Today there was a new board, a big board right in the middle, with pictures of families bicycling in helmets. It looked like they were in the treetops or something. Anne got up, intrigued. This was something new. This was rarer than anything yet.

Six miles of new bicycle track, the board said. *Healthy living in the forest. Walk and cycle safely.* It had pictures of butterflies and deer. *The rare black hairstreak butterfly. If you are lucky you may see a shy fallow deer.* Then there was a photograph of a shy fallow deer, but in another place altogether, from the look of it.

The next part of the notice had a picture of a long wooden tunnel on stilts. *400m of walkway,* Anne read, *designed to take visitors, including those with pushchairs and wheelchairs, into the majestic oak canopy to feel close to these magnificent trees.* She studied the picture. She would like to ride a bicycle in the tree-tops, if that was what was on offer. There was a photograph of a walkway in New Zealand, in the rainforest. The trees were different! Anne saw, and packed together, not breezy and open like here. It looked thick and bursting. The walkway had huge steel legs like a pylon and there were tiny people ranged along it, pointing with eager faces. At what? You couldn't tell. None of them was on a bicycle, as far as Anne could see.

The walkway will be a spiritual place to view our natural world from a different vantage point, to pause for thought, to get closer to nature.

Right.

Anne sat down again to digest.

Ah, our lady of the litter.

She hadn't noticed Nigel. He was balancing a herbal tea and a plate with a slice of carrot cake the size of Anne's foot. Nigel was rude. He always came and slurped his tea at her table. He never offered her anything these days, just ate whatever he had, right in front of her. He put his cake down so it was close to Anne. She found herself unable to look away. I take it you aren't in favour.

Anne looked up from the cake. In favour? Of eating cake? She was very much in favour of cake. That cake in particular had a very favourable look to it.

But Nigel pulled the plate towards him. No. Anne had said

the wrong thing as usual. He was concerned with the wider welfare of the wood. Not trivial concern, Anne. Not trivial concern. But trivial or not, Nigel seemed happy today, fizzing even, pushing carrot cake into his mouth and pointing at the board, crumbs everywhere. He had no manners. Fiddling in his dirty old bag for papers, all at the same time. He wanted to slow down, Anne thought sourly. He'd have a heart attack at this rate.

Of the walkway, Anne – the treetop walkway. As our only resident, I take it you aren't in favour. Gulping. You'll have to sign up. You could be a valuable campaign member.

Nigel's eyes darted sideways. Good morning, madam. He'd seen a woman now. A woman had walked past with a tray full of Ribena boxes and Nigel was up – maniac – spouting crumbs. Are you against the urban vandals of Whitehall? Are you against the despoliation of our beautiful woods?

Anne watched him. You didn't just talk to people you'd never met. You didn't just go up to anyone you felt like and start talking, not like that anyway.

The woman looked puzzled. She was trying to work it out, what he was on about. You could see that she didn't know if he was a nutcase or not, but the long words got her. Nutcases didn't say despoliation. Anne had head-spin.

Nigel had papers and petitions. He had a kind of awful way with him. The woman was like a rabbit in the headlights. Her children pulled pieces of clothing, that should have been up, down. They clung round her.

Mum I'm really thirsty Mum.

You said we could have something nice. Ribena isn't nice it's boring Mum. You said you promised.

They were round her legs so she wobbled the tray. She would have signed anything, Anne thought, just to be allowed to put the tray down and pull back her clothes and quieten the children. Nigel put his papers on her table.

You are a woman of good sense and conscience, he said as she signed her name on his petition, and you have three beautiful youngsters. Enjoy the forest, he said, filling his own lungs and tapping his chest. It's yours to breathe in. The children stared at him, thirst gone.

The woman caught Anne's eye and half smiled and turned her back. Confusion. She was barely head-above-water, Anne thought.

Mum, *look*!

Mum. Mum look at that lady. I seen a lady with a beard Mum. That lady –

The children were shushed. Anne saw the woman's shoulders jerk with anxiety. She was no way in control, as Peter Parker would have said. Anne got up and sat down a little further away, partly to relieve the mother of what she couldn't control and partly for a bit of space. It was particularly busy today. She watched the little birds hopping closer and closer to the tables. In front of her was a tray, covered with crumbs that she shook off onto the floor. Out of the corner of her eye, she saw Nigel, still at it, moving round the outside tables, like a cleg, swatted away by person after person.

Fragments of conversation drifted back to her. Well, they can do what they like if they've got the planning, Anne heard. It was a red-faced woman sipping from a sports bottle. She had purplish hair that stood up as if it was wet. I don't really have a problem with it, one walkway in a forest this size. Her clothes looked as though they had grown on her.

Anne raised her face to the sun and closed her eyes.

Have to move you along today, Anne. It was Sue, wiping down the table and taking the tray. We're getting busy for dinner time now. Otherwise I wouldn't ask, you know me.

Anne got up. She thought she'd go back by the skips, check for anything useful.

On the edge of the car park Nigel was talking to a man and a woman now. They were holding hands and making small moves of impatience. They only had the lunch hour. Nigel didn't notice.

Anne heard, Public body, and, Checks and balances, and, Damaging in terms of habitat. The problem with Nigel, Anne thought, is that he speaks a language no one understands. The woman interrupted him. She'd had enough. Yeah, well, if it gets some of the kids off the streets and into nature then I'm all for it. People come before wildlife, in my book.

Anne thought of Peter Parker. Was Peter Parker a kid off the streets? she wondered, as she peered into the car-park bin. Just polystyrene cups and sandwich wrappers. Anything that was good for Peter Parker was good in Anne's book. She was going to look in all the skips for bicycles and then she and Peter Parker were going to bicycle into the treetops.

Lazy summer days meant Anne didn't sleep so much at night. You didn't need to sleep in summer. It wasn't dark for long enough. Anne went night-walking, to the oak stands, on the other side this time. The boards in the car park gave all the coppices names. She went to remind herself of the places that fitted the names and she went at night because the light summer nights were too good to waste. Also the wood was different at night. Things changed their geometry in the dark. They made up new rules. Insignificant things tripped you up or snagged or soaked you. Distances you knew to be short stretched as long as they felt like it. The owl's flight disentangled itself and grew unerring, and the bats who had no eyes to speak of flew faster than thought and never bumped or cramped. Walking at night made you small.

She walked round the edge of the wood because mostly the understorey was too thick in darkness. No one wanted to be struggling through a thicket in the night. The sky lightish, great ridges of cloud tonight like sand bars on a dark sea. There were one or two stars, in between, and the moon weightless and slim again, newly delivered of one more blind white child. Over the stile and into the land beyond Smarty's, stinking of barn-reared chickens and the barns themselves, long and low and black, where the foxes came to nose the locked doors and the paper cracks and smell blood and feathers and dream their wild and beating dreams. This was a good rabbiting field, where Anne set her snares in the ditch at the wood's edge. There would always be a fox there, looking at the sheds as she checked her haul, turning away bested, licking his black lips with a long tongue. Dream on, she'd say to him, gloating. Try rabbit for a change.

Madiron Coppice, Crabtree Thicks, these were the oldest of the oak stands. Quinton Tongue Coppice, Rolls Mere Coppice, Stony Coppice and Great Straits. She didn't know which one she was in and she didn't much care, rolling their names around in her mouth and barging through the thorn backwards and into the wood again. Lovely. The night smell of it up through the ground, and soft underfoot. Tawnies faint on the other side, calling on the wing. The long straight boles of timber-grown oak. Trees are warm. It's a low, slow warmth, imperceptible like their growth but it's definitely warmth, or that's what Anne thought as she moved rustling among them.

She was looking up into the patterns their canopies made, black against the sky, polite how they made room for each other, not wasting any light but not encroaching on each other either. No overlapping, or hardly any. If she hadn't been looking up she might have seen him before she heard the shot, the low whizz and crack of a rifle. Close by, a deer buckled among the hazels. Anne's heart leapt to her mouth. She almost cried out. She might have walked right into it, two seconds sooner and she might have been shot herself. She dropped to her knees, flattened herself like the hares in the field, tried to control her breathing. Someone came shoving through the undergrowth. Heavy feet. Anne could see a flashlight, arcing back and forth.

She'd never seen a poacher before. She had no idea what he'd do to her if the flashlight pointed her out, crouching like a criminal herself, watching. What colour were her clothes?

But he knew where he'd shot, obviously. He found the deer. Anne saw the fine head caught in the beam, the black eye open, still registering that split second of surprise. A young buck. Then the man came up to his kill, put the light down so he could paunch it. He pulled a knife out of a leather sheath, strapped on his belt, and she saw the blade gleam. She could make out the sandy-coloured hairs on the back of the poacher's hand, the green of his jacket sleeve, his boot, close to the deer's head. Then, as he bent his head into the light's arc, she saw Ranger.

He was quick about it, but even so she had cramp when she finally unfolded and creaked upright. She had watched him tie the back legs to the fore, drag the carcass out of sight, to his truck. She listened for the cough of the truck's motor and the whine of it reversing, wheels catching and spinning once or twice before it was gone. She gave the wood a good chance to regain its silence, to plug – with darkness – the hole Ranger had made, to seal itself into itself again.

She was cold so she walked back faster than normal, not the way she'd come but on round, and because of the speed and because she was digesting this new fact, that the Ranger was also the Poacher, she walked slap into her next surprise. Plastic tape at hip height and it snapped against her so she almost tripped. What on earth? What now? It was so unexpected, tape stretched, now she felt along it, on and on, between the trees. She followed it round, a hand on the tape, up to the next tree, where the tape was wound once round the trunk, and on again, miles and miles of plastic it felt like, although when she came to the end of it, she realised it was a horseshoe shape. She was back where she'd started pretty much. Baffling.

Perhaps it was marking off Ranger's shooting, for the safety of people like her – who knew. Perhaps the shooting was legal after all. Would you cull like that, alone, at night?

Anne felt heavy. She shook her head as though to dislodge something. She muttered. Night was more different than she'd remembered.

She left them behind, the taped trees, the poaching ground, back to her own parts and there was comfort in that. She walked all the way round to clear her head properly, through the field of dozing cows, their jaws working through green dreams. Nice smell. Across Steve's old track, now the path to the housing estate, through the hedge and into the hayfield beyond. She flicked at her face to brush something away. A bat. Close to, like that, she always thought she had something in her eye. Through the gate and into the different world of the wood. Smelling the trees thinking about rotting in high summer, the fusty comfortableness of the habit of leaves, like middle age. In the hut the stove had gone out. Who cares, she thought, it wasn't winter.

*

He turned up again two days later, Peter Parker.

Anyone at home? Come on then. We're going hunting, remember? You promised.

Anne was on her second day of worm preparation. She didn't look up.

Oh man, what you doing?

His disgust always made her laugh. He had no stomach for anything. She was grinding dried worms, obviously. He squatted, looking serious for once. Don't tell me you actually eat that. He couldn't get over it. He put his head close over the stone where she was working. His cheeks had tiny gold hairs on them. He was like a peach. He'd watch for a bit, then he'd put his head down to one side. Ugh. Ground-up worms. I don't believe you. Then he'd watch her again. She swept the powder carefully into a jar, picked up some more worms off the drying stone and started again.

You eat everything, don't you? Do you even eat sticks? Go on, eat a bit now. Eat some worms then.

Anne licked one finger, dipped it carefully in the worm powder and licked it off. She put out her tongue so he could see the powder on it.

He was up dancing round her clearing, his nose in the crook of his elbow, shaking his free hand at the ground as if there was something on his fingers. Oh man, he kept saying, I don't believe you. Dried worms. And he jumped about again. What does it taste like?

Anne didn't eat them like that. You didn't just eat worm powder. You used it to thicken stews. It was protein and vitamins. You needed those things to keep you going. She looked up at him. It's a supplement.

How did she know what to do? Who told her about supple-whatsits? He was back next to her stone, watching again.

She had a friend once. He told her. He knew all about survival and he told her. Anne looked into the canopy of her trees, her hands still, the worms forgotten. And the memory of Steve caught her and drowned her, like a wave. She wanted him back so badly. Peter Parker watched her. He never missed a trick. What was his name, her friend? Was he her boyfriend?

Steve. He was called Steve. And no he wasn't. What a stupid question. You don't know anything you don't. She gave the worms a bang.

Alright, keep your wig on. I was only asking. Give us a go then. Let me have a go at that.

She gave him the flint that she used for grinding. She'd found it in the field at ploughing time, a long white unbroken flint with a round end, like a pestle. Go careful. You don't want to waste it. She put a little pile of dried worms on the stone for him. It's just a small movement. Just kind of rock it back and forth. Mind you don't jog them off the stone.

He was quite good at it in fact. Anne got up and fetched her spade. She made an incision at the edge of the clearing, turned the clod and picked through it. She was quick, like a bird, for all her size. The worms she found, she dropped into her tin, on the drying stone. He stopped grinding. What are you doing now? She had a worm between finger and thumb.

Squeezing the mud out of it before it dries. I don't eat mud, you know.

His eyes were wide. You're cruel.

Another day. She didn't know why he kept coming back. He just appeared. Sometimes it felt to Anne as though he was drinking her, when he was focused. The number of questions he asked and the directness of his glance. He was thirsty for something. And he kept on about the hunting.

When do you go then?

Depends. The corn was high and ripe and Anne was boiling up birdlime.

What is that? Are you going to eat that and all? He looked into the pot. Holly leaves? That'll make your throat well sore.

What if I'm not going to eat it?

He shrugged. What's it for then?

Catching jackdaws. Ever eaten jackdaw stew?

He didn't know what a jackdaw was. But then he didn't know anything. He didn't even know the simplest things. Robin, he'd said to a bullfinch once, when she'd asked him, and blackbird to anything, a magpie, a crow, a swift on the wing. Imagine that, not knowing a blackbird. Confusing that dapper little singer with a crow. She'd shown him a crow see-sawing on a post, coughing up his coal-lump croak. Same difference, he'd said with a shrug. And to the flowers that Steve had loved, yellow archangel, woundwort, tansy – I dunno, daisy? Then, in triumph once, over a blaze of ragwort, Buttercup. It's yellow, isn't it? Anyone knows that, buttercup. So Anne told him the names, in case he ever needed them, like Steve had done for her. Heartsease, bittercress, she told him, forget-me-not.

She thought she'd show him everything she knew, in its time, how the goat willow lit the wood like a torch in spring, how the seedlings pushed blind and hooped through the earth, how the birds lived twig by twig, every year starting over, with unquestioning artistry of moss and down, each one different. She thought she'd show him the flowers and seeds, which to eat and which not. She thought she'd show him what she knew of the papery eggshells, hatched or broken or burgled, what she knew of who ate what, the snapped neck, the small spat-out bones, the frozen body on the ground. But he's always looking at something else when she tells him, banging at the trees with a stick, shooting with his fingers, hopping around. Loser, he says to the pigeon flattened on the road. Same difference.

So? What about the hunting?

She set the traps at night. He couldn't go with her.

He could so.

Well, I'm not having you. You'll make a noise. Scare everything away.

He was injured. He would not. He was quieter than her. Lumping great feet she had. Hear her coming a mile away. Anne went on with what she was doing, not answering.

When d'you check them then? I can come for that.

Early in the morning. Before you're up.

But he was up, the following morning. He arrived just as she was leaving. He had a rucksack on his back, for school. I'm going to school after. And he wanted a spear. Just sharpen the end for me. I got to have a weapon.

He was so excited, dancing around, making feints with the stick she'd sharpened. This is wicked.

It was more of a walk than he'd expected, round to the chicken-shed field. Several times he said, Come on, what about here? There must be loads of rabbits here. Why can't we just stop here?

Can you see a rabbit?

No.

Finally Anne stopped. He was driving her mad with his constant jumping about and his complaints.

Don't you ever *look* at anything? Peter Parker opened his eyes at her, as empty as the sky. She made an impatient gesture with her arm, taking in the fields, the feathered line of the wood's edge.

It was a morning to match him, not that he noticed anything. It was gold and pink, with light clouds and a sky palest blue. Soft and warm already. There were comma butterflies along the edge of the wood, a cuckoo calling in the depths. On the tips of the grasses the craneflies gangled, impractically chinooked some of them. The pigeons were winging to and fro and at the corner, where the wood turned uphill, there were swifts, stunt-flying low over the long grass, in a frenzy of feeding.

Anne leant forward into his face. I'm going to check my traps, she told him slowly and for the last time. There's nothing to check here. If you don't want to come, then get lost why don't you.

They went on in silence, for several minutes. Then Peter Parker started up again. He kept throwing his stick forward at nothing. Nearly had something then, he said every time. I was like – he made a gesture with his finger and thumb – that far away.

That far away from what? A dock leaf?

No. A fox.

Anne made a noise in her throat. He'd be lucky if he could spell fox, let alone catch one.

F. O. X. See? He threw the stick again. You're just jealous.

But he held his nose through the chicken-shed field, so Anne had some peace then. He was horrified by the smell. Into the wood, near the warren, she stopped noticing him. She was busy looking at the ground. She went slow, picking up dry second-time-round droppings and putting them in a bag. What are you doing? That is so wrong. He had his hand over his face. That's poo you're touching. Anne had almost forgotten he was with her. She turned round, shushing him threateningly so that he was properly quiet for the first time.

She went on again, head down, checking for trails, for fresh droppings, looking at the size of a new tunnel through the grasses on the ditch, judging who'd made it. I'll do one more lot, she said, more to herself than him, then leave it for a bit. He was following her so close, trying to see what she was doing, that he bumped into her when at last she stopped. We'll try a couple here, she said, the excitement getting to her. You're more likely to catch them where they've got to go round something. She measured a hand's length from a fallen branch and drove a peg into the ground. Then she measured the length of the wire noose and put two sticks in, forks up to hold it. So the rabbits get used to it, she told him. He was all attention for once. I'll put the wire on tonight.

Can't we stay and watch it get caught?

No.

But when they went to the set snares it was a different story. Two were empty. Anne pulled them up. The third had a rabbit by the neck, still but not dead. As they approached, it beat the ground with its back leg in panic but it was exhausted, you could see that. Peter Parker didn't like it. It unsettled him, the thumping contortions, the bulging bloodshot eye. He looked at Anne. She was busy. She didn't notice. She was breathing heavily as she bent down and as she worked the wire loose she put her tongue out at the side of her mouth, like a spastic, between her teeth. Peter Parker put his hands up to his head. She whipped the rabbit up by the hind legs and coshed the back of its neck. Not easy because it writhed and bucked in the air, even upside down.

Limp now. Just the frozen eye, staring out its last emotion.

He looked from her to the rabbit and back again. Aghast.

Well what had he thought it would be like? Killing is killing.

He didn't say much on the way back and he didn't throw his stick. He might have just been tired.

Anne didn't notice if the rabbit knocked its head against things when she walked. She held it by the legs, head down and swinging. She dropped it on a stone near the pool. Peter Parker sat uneasily, a little further away, but never took his eyes off the rabbit. She came back with a knife. He was whitish and when she paunched it into the nettles, purple and viscous and still warm, he retched. It's the smell, he told her, gets right up your nose. The rabbit had been pregnant. Anne showed him the little babies, eyes seamed shut, slimed among the gore.

He hung around, kept going back to the guts to look again.

I thought you were going to school, Anne said to him, as she skinned the rabbit.

Well, I ain't.

He didn't like the look of the flayed rabbit but he hung around looking at it. He didn't like the smell, when Anne jointed it and put it on the stove to cook, pretty well straight away, so it couldn't go off in the heat. He hung around the pool while she scraped the skin with her knife and pegged it out over a flat stone. What's that for then?

To make a blanket for me in the winter. When I've got enough.

The day burnt on. There were flies now, over the guts. Peter Parker had a sulky face most of the afternoon. He kicked the baking stones and he threw things into the pool. He was rough. That is wrong, that is. He said, looking at the guts again. I couldn't live with that anywhere near my house. Why don't you put it in the bin?

It's far enough away and it'll be food for someone.

You're rank.

Anne felt sorry for him. She didn't know if it was her weakness, or his own, that made him so cross. What do you eat then?

Peter Parker shrugged. I don't know. Steak sometimes. Burgers.

Anne opened her mouth. Steak? And he couldn't take a rabbit?

CHORUS OF TREES

Heat. Summer well advanced, and the wood rustling like tissue paper, trying not to transpire, while every bird sings liquid from its branches. Close your eyes when you next listen to birdsong and you'll hear green in every note. Lushness pours out of their throats.

Birdsong in a dry summer can be a torment.

This is a killing summer. No movement at all is best. If you want to survive. The trees along the wood's edge patiently holding branches out into the fields. So light and dry. Little weight to carry this year. Closing stoma, holding stiff the tough little leaves, small size, thick and in-turned.

Down in a thicket, on a hot day, Anne and Peter Parker hiding from Ranger, sitting on their haunches in the only damp, sniggering, and the Ranger standing, hands on hips in the baking clearing, looking this way and that. He is annoyed. He has sweat patches under his arms.

When Ranger goes, they crawl out stuck with goosegrass. Peter Parker is fussy, picking away at his shirt, complaining while Anne wades into the pool calf-deep. His voice floats up through still air. He doesn't want to get his clothes wet. These are Lacoste, he tells her. Anne isn't listening.

Inside, the trees hold greener summers. Summers when you hear it drop, drop. Feel it slip around branch and trunk, gathering in the elbows, the snags, the rot holes. Running off the smooth-barked trees, seeping round the roots.

Green summers before, when the rain was drinkable, dropping through layers of leaves and the length of us, root tip to shoot, sipped, sipped. Moss furring everything then. You could hear things growing, the ferns, the hazels holding their green pennies to the sky, the slow push all summer long. Effortless multiplication of cells.

We hold our memories. Not in the pinched rings of a hard season but in rings that are wide with growth. We can remember that.

Nothing like summer rain in a wood.

Now, look into the burning eye of the sky and try not to feel that we are light-headed with drought this time.

Stand, reaching branches over fields that are browning already, filled with rushed seed heads and thistle, and think of grass that is green and beaded and bending.

Outside the wood a kestrel on the telegraph wires, sleek in a pink cloak, scoring the grass fields for food, hunting by itself already. Swivel, swivel. It has an eye like a bradawl.

The ground hard, the puddles dry, earth cracking under a brilliant sky. The kestrel rises, sweeps sickle-backed across the field to a minute movement. He's a brazen bird in a world that glints like metal. Stops in mid-air. His other name is windhover.

TIMBER I

They were extending the Woodpecker café. There was a big skip at the car-park entrance. Nigel was slumped over another carrot cake. No one could say I haven't tried, he told Anne. At least I can rest easy. Anne looked wearily at the cake he wasn't eating. As though eating cake was a duty, she thought. I've shouldered my lance so to speak. He looked accusingly at Anne.

There's tape around the trees, she said, although she said it more to herself than to Nigel. That was how their conversations often went. As though each one was thinking out loud and the other simply overheard, both of them disowning their brief communications almost before they were spoken. They've taped off loads of trees.

Of course, Nigel said, of course they have.

I walked right through it. Anne talked with her eyes on the cake, she couldn't help herself.

Nigel stood, he'd seen someone approach, but he looked at Anne in surprise, when she spoke, his mouth open so she could see all the pinkness and spit. Good on you, Anne. He raised a fist. I didn't think of that. Civil disobedience. Why didn't I think of that? Civil disobedience is the way forward. It's obvious. The more we cut it the slower they'll be to start. I'm relying on you, Anne. Cut, cut, cut.

He gathered his tattered papers. Ah well, bloodied but

unbowed, he said, making for the new arrival. How was it he never noticed people step back from him as he approached? No one ever wanted to talk to him. That was obvious. Anne watched him go through his patter. Nigel was a nutter. She thought about taking a bite of his cake, but he was coming back already. It hadn't gone well by the looks of things.

He sat back down sighing and ate the cake in two mouthfuls. He hadn't lost his appetite after all. Ranger crossed from the car park, clean and brisk, sleeves rolled up, sandy hair bright in the sun. Morning, Ranger, Sue said, like he was something special. Anne goggled at him. I know what you're at, she said to him in her head. He held the door open for a lady with a tray. With more than half of herself Anne admired him. She hadn't known that he could shoot. How much do you get for a carcass? she wanted to ask. I'll bet you're making a tidy bit on the side.

He never acknowledged Anne when he saw her at the café. She didn't fit with his clean and tidy image. He was a tosser after all, Anne told herself in Peter Parker's voice. She got up and went to look for bicycles in the new skip. But she brushed past him, as she went, on purpose and uncomfortably close. She thought he ought to know that she knew. Ranger looked surprised. She usually kept her distance. You want to look where you're going.

Anne gave him a little smile and kept her mouth shut. I've seen you. I know what you're at.

The skip was like a mini dump. All kinds of people pulled into the lay-by in the early evenings, men mostly. They'd get out, looking a bit shifty, and put something quickly in and drive on. Anne checked regularly, hoping for bicycles. It was electrical stuff mostly, useless, plus some kids' stuff, an old pushchair once and a giant glittery teddy with staring eyes. She did find a telly, but that was elsewhere, among a load that had been fly-tipped on the other side. She went and fetched the wheelbarrow and wheeled it back. She knew it wouldn't work but it was something to look at and she could imagine.

What the heck use is that? Peter Parker asked when he saw it.

Anne shrugged. She didn't have to explain everything to him. Do you have a TV?

He stared at her. Like. No. And we cook our food on a fire.

He'd skipped school again. It was well boring. He took a packet of cigarettes out of his pocket. Want one?

Anne was mocking. I've seen you, coughing with your little mates. What d'you want to smoke for?

Now it was his turn to shrug. He pushed the cigarettes back into his pocket. I nicked them off of my stepdad.

Anne went and sat by him. He'd seemed quieter recently, moody. Maybe it was just since the rabbit, she couldn't tell. Go on then, she said. I'll have one with you. My mum used to smoke. He looked up, flashing a smile. Why? Why should it matter to him if she smoked with him or not?

He took the cigarettes out again, old hand. Got a light?

Anne went in and fetched one of Steve's lighters. Well, it was a special occasion of sorts. She'd never had a cigarette before. The smoke looked blue and alien in the clearing. It made curious patterns before the air got it. Anne didn't breathe it in much.

You've got a bike, haven't you? she asked him after a bit.

And? Peter Parker said. You're not borrowing it if that's what you're after. I'm not having you trash my bike. Your weight.

It came out rude but he didn't mean it like that. Anne

smiled to herself and blew smoke. She wasn't telling him. It was a surprise. For when the walkway was up.

Are you inhaling? Peter Parker watched the smoke out of Anne's mouth. He was sitting with his elbows looped on his knees, old tracksuit bottoms and a football shirt. It makes holes in your clothes if you drop it on you by mistake. You're not smoking unless you breathe it in. Look. He squinted his eyes when he sucked. He looked hard and soft all at the same time.

Anne inhaled and he watched her. Her eyes swam.

Makes your head buzz, don't it?

They lay on their backs with their heads buzzing and felt ill side by side. Anne said the names of the birds as they crossed, so he'd know. Jay, blackbird, tit, tit.

Peter Parker rolled onto his side giggling. Oh man.

Flycatcher.

Alright, alright. He was hungry. He wasn't going to eat her food. He wanted to go to the café. He'd got some pennies. Get me some crisps or something. I don't want no one to see me. On the way they passed wild raspberries. Anne picked a handful. You don't eat the red ones, he told her. The red ones aren't ripe. I know that, my nan told me.

He didn't know anything. He wouldn't survive for five minutes. Anne crammed the handful into her mouth. She was grinning at him all the time.

You're crazy. He looked at her slantwise, like he always did, his lips slightly curled. You're probably going to die, one of these days, you know that?

They're raspberries. Don't you even eat raspberries?

I don't eat nothing out of the woods. I told you. I'm not an animal. Sometimes he didn't find her funny. Come on, I want my crisps.

When they got near the café, he gave her the money. Don't take none, mind. I want to know what it costs and I want the change, alright? If there's enough, get me a Mars and all. He ducked down in the undergrowth.

Anne went on a little way into the Woodpecker clearing. She hadn't shopped for ages. She opened her palm and looked at the money that was strange to her. She looked across at the café. What had he asked her to do? She couldn't shop. She couldn't remember what any of the coins were. She couldn't do it. She turned and looked back at where she'd left him. No sign. And then there he was, head up and signalling. He was so obvious in the light. Anne looked quickly over her shoulder to see if anyone else had noticed. He was frantic. Get on with it, his hands were saying. I can't wait all day.

Alright, alright, Anne thought, in his own words and turned and went into the café. The things I do for you.

But it was easier than she'd thought. It wasn't Sue, it was one of the young girls. She didn't even look at Anne when she served her. One thirty-seven thank you. And, although Anne was sweating and shaking, and although she dropped a coin on the floor and someone else bought a drink over her while she looked for it, she managed. Then she nearly bumped into Sue on the way out.

Oops. Takes two to bump. Won the lottery, have we? Never seen you buying before.

Anne mumbled and scuttled. I've got a friend.

That's nice, Sue said at her back. Enjoy.

She didn't care if Sue raised her eyebrows at someone at a nearby table. She didn't see or want to see. She did a funny lolloping walk, only just managing to stop herself from running in triumph across the clearing and back to Peter Parker's head in the bushes.

He put his thumbs up at her and grinned. Worcestershire sauce flavour? Yess. He kissed the packet. He gave her two crisps for going to get them and a bite of his Mars bar.

They walked back down one of the quieter rides.

What do you want me to do then? Go on. Shall I climb up that tree? I bet you I can get as high as that nest.

That was how he was nowadays, buzzing one minute, taking risks, gooning about for her, and then for no reason he'd be quiet, like she was invisible. It made her cross sometimes because she'd want to say, What do you come all this way for if it's just to be mardy? Spoiling a sunny day with one of his sulks. Anne never asked, but she could see. She was no fool. You didn't have to be a rocket scientist.

Don't go that way. I'll be for it if anyone sees me.

For what?

If they find out I'm here again. You know. I'll be for it.

So, trouble, obviously.

What do you come for then, if you get yourself in the bad books?

Peter Parker rubbed his hands and took a jump at a low branch, swinging upside down like a monkey, then up and crouching on it on his toes. He wasn't even holding on.

But it was a stupid question. Why had she asked him? She'd come, hadn't she, all that time ago; she knew. She could remember.

I came to the wood once. Her voice was anxious and appealing. Come down off that branch, was what she wanted to say.

He flicked his hair back. You're still here, he said. In case you hadn't noticed. He jumped down beside her. Sometimes you're so lame.

Anne just laughed.

He didn't always come. Sometimes there'd be days between visits, when Anne would enjoy the solitude, wondering about his separate life, as she busied herself about the clearing, patching, making, putting things in order. Or she'd feel well and bursting with it, because it was summer maybe, or because she knew her place and she wasn't alone. Then she'd walk just for the sake of it, with some slight errand in mind, wide of the wood, at dusk usually, at the changeover from swifts to bats, the moths bumping about and the smells leaking from hedgerow, from cut grass, tree, track, barn or abandoned machine, as if everything, so distinctly itself, waited until evening to give up its identity. Did she smell more at this time of day? Anne wondered.

There was hay several fields down; that's where she was going. She had string looped over one shoulder and a bag tied on at her waist. She was going to see if the field had been tedded. Hay was her luxury in summer, new hay for a mattress. It made the hut smell lovely. But you had to be patient. You had to wait for the tedding for two reasons. It was easier to take then, without it being obvious, and you didn't want it before it was properly dry. They baled usually a day or two after tedding. You had to be quick. You took a line, somewhere near the middle of the field and just rolled it off the top. The tighter you rolled the more hay you got and then you tied it and lumped it back. Two or three journeys Anne usually made, depending on how much she wanted and how much energy she had. Sometimes at the edges or where the tractor had turned quickly, there was grass still standing. Anne pulled at the heads absently, identifying them in the dusk just by the feel of them, and even without Peter Parker, she said the names to herself out of habit. Timothy. Burnet. Rye. If there were wild oats she picked them carefully and put them into the separate bag.

Quiet. And the smell of hay. And one car sweeping past on a road on its way home.

Then, walking back, bent under the first load, Anne glanced up to see her barn owl, ghosting out of the ditch with his own burden, something small and bulky in his foot. He raised his eyebrows in recognition and surprise. Fancy seeing you too, Anne told him, light-hearted, and she watched him away. It was a field mouse. She could tell that by the length of its tail. She was thinking of what the owl never considered, that rushing exchange. Changing the thick, known world of grass and earth, for the horror of air.

She rubbed her back, sore from the bending. The light dark of a summer night. The first bats stunting overhead and the mouse with new noises in its ears, over the hedge now, in its last confusion of flight and death. A black silhouette, just the small J of the tail hanging down in a curl, while the great wings beat above it. Anne turned to the outline of the wood. And that happens every night, she told herself.

She thought she'd go for one more load, though the dark was fallen. She wasn't ready to sleep. Might as well. She went through the gate and round to the housing estate field. All the lights were on in the estate and as she came through the hedge she was in time to see a car, on Steve's old track, explode into flame. What Ranger called a take-and-bake. There were boys on the haylage bales, dancing about, effing and blinding, watching. She could see them frenetic against the sky. Bad boys. Then the breeze shifted and the noise of the flames and a great plume of smoke, thicker than the night and blacker, reached towards the edge of the wood. Acrid stink in the summer branches, catching in Anne's throat. Something horrible burning. She got up to move on round, still watching the fire and now, at the edge of the estate, the blue lights of the police pulsed.

The boys' heads turned.

Fucking lose yourselves.

They were smaller, more runtish, than they'd looked on the bales. Slithering down the sides, falling and stumbling. I'm out of here. One of them kept tripping over, pushing at the backs of the ones in front, waiting to go through the hole in the hedge. Across the hayfield now, their movements jerky and inadequate. This way and that. Their high, half-broken voices floating back to her through the darkness, panicky and foul-mouthed.

Anne waited a while, to watch the police talk into their walkie-talkies by the car. They looked around a bit but they either didn't see the boys, or didn't bother going after them.

In the distance Anne heard a fire engine wail. She turned to go into the wood.

Anne had carted the hay. She had unrolled it in her clearing, to dry off the evening dew that would have been on it in the field. And still Peter Parker stayed away. She had rolled the hay up again, but looser, and dropped it into the box sides of her bed. She had slept on it for two fragrant nights. And now she began to feel restless. She wandered about in the wood during the day, hoping to bump into him, wondering where he was. She would have gone to look for him but she had no idea where to start. How many days, four? Five?

So, now, without thinking, down the path towards the new area, and it was pretty noisy, Anne noticed. There was another new road, at the intersection of two coppices, an old ride that she remembered as a scooped green lane. It had been soft almost all year round, with the trees arcing over. Walking down it used to be like walking through a loop of green light.

Anne stepped out onto the road. It was lumped up for drainage. Very clean, very hard. Grey granite chippings, with new posts along the way to sign you in case – what? What could happen in the thirty yards between that post and this? Anne had no idea. She stood on the road and looked at the posts. She missed the green shape of it before. She thought, like she always did, of the earth under the road, under her feet – useless now. Never grow anything any more, and the worms struggling through the sterile dark, puzzling at compaction.

And as she stood there, Peter Parker forgotten for a moment, many people passed her. People buzzing along, in tight clothes, on bikes, running, and two women in particular, walking in a funny way, talking, with their elbows bent, fists pumping. They all travelled fast, as if they were going down a tunnel, hardly a glance to left or right. You walk differently on a road, clearly. They skirted Anne briskly, as though she was invisible, until a woman with two Labradors, they bounding and she wheezing behind, saw Anne and said, Good morning, and, What a privilege to be in the woods on a day like this.

Anne said, Yes. Absently. But *in*? In? she thought. She looked down at the clean granite surface, holding back the trees, stretching away and away, wider than need be, separating you from the trees, the ruts, the snatching under-growth laced across with threads of cobweb, the hanging caterpillars spinning themselves down from the trees and into your face by mistake. This isn't *in* anything. This is on. She walked away down its grey length, her queer and rolling walk out of sync with the road, moving at wood pace, flexing at the knees and lifting her feet because of the habit of mud. Why do you walk funny? Peter Parker had asked her once. You look daft like that.

Where was Peter Parker, and where had all these people come from suddenly? How had this side of the wood filled up so quickly without her noticing?

Anne walked as far as the tape at the poaching grounds. There was a mess. There were big Portakabins with fat men in and out of them in hard hats carrying cups. Their trousers were falling down. There were machines the size of Porta-kabins parked about and piles of treated wood on the ground. But the trees were still standing. No sign of a walkway yet. In front of Anne, on the tape, was a yellow sign with a black hand in its centre. *Woodland operations in progress. Keep out!*

Anne went back to the clearing and waited for Peter Parker. How many days now? She notched sticks, lost count, notched twice in one day by mistake. Was he alright?

When he did come at last, it was late for him. Dusk. Anne had been sewing her rabbit-skin blanket, had given up with the light and was sitting watching nothing in particular. He was so unexpected, now, at this time of day, Anne thought she was imagining him. Only he looked different. His hair was shaved like the hayfields.

She jumped up, unable to disguise her pleasure and relief. Then she felt a fool, and sat down again and went back to her sewing like she didn't care.

What have they done to your head?

Peter Parker ran his hand over the stubble. Number one. Me stepdad done it. It's discipline.

Three syllables to that word. Anne rolled it round thoughtfully. Discipline.

He was in the army. I wish he still was.

Anne looked up at him standing there, stick in hand like usual, thin. It's nice to see you, Peter Parker, she was thinking but she didn't say it. She would have put her hand out to touch him but she didn't do that either. It looked like it was going to be one of his angry times. Talking was all she had to offer, to soothe him, to keep him there. Steve was in the army, she thought. Then, I've got an army coat, she told him, to keep the conversation going.

Peter Parker hit his shoe with the stick. Fuckin squaddie. I hate him. He came and sat down. Got anything normal to eat?

Anne had an egg. Would an egg do? That was normal wasn't it?

He looked doubtful. What kind of an egg?

Fried? I don't know, boiled?

He'd have a fried egg then. But mind it was clean. He wasn't eating no forest muck.

Anne cooked him the egg and gave it to him on her only plate and he ate it, although it tasted weird and she didn't have anything like toast or ketchup.

How do you live? he asked her when he'd finished, incredulous. No toast and no ketchup and only weird eggs. He put his hands to his shorn head. But it was the first thing he had ever eaten in her clearing and she'd cooked it for him.

They sat in silence for a while, just the tapping of Peter Parker's stick on the ground where he was hitting things. Then he stretched back with his hands behind his head. Where's the Milky Way then? Bet you don't know the stars and all.

You can't see it from here. Not at this time of year anyway. Anne was picking up her things, the plate, the rabbit-skin blanket. She didn't bother looking up. That's Orion if you want to know.

Yeah right. He laughed.

You're late out anyway aren't you?

He rolled over. I'm grounded, that's why.

Grounded? Was he staying out here all night? What on earth was grounded?

Are you taking the pee? Peter Parker shook his head at her. What planet are you on, man? Grounded. You know. Anyway, I come out the window. He's not keeping me locked up. I'm going to ring Childline tomorrow see if I don't. He put his hands up to his eyes, curled like binoculars. It's fucking dark. Do you get night vision if you live in the woods?

A bit later he got nervous. He thought he ought to go back and started off, but he'd turned round again before he got to the end of the clearing. He couldn't see nothing. Would Anne go with him? His age telescoped suddenly. A little boy. He needed to get home.

They set out together, Anne leading the way and Peter Parker walking so close behind her he kept treading on her heels.

Budge up then and let us walk beside you. It's freaky back there.

They bumped along side by side till they came to one of the surfaced roads where there was more room. Once an owl crossed in front of them making its hunting shriek. Peter Parker jumped and grabbed at her sleeve. Anne laughed.

Only the barn owl. Haven't you seen him before?

Woh. That was close.

He'd thought it was a ghost.

When they were walking he was alright again, chattier than usual, even, talking maybe against the dark. Anne remembered her first night in the woods, much older than him. She'd been scared silly. They came to the edge of the wood, by the dell, with the path back to the estate stretched out in front of them clear enough. Peter Parker hesitated.

Come on Anne. Walk us a bit further. There could be anyone out there. There could be freaky people in the shadows.

Anne snorted at him. What kind of freaky people? Honestly. And he looked at her, his teeth white in the moonlight. He gave her a nudge with his elbow.

People like you. Anne could see he was smiling. Go on Anne, just walk me to the estate. Please?

When they reached the estate Peter Parker stood under an orange light. He offered Anne his right hand palm down, thumb out, and Anne took it without thinking, by instinct. Then she walked back to the wood with her hand still open. A couple of times on the way home she looked at it and wondered. And later, in the hut, she tested it against her softest places, to see if he had felt it to be rough, and hoped he hadn't noticed. I'll take you bicycling Peter Parker. You wait. You'll like that.

Into the eye of summer now. August, when the sun burns a hole in the sky and the leaves turn in on their own stillness.

Anne went out among the cows in the morning and lay full-length in the dew, luxuriating in the cold and the wet for as long as possible. From her back she saw the sky, which had got up this morning thick and mazy, lift and lift, turning itself as it went, into something its opposite, hammered out flat at an impossible height.

Birds in the insect superhighway. The sun angling itself up the sky, staring down through its shaft, at the world that had climbed to reach it, while the world, which had got only to its own top again, saw nothing but the helter-skelter descent, down its other side and into winter, and stared at that, in stillness.

But it was stupefying, the stillness that Anne felt too, drugged by heat and the moment, and for herself, now, by the fat sway of udders and the splay of feet near to and from underneath. That's what high summer means, she said to herself, looking at the sky. She made a telescope out of her fingers to circle the early buzzard. He was almost a dot in the extra space. Hungry already, although he too looked lazy.

That was the only bird Peter Parker took any interest in, the buzzard. You should get up earlier, Anne told him in her head. See him now. They'd come upon him once sitting on a post, huddling in his cloak of feathers. He's raging, Anne had said, and Peter Parker had been scornful with a stick as usual.

No he isn't. You don't know.

Yes he is. Look at his shoulders and his eye. He's brooding he is. He's getting angry enough to kill and eat.

Because it was easy to be fooled, Anne had noticed, by the buzzard's height, by his lazy circles and his blunt wings, into thinking he wasn't bothered one way or the other. He's furious up there, scoping down through that yellow eye for something warm and unthinking. They had seen him, after, ripping at his prey with that fish-hook bill of his. Pretty savage. And Peter Parker had said, Woh, and, I see what you mean.

The buzzard's eye is related to the sun. Anne followed him with her finger telescope. That's how come he can go so high and not get burnt.

By the time she got up again, with pats in her hair, it was hot already. Back into the wood's cool, grateful. Down the old path that hadn't changed, although now, as so often these days, a heavy-breathing jogger dodged past her. Early. The early ones were the fittest always. She'd noticed. She was looking forward to her bath.

But her animal sense prickled. There were people in her clearing again.

At first she thought it was just Ranger. She could see the truck parked in its usual place. But another man, with a clipboard walked out from behind the hut. He was standing by the chickens. Looking it all over. Then he looked back at the pond, at the clearing, said something to Ranger that Anne couldn't hear and they both started to move towards the truck. He had mirror sunglasses and he lifted his feet higher than he need have done, as though there was something unpleasant. He had a bad atmosphere. Anne didn't want to be seen. She stayed behind one of the trees at the edge, but, as he too turned to the truck, Ranger saw her. She was sure of that. He glanced quickly away and he looked shifty. He looked like he was hurrying, his hand behind the other man's back. They got into the truck. Ranger backing more carefully than usual. The smell of diesel hung among her trees.

Anne walked in their footsteps, checking all was well. The chickens croodled undisturbed. The pond, shrunk in the heat to leave its edges naked, still hopped with insects. Inside, all was as she'd left it, the bed rucked, with the press of her body on the opened-out sleeping bag, her stacks of pots and tins piled by the stove, the dusty trophies hanging. So nothing had been touched. Why had they been? In the pit of her belly Anne felt unease. What had they come for then?

She thought she'd have something to eat. That was sensible. A weird egg maybe. The corn was standing, ready for reaping, just about, and she'd been cutting every day, so she had flour for once. She trundled about, out to the pool for two scoops

246

of water, one for the flatbread, one for the egg. Fussing at the stove. Riddling. Clanking pans. Stone up that covered her coolstore in the ground. Egg. Trying to bury her unease in familiar things. All her little routines.

Then it started. No warning, just cough, cough and then roar. Like the wood was tearing. Chainsaws. Anne stopped what she was doing. What were they up to now? It wasn't the time of year for felling. Felling happened at the back end. Anne stood and listened. It was coming from the poaching grounds. That was the walkway. They must have started on the walkway at last.

CHORUS OF TREES

Twilight at the walkway, following a day of heat and noise. With the falling of night, the lightest of summer breezes has sprung up. Quiet now. The saws oiled and locked away. Around the new breaks in the wood's canopy the trees flex and bend into the extra space. A tawny crosses and settles on the far side, blinks at the change and swivels. He swoops on something unseen.

Witness, say the trees through the breeze in their branches. Witness the change.

Watching, down the centuries, you could see it all. The little, bitter fields expand into doctored lushness. The buildings rise. The church, new-dressed with every fashion, floats its message over the villages that are becoming towns. The dead plague times. The mud everywhere. Muddle and panic and superstition. Civil war, robbery, scuffle and rush. Spreading branches to canopy the wounded, the whimpering fugitive, the outlaw. The hunts, the lone plodder hock-deep in the unimproved rides, the titupping ladies in summer.

Ask the milking oak how old it is. The milking oak will tell you – the things you think of as your own, that aren't. The things you never knew. The corncrake gone, the orchid. The arrival of the rabbit and the foreign pheasant. The little owl, the muntjac – how it watched them settle, how it saw the last red squirrel die. And once, grass slender and in tender green, how it saw the fallow deer, shaken out of their Norman crates, raise muzzles to the earthy air and leap – now here, now gone – perform their vanishing trick for the first time, under a quieter light.

So what.

There used to be ditch banks, hand-dug, along these rides. There were dead hedges and wood pasture. There were quarters painstakingly coppiced by a man whose hands were as dead cold as his blade, working on through the winter's silences alone. Shaking crumbs from numb fingers at dinner time, to feed the birds who were his only companions. Cutting, stripping, binding. Not a lot wasted then, if that is any consolation. Slow and solitary, lighting a fire for warmth when he stops, and then on again, numb-knuckled into the dark afternoon, so that ten summers later you could walk down this green nave.

Now another man works alone, a different way, clearing stands in this hot, late summer, high up in the seat of the Timberjack, among the timber-grown pines, pulling levers all day. A giant elbow, crooked towards the sky, swings its metal knuckle round, swivels, locks sideways round the trunk of the tree and then a small noise, only just louder than a whirring sound, for what – a couple of seconds? – and the pine falls. Roll forward a little. Lever. Slide along. Lever. Grip. Lever. Another whirring and the end of the pine falls neat onto a stack. Roll back. Lever. Shoot another length through the metal knuckle. Lever. Whirr and drop. And so on, for three or four lengths, and then the elbow hoicks the brash away, and the Timberjack rolls over it. Takes another pine.

You can do ten months' work in ten weeks. It's a nice piece of kit, the Timberjack.

At dinner time, on the mobile phone, with the crows

watching. I'm in the Forest, can you hear me? Finish late. It's a dodgy signal. He eats in the cab, with the radio on, because the cab's got air conditioning.

No stopping, even with the dark, because they're under pressure to finish the job. They are reinstating wood pasture, beyond the walkway. Headlamps like monster eyes among the tree trunks, and the Timberjack eats, and spits, and eats again, and the man goes on, far into the night, pulling the levers, in the dark, alone.

And the trees watch, and go on living, till the Timberjack gets there, or the chainsaw.

Above them, briefly, a falling star, scoring down the summer sky. The sky holds its history, just like us, their full heads say. A star falls and the sky keeps it, opens its palm to show us, light years later.

TIMBER II

Another day and the saws still going. What was up with Ranger? Anne saw him standing by the far ash, on the edge of her clearing. He'd come on foot.

He never went anywhere on foot.

She was sitting with her legs out, making and mending. She knew by instinct when someone was in the clearing, so she looked up and saw him there, trying not to be seen.

Blimey, she was sharp, she was.

He kept coming back. He brought her presents, a cup from the Woodpecker gift shop, with a woodpecker on the front of it, in case she had company, a packet of tea once, a bar of chocolate. He sat with her, different from before. He made conversation at her, which she wasn't used to. His wife Madeleine was expecting again. Mr Stallard was coming down. Visitor numbers were up. How did she manage things in winter?

He'd never asked before.

What did she think to an allotment? If he could get her one.

It was inconvenient, all these visits, although he was being kind. A lot needed doing. Cutting the corn from the edges of the fields and down the sides of the tractor tracks. Plenty of jobs before winter came, things to sort and store. She hadn't got time to sit around chatting all day. And if Ranger was going to turn up, she didn't exactly want to be caught coming back with game or with armfuls of corn however much poaching he did. It was awkward. So they sat, in silence, often, when he did come, and listened to the chainsaws working on through the oak stands.

She came to hate the noise of the saws. The sound of air ripping. That was the first thing. Sweet and soft, the morning air, and the chainsaw raw against it, which is just the sound of appetite. Then the settled sound of the saw put to the tree, like something slaking itself. Gulp, gulp. Bark, cambium. Choke, rest and then feeding again. Sapwood, slower, through the sapwood, into the heartwood and out the other side. Then even above the saw, you heard the tree's last silence. The silence of it holding, holding, pause and the chainsaw ticking over.

Sometimes a groan as it went.

Then thump, like a muffled bomb and the ground reporting shock. And afterwards, sometimes, Timber! and a laugh.

It was hard to listen to it all day long, day after day. And then Anne would look up, nearly at her wits' end with irritation, and see Ranger staring at her, with that uncomfortable look he wore when he was with her now, saying nothing. Drive you mad.

Once there were some people walking, who came into the clearing by mistake. Look, someone's actually living here. Oh my gosh, look at that. Gawping at Anne and Ranger. Is this bit private then? Sorry. Ranger got up and he looked so awkward and he whooshed them away quickly. Is there a quick way to the path? Anne heard them ask and, I suppose you could say we're lost in the Forest. A laugh floated back as he shepherded them out. Lucky we bumped into you.

Anne tried to concentrate, get her jobs done. She did everything in a rush now, when she could be sure Ranger wouldn't turn up, after he'd gone home for tea, or in the early morning. But on the fifteenth day, or maybe the fourth, who knew? – the noise and his company got to her at last, and she stood up and walked over to the busy side, like she was drawn to it. Down the unquiet rides, with her rolling gait.

Where are you off to?

No answer.

Just Ranger, puzzling, among the trees in the clearing, by himself.

Anne saw their backs first. A group of people, the scene of an accident, craning to see. There were mothers and children there, watching, and the children were dancing with excitement, like Peter Parker, because it's wicked, seeing a big one go. Massive, and it goes with this crash.

People tended to move away from Anne, so she got to the front quite quickly, among the children. The site alive like an ant heap. Everywhere, men with hard hats, who are experts, so they say. Who say it's dangerous work. Wait till you've got your chainsaw licence, sonny, as they lean on the rails of the Portakabins or the sides of the dump trucks, drinking tea and watching themselves. They wink at the young mothers and swagger because of their own importance, because there is tape separating them from ordinary people, tape with a sign on it, showing a black hand and *Stop! No entry to unauthorised persons*. They are authorised. That's the difference.

Anne got tunnel vision. Suddenly she couldn't see anything, except the new hole in the roof of the wood, like a punched tooth. And confusion. She felt the confusion going on along the fallen limbs and in the gap above. The mapping systems of the birds disorientated. The exodus of so many tiny things scurrying through a still trembling profusion of leaves.

And the leaves.

The leaves that were made to angle cleverly and rotate, to catch and store light, to be obstinate in wind, mashed into earth with the force of the fall. All this Anne saw for the first time. And the neighbouring trees, stripped, in passing, of branches and side shoots, held out their torn limbs and gaped with her.

She watched the men working into another. But she felt it now as if it was in her own body. This is us, she said with the trees. Bite. Bite. Crack. The thump of it as it hits, and the shock waves the earth sends through her own feet.

She blundered unseeing through the tape, which snapped against her, and across the site, arms up against the undergrowth, legs kicking like a swimmer, over bramble snag and fern.

Oi! they shouted at her. Oi! Clear the site. This is a hard-hat zone.

But Anne can't hear. She is listening to the trees. So someone comes, someone is detailed to escort her out of danger, because they realise now – she's the lady from la-la land – and the others, not escorting, wink at the young mothers again and look strong. Always protect the public.

But she was going anyway.

Anne walked faster than she'd ever walked. She put her head down and she didn't look up until she reached the clearing. She sat down, heaving a little, the sweat from her exertions making grimy tracks from temple to chin. She leant against the pollard, and put her hands down without thinking, on the knobbles of its feet, and looked up into the green of its feathered profusion. Well, she asked it silently, what do you make of that?

It reached out broad, either side of her, impassive.

The bandsaw, the cross-cut saw, the saw that roars, teeth whirring. Nothing new to a pollard after all. They've watched it for eight hundred years and upwards. They've stood and weathered it, maybe three hundred since they were last cut. Frozen, in attitudes of shock. Standing till they drop to pieces. The Queen Hive Oak, the Church Path Oak, the Milking Oak, the Meeting Ash, the Holy Ash. The only ones to have names, as if they were human. These trees are age-old.

The pollard just rustled, inscrutable.

A squirrel crossed above Anne's head and the leaves shook. Look how I'm cut. The pollard held up its thick arms. It's no big deal, cutting in a wood. It's part of the cycle. The stump either rots or springs; both ways are life.

And still, on the other side of the wood, the saws whined and overlapped and stopped, and stuttered into action again.

What's the worry? Leaves shifting in the updraught. Haven't you the strength for what is asked of you?

And small things dropped to the floor, in the stillness. Seeds. Twigs. Rot. The white rot, the brown rot, the soft rot. The trees' close relation to the soil, which for most people is a dirty word.

Decay is not the end. Collapse or felling, breakdown, re-absorption. Trees take a longer view. They are intimate with the constituents of their ancestors, feeling with fine-haired fingers through the mould and matter. The bark gaping black on that veteran, frilled with fungus. How much longer have you got? Do you know?

Why so accepting, Anne asked the quiet trunks – why does nothing register or protest?

The circle must close somewhere. Trees practise dying every year.

Anne put her head back against the boll of the tree and looked up and watched the river of bark flow over her head and out into the branches. The scale of that. You're a monster, she said to it. She put her hands down among the roots and the mulch. I could root here. I could put my feet down and anchor my bulk here and reach up for the light. I'm bark-coloured. I'm slow. I could adapt if they'd leave me alone.

The distant vibration of the saws. Did she imagine it, or did the leaves tremble on the still air? She pushed her fingers as far as they'd go. Roots are busy. Skirting the systems of the other trees. Metering change, in temperature, in water. Registering the pulse of life, the minute shock waves of the burrower, the walker, the unthinking driver on the road the other side.

Shock travels miles if you know how to listen, say the leaves on the trees.

But trees are absorbed and dismissive. Anne gave up trying, put her hands in her lap and closed her eyes. And in the dark, unseen, the trees went on, catching water in the net of their roots. Working with the most disregarded of the elements. Water's ugly, commonplace, sister. The most heaped up, pushed aside, taken for granted element. Mud.

It isn't all the glamour of the wind in your branches.

Anne got up and moved across the clearing. I need a bike now, she thought, still listening to the saws. It won't be long now and I really need a bike.

On her way past, she looked at the woodwasp's ball of spit and paper, hanging like a lantern in the dogwood there, went round it on quiet feet, admiring. The wasps were in and out endlessly. They were too near her hut and they stung without provocation. She should have smoked them out maybe, but she left it. It took a long time to build that after all. She'd become so careful now, of all the wood's creatures, of the billion things, with feet, that live in the bark, the holes, the mulch of leaf and decay, the things that were nameless and pale, jointed like plumbing, the scurriers, the biters, the still things waiting for change.

She could borrow her dad's bike, if she could get into the shed, or she could ask him, one morning. He didn't work Saturdays or Sundays, if she could find out when they were. Almost without thinking, she bent down, picked up a bag caught among the nettles and moved on, gently along a winding path, collecting the unwanted things, the wrappers, the cans, the bits and bobs. I'll look after you, she said to the wood, cleaning it, tending it. I'm good at looking after.

Even so, Anne felt uneasy. For a couple of days. She worked harder, whether Ranger came or not. She sang constantly, to keep her spirits up, to drown out the saws and stay positive. But still, something else, some other change. She couldn't put her finger on it. There was an emptiness, a loss somewhere in the noise and muddle.

She stopped working one day. Just put down her hoe and stood with her mouth open which helps your hearing. Pricked, alert. But there was nothing. Nothing unusual, except this unease.

And she left the clearing and set out, she didn't know where. Walking the wood wondering. And the wood seemed dead . . .

Where were the deer?

She hurried everything, in the days that followed. Hurried her most necessary jobs, hurried her garden, hurried her milking, to look for them, like she had before, in her first winter. She went to all their favourite places, too early for beech mast, too late for the thickest fawn-protecting cover.

Panic.

In and out of the old dells and glades, into the fields where they grazed or played. But each place she went was empty and the wood so full. Noise and dogs and people. Everywhere she went, it seemed, dogs bounced out at her. Everywhere, she heard people calling them back. Bonnie! Bonnie! Come here. Carter! Lola! Gypsy! Buzz! Cheerful morning walkers, who stride out and talk while their dogs sniff each other or yap. You couldn't breathe. Everywhere signs that needed reading. Bicycles, horses, runners. And on the far side, one evening, two boys on scramblers, ripping through the undergrowth, illegal.

Days of looking.

Then tired and dusty from wandering so long, Anne gave up. Early dusk, by the boys' dell, and she dropped her shoulders, sagged back to lean against one of the overhanging trees. Gone then. She knew that. That's what deer did. Select a place, pass on, like mist or wind. They would be in the corner of someone else's eye now, flickering between other trees. Anne thought of them in new feeding grounds, browsing, necks extended, doing their delicate damage, rooting, stripping the green bark, leaping other bounds. I hope it's nice.

A silent autumn without rutting stags, what a thought.

And what about the rest of them – her old familiars? Would they still find space for themselves – the fox, the barn owl, the woodcock odd and still on the wood floor, the flinging kestrel outside, that mad buzzard. Anne thought of an exodus huge and slow, like the ark only one after another. Soon there will only be me left.

In the days that followed, she moved like lead around the confines of her clearing, corralled into smaller and smaller spaces, and felt jittery in her head.

Peter Parker came back, dull, stale. He'd climbed out of the window again. When dusk fell, he didn't go back, just sat on the ground, outside the hut, throwing stones. His stepbrother was coming to live with them. It was going to be really bad. Anne went about her twilight jobs, not knowing what to say to him.

Later, they lay on their backs, in the first real dark, smoking and making wild plans.

Come on, we've got to work out how to steal the duck.

She'd been horrified the first time he'd mentioned it. I've never stolen anything. Propped on one elbow, looking at him as he lay outlined, knees up, one leg crossed over, resting on the other.

Yeah right, he said without looking at her. So old Smarty said you could just like help yourself to all that milk and hay and oat stuff or whatever?

Then he turned and she could see his eyes glinting and the third red eye of his cigarette, which he liked to wear now clamped in the corner of his mouth because he thought it made him look hard. That's what he thought anyway.

And the wood for this hut, he was saying, and the rabbits and all the rest of it most like. You've been stealing all your life. You're like a total burglar you are. One duck – what's the big deal?

He was getting hard to manage. Come on, Anne said, forget the duck. I'll teach you Roadkill.

They lay in the ditch. You stay there, she told him. Watch this.

To do Roadkill you went on the uphill side. Rabbit or squirrel? she shouted at him.

What? You're mad, you are.

Rabbit or squirrel. You have to choose.

I dunno, squirrel, whatever.

Anne lay down on the road like she'd seen the squirrels, not cuddled in death like a rabbit but spreadeagled like you don't care, neck twisted, parts on show.

Oh man, get up can't you? Then, when Anne didn't move, What the fuck are you doing? He made to get up and go himself, only he didn't because he was scared of the dark.

Anne knew that. The road giving back the heat of the day, thrumming while the car was still unseen.

There's a car coming! He was standing now, shouting at her, pointing. No way! You're crazy!

Anne lay staring at him as if she was deaf. She could feel the car vibrating in her own body. Sweeping round the bend, intent, its headlights fingering the road ahead.

Get the fuck out of it! He was screaming at her.

Anne thought, watching him from the tarmac, he must have cared after all.

He didn't realise that the car sees you. You're lying uphill, so it slows, doesn't it? It was power, making them slow down and look in the night, shocking them. He was nearly crying. Please Anne please. The car was almost on her. Anne held her breath an extra second for bravado.

Sudden and animal she rolled into the ditch. The car swerved, crawled past and was gone.

Peter Parker was hysterical, holding his head, his eyes like plates in the moon. You're crazy. That is so bad. You're mental.

She thought if she touched him she'd get a shock like off the stock fences. She lay on her back in the ditch.

Look at the moon go.

He was shivering. It's not the moon. He snapped at her. Stupid. It's a barn owl. You told me that.

Anne smiled her yellow smile in the dark. She felt invincible. He didn't know anything.

It's the moon.

But the question of the duck wouldn't go away. They played Roadkill a couple more times, although it lost its power to hold, after that first unrepeatable success. So Anne gave in and took Steve's old chicken basket and they set off for the pond, which was in the old village beyond the estate. Too far to walk, desultory in the dark. Neither of them really interested in the project anyway. She didn't know why he'd been so insistent and she didn't need a duck. So they walked in silence mostly. A grim last rite. Till they came to a small pond, odd under the sodium lights, with the ducks round it, some asleep on one leg, some on the ground and the pond oozing its compromised smell and looking thick like jelly. Why did they have to be so obvious, the ducks? You didn't even have to try to find them. No challenge. And something decadent about them not hiding away to sleep. Like drunks on a park bench.

Duck are muffins to catch. Tame ones are anyway, if you leave it till night. They put their heads under their wings and you just pick them up like a loaf of bread. There was no quacking, no drama. The one she chose didn't even flap, just gave a sort of squeak of puzzlement, the sort of noise that might come from a piglet. Anne plopped it in the old chicken basket. It panicked its neck forward once and hissed at the corners of the basket, but that was all. She soothed the feathers on its back with one finger and shut the lid. I'm taking you to a better place, she told it doubtfully in her mind.

Peter Parker was disappointed and scornful, dragging along, kicking things into the gutter. He'd expected something, tension, a police chase, Anne didn't know what. They didn't talk, but she could tell from his walk. Half-way across the estate he said he was going home. See you. And he left her there, alone under the lights, with a duck in a basket.

She took a wrong turning somewhere, up or down one of the endless rises. The roads so unfamiliar. Looking at the sky to tell which way she was heading. Haywain Close. Fieldgate Close. Dainty Grove. Hilldrop Rise. So many houses carefully built to look different and they watched her pass with artfully dead faces. Cars parked in driveways with their meaty backsides turned. This is our place.

It was far into the night when she reached her clearing.

She let the duck out in the morning and fed it corn. It fed, greedily as if nothing had happened, and took to the water. Anne watched it white and alien on her pond, swimming round and round. Little rushes here and there. Slow, dim puzzlement.

Do you know anything? Anne asked it. It had so little feral sense. She called it Peter Parker in punishment.

He came round in the day this time. The grounding was over. Anne hadn't seen him in daylight for so long she almost forgave him. He watched the duck with pride, hand on hip; made like it was his achievement.

I think I'll call it Triss.

It's already got a name. It's called Peter Parker.

He looked at her, put out. Could of waited till I came.

Still, it was called after him, and that was kind of pleasing. You could see that. He walked round the pond considering. Anne couldn't resist rubbing it in.

Well, she's good for nothing without a drake. She might not even last the winter anyway.

She?

Anne just smiled. He deserved it.

How do you know it's a her anyway? Could be a him. Could be a boy.

Oh for goodness' sake.

Peter Parker's stepbrother was called Joe. He was alright, as it happened. Anne didn't know if it was Joe or the duck, but Peter Parker had pretty much stopped coming to the clearing. She saw him around sometimes, with a new crowd, older. They were loud and they smoked openly. He looked fragile and different from them, though he didn't seem to notice. She didn't mind. So far.

Nothing stopped Ranger though. He still came with his presents and made conversation about the world outside the wood. Had she ever been into town?

Now what on earth would she want with going into town? Sometimes he was so stupid, she didn't even bother answering him. It was as if their roles had changed, as if he wasn't in charge any more. As if he respected her, her strength, her expertise, moving deftly round the clearing in the heat, burnt dark brown, wearing her clothes loose. He watched her all the time. How long you been here? he asked her once. And that was another stupid question.

Only the duck – the duck nearly brought back the old dynamic.

Where'd you get that from?

Anne stared him right out. It dropped out of the sky. She made an arc with one arm that embraced the staring blue above the clearing. It was Christmas time.

It will be bloody Christmas and Easter and all for Mr Stallard if you start nicking stuff. I'm telling you. You're not a pikey, are you?

Anne turned away making a snorting noise. Ranger was no substitute for Peter Parker. He really irritated her sometimes. What about your deer? she wanted to say. Where are your deer then? Shot, by the looks of things, or chased away by all your halfwit visitors and their dogs. You don't know anything. But she kept her mouth shut. She just walked into the pool in her clothes and lay down till she was soaked. Then she waded back out again with the water streaming off her, to sit at the foot of the pollard whittling pegs for snares. Not even the whisper of a breeze today. Above their heads, even the trees, who moved so little, were shocked into absolute stillness. Leaves held up rigid, conserving everything. How soon before we can drop them? they seemed to be asking. Snick, snick, snick, said Anne's knife in response.

You see that little mate of yours?

Anne looked up, wary now. Not for a while, why?

He's going to get himself in a bit of bother and all, if he's not careful. Messing around on the machinery at the walkway site – him and his new crowd.

That's his stepbrother, I think. Anne was interested in this at least. Joe.

I know what his name is. He's a right little so-and-so that one. He's on a warning from the police already. That's why he's come to live with his dad. You want to tell your friend, if you're seeing him. Stay away from that lot. They're a bad bunch. Driver only got out to have a slash and they were in the cab, weren't they. Drove it into a bloody tree.

Anne couldn't help laughing.

But it wasn't a laughing matter, apparently. I tell you what, this isn't the job it used to be. Bloody kids everywhere. Bloody complaints. Dogfights, litter-picking. D'you know how many times I'm emptying them toilets at the Woodpecker café? Anne looked up from her pile of pegs and shavings, shook her head. Twice a day. Twice a day. He was standing with his hands on his hips now. Ranger? Bloody toilet attendant, that's what.

Anne was sorry for him in a way. A dog jogged into the clearing, found the pool and stood in it, slurping up the precious water, drool hanging down from its muzzle when it raised its head. Anne picked up a stone and threw it from where she was sitting. She had a good aim. It caught the dog square on the hindquarters. The dog yelped and ran off. Ranger put his hands to his head. He looked every which way to see whether the owner had spotted them.

You can't do that.

Anne grinned.

They'll have you for that if they catch you. Cruelty to animals. You're a liability, you are.

But it worked. He didn't hang around after that.

Sue had been kind recently. She'd been giving Anne ice when she went down to the café, a whole glass of it for no charge. Anne really appreciated that. She took Sue some eggs in return, in a little basket made of willow. Ooh, Sue said, don't they look the real thing. Are they safe to eat?

Nigel sat at another table, grey and sweating. He waved a hand at Anne and gave a picturesque sort of bow. Sue whispered that he mustn't be disturbed. He was writing something for the local newspaper. He's a real one-off. Like you. Sue wanted to be kind, although it was difficult for her to hide her distaste of Anne. He's got such a way with words.

Peter Parker and the new boys swaggered into the car park. They were loud. About nothing. One of them went up to the counter, where a new girl was serving. Sue bustled inside. I've told you, she was shouting, could you please leave? We are not serving you here. Could you please leave? There was a mild ruckus. The boy opening his hands. What have I done? Alright? I haven't done nothing.

They turned to go, with the big boy swearing. Let's get out of here right. That fucking bitch is tight, man.

Peter Parker gave Anne a sort of half-look, then thought better of it and spat to one side and hitched his trousers. Sharp little cheekbones, Anne thought, and he was all gold, however ugly his clothes, gold hair, golden skin. Don't go with that lot of goons, Peter Parker. But she didn't say it. She just watched him leave, chicken-bone shoulder blades moving under the skin of his back. He was wearing a white vest and his arms were thin.

Sun, reverberating in the sky like a gong. There were early blackberries knotted in all the hedges. It was a bumper year. Anne picked dutifully, all the way back to the hut. She wished she had someone to pick with. They could have had a feast. She could have milked extra, and let it stand in her cold store, and skimmed the cream. And they could have had a blackberry banquet. If she had someone to have it with.

If you make it to spring I'll get you a drake, she told Peter Parker, who was wagging out her tail feathers on the pond. Anne put the bag of blackberries down in the heat, where they got flyblown and crushed together and their juices ran away through the safety holes in the carrier bag. She watched the duck and did nothing. Worrying about the real Peter Parker. Missing him, apart from anything else. The rabbit blanket was unfinished. She hadn't been hunting for days because of the deer. She was living off eggs and parched vegetables. Nothing was right. It wouldn't rain. If *you* make it till spring.

When night fell, she got up and she walked. She walked far into most nights and she slept until midday. Over to the walkway once. It was nearly finished. Big black hulk, square-cut, steel legs, like something over a motorway. Funny how wood could look so unlike wood. She walked right through the tape and on up the ramp. She'd chosen a moonlit night on purpose, though as she walked, so easy and so gradual, up into the trees, she thought of her own face, her old fat face, upturned to the sky, rising above their crowns, a second light for the night.

Out through the tops of the trees, and it was so easy to be a bird after all, or a small planet. Everything laid out before you like the promised land. No noise, just soft hootings echoing back and forth and the swish of a car now and then. Far out on every side, the wood stretched. Billowing tops, that lapped their black foam, a hand-reach below, and the walkway rocking, as though on a sea.

She raised her face to the night breeze. She hadn't expected so much, such loveliness, so effortlessly gained. Spreading away, wide on every side, and the lights of the town, that seemed to have the upper hand in the day, were tiny against the wood's great dark. She thought of the foxes and the badgers, all the night-time activity that the canopy hid. There's room enough for all of us to live, after all, she thought, looking at the wood. Plenty.

She stood there a long time, just breathing in what the trees breathed out, and the cramped feelings of the past days lifted off her like mist and her love for the wood overwhelmed her, so the stubborn rain, that hadn't listened to the cries of the fields and trees, rained instead, salt and small, down Anne's cheeks, in gratitude. As if she was dissolved into the whole, thinned and absorbed into wood and sky, with the metal of the night air and the must of the wood floor both on her tongue together.

After a bit she walked slowly on, one hand on the top rail. Maybe things would work out. Maybe Peter Parker would settle, and the deer come back. When it was finished.

She thought of her old plan to bring him up here on a bicycle. Bicycle among the treetops. That wouldn't please him now. He'd grown away now. Even so, Anne looked out, across the canopy, cupping the promise of this new perspective, like something precious, spillable, inside her. Keep it safe. You never know.

Then the walkway ended suddenly, and the wooden rail under her hand gave way to the cold of scaffolding poles, criss-crossed and jointed. Anne was open-mouthed with surprise. It might have gone on forever. Abrupt this ending, without logic. No warning. Just the chopped-off platform, still strong, and the square chute, dizzy, into the dark.

Anne looked down and felt the pull of nothing.

She slept when she got home, a deep sleep, and, when she opened her eyes the next morning, the size and calm of the wood from the top of the walkway was still with her. She felt washed clean. How much time had been wasted in anxiety? She lay for a while, relaxing into the memory of space, and watching the early light finger her collectibles. Then she sat up and got out of the bag, making all her movements smooth, so as not to jolt the vision out of focus. If she could just keep it clear . . .

She swept out the hut. She washed her clothes. She cleaned

274

and reset her stove, soaking the ashes, until they stopped
fizzing, with buckets of water from the pond. You had to walk
out now, across mini mudflats, to get to the water, the pond
was so shrunk and the stream down to a trickle.

She spread the soaked ashes on the vegetable plot. Watered.
Starting to lose the morning's cool. Anne looked up, through
the trees. Heat flexing above the wood already.

Milking time. Two walkers even this early and at the
milking gate a dog that barked at her and wouldn't let her
through. What are you talking about? Anne asked him. Get
out of my way, I've been coming here for years. She could
have given him a whacking great kick. He didn't do anything,
just barked, and she reached over, gingerly, and opened the
gate. From the other side, she leant over and barked back,
with all the savagery she would have put into the kick. Bloody
dogs.

Topsy! from somewhere closer than Anne would have liked.
Topsy! And a thin whistle. Anne lay down and waited for
quiet. Someone had nailed the buzzard to the sky. His wings
flamed translucent.

There was a person leaning on the gate, looking at her.
Topsy's found someone. Good girl. Clever girl. Michael!
Shouted very loud. Michael, someone's had an accident.

Another person at the gate and the gate opening. Wheezing
and fat concern on two faces. Moving with difficulty at speed
across the field. Alright! We're coming. Michael, hold Topsy.
Are you alright?

The buzzard unnailed himself and slid off sideways.

They leant over Anne. Are you hurt? Michael's got a mobile
phone. We'll call for an ambulance.

I've got a mobile phone.

Louder this time.

They waited for Anne to respond and, as she stared back at them, flat on her back, doubt and then disapproval took the place of concern in their faces.

I'm lying down, she told them.

It explained nothing. They looked at each other, mouths set in indoor faces. She had caused unnecessary alarm. They straightened up and they left. She watched their backs to the gate. Topsy was barking.

Anne heard, Topsy found her, she really has empathy that dog.

I think she was drunk, she wasn't hurt.

The words floated back tinny, on air thinned with heat and dryness. Anne stared hard at a spider bunched up like a grass seed, in the middle of her dew-decked web.

After milking, she walked slowly back, scrabbling in her mind. If she could just get back that feeling. If she could hold the walkway's new perspective. She concentrated on the warmth of the milk and its coating of mucus in her mouth and throat. Comfort in that surely.

But the wood was teeming. Maybe if it rained, Anne thought, in desperation. There would be fewer people in the rain. There always used to be.

There was a letter pinned on the door of her hut.

CHORUS OF TREES

Much later now. Thick summer dark, like a blanket wrapped over your mouth. The hut and the clearing deserted. Just the trees watching the night sky and waiting. Passing time. The circle must close, say the trees, standing round.

And busy with their cycle, they go on the same, despite the saws and construction machines, or the heat, or the change. Withstand, they whisper. Do you not have the strength to withstand?

Tracking above them briefly, a falling star. Burns across the sky. Is gone.

Who is this, down below, restless down these rides – walks incessantly, tripping, dazed, over ground as familiar as her own body? Why doesn't she stop and rest?

And what is it she carries in her hand, raising, scanning, dropping, as she walks, a small and fevered flux, of up and down, and round and round? A scrap of moon-white paper.

Under the trees' still leaves, a black shape, breathing, hurrying, bumping against trunk and root. All through two days and round one night, without stopping.

As if something from the outer edges of the sky, had fallen, charred, through great resistance.

Anne.

Holding the letter, fighting darkness, moving onward down the ride.

DEAD WOOD I

There were words in the letter.

No rain, Anne told herself, halfway through her second morning of walking. Fagged, disorientated. That was the matter. That was all it was. Her mind buzzed dry like a fly in a web. Rain would wet the words and they would flower into understanding.

Clatter clatter clatter. She held the paper up again. *Unlawful occupancy. Liability. Forcible eviction.*

And where was Ranger now?

Dog-tired, she walked, like she was sleeping on her feet, to the café – by accident or on purpose? – the long way round, through the harvested fields, where she should have been gleaning.

Coöperation. Immediate effect.

Through the barn owl's hunting grounds, not seeing. Jays screaming in the wood. And faintly, but still there, the words buzzed with her mind. *Personal security. Community housing. Allotment.*

Nigel was at the cafe, his ponytail like string, his face white, crumpled over his carrot cake. Anne sat down at his table. Hello. Hello Nigel. The syllables thick and slurred.

Hail! Hail! But after his greeting he stopped, because he must have noticed, for once, how she was. He looked at her, and he saw the exhaustion, her mind falling. We live in puzzling times. He said it companionably, as though their troubles were shared, as though it was just the building of the walkway that was the matter, or the filling up of the wood.

So she passed him the piece of paper, crumpled and softened with handling, the letter from Mr Stallard that she'd found pinned to her door.

Two birds hopped in the silence, while he read the letter. Sun-soaked clearing.

Nigel brought the palm of his hand down flat on the paper. He said Anne's name three times, and each time he said it he pulled himself straighter in the chair as though there was a string from the top of his head tweaked by something unseen. She watched his mouth open and shut, the sounds coming out of it like bubbles.

This was an abuse of human rights. This was oppression in the raw. This was an urbanised beaurocritised state steamrollering the individual.

It was raining words. Anne stayed silent because she was waiting for them to drop on solid ground. But there was nothing there. Nothing underfoot after all.

Nigel reached across and put a hand over hers.

Never fear, Anne, never fear. Trust me, I am a seasoned campaigner. His hand was clammy. There was no comfort in it.

She needed tea, that's what Nigel said, and he got up to buy her some, like he was offering her a fur coat. Anne sat still for the first time in days and felt herself to be still moving and watched the people. They were eating ice creams, playing, enjoying the beautiful weather. Gorgeous, isn't it? Aren't we lucky? They hadn't had letters.

Ranger crossed the car park, hands in pockets, sleeves rolled up. He hadn't seen Anne. Nigel barred his way into the café, with Anne's tea on a tray. Ah, Ranger, a word in your ear if I may. Ranger was obliging. He made some remark Anne couldn't hear and laughed. Only when he realised that Nigel was taking him to Anne's table did his composure falter. She heard only part of what Nigel was saying, National newspapers, and, Taking this higher. And then Ranger's strangled responses. To be honest, Nigel, she's not safe there. Hooligans. Broken it all up before. Best interests. And, I've put in for an allotment for her. Mr Stallard.

She drank some of the tea and it almost drowned her.

Anne stood. She said to herself but out loud, I'm a survivor. It didn't sound so solid any more. The men turned and her eyes met Ranger's for the first time and he was a small man after all. She took him on.

Where are the deer then? Loudly. Where are the deer?

And everyone else heard and looked round, at the friendly Ranger in his uniform and the two odd ones buzzing at him, a couple of papery old hornets.

They've gone, haven't they? You've shot them all. Or they've been pushed out. There's no deer in this wood any more.

Nigel was standing at her side now, nodding and repeating odd bits and bobs, just like Mother.

This was their place before you came.

Their place indeed, Nigel echoed.

And you've driven them right out.

All the people watched and waited for the Ranger's response. The Ranger put his hands on his hips, now he had an audience. He laughed a good-natured laugh.

Oh they're there alright. We know where they are, don't you worry.

Anne made a hornet noise in the back of her throat.

Fibber. She spat on the ground to one side.

And Nigel slipped his arm through Anne's, very stately, and escorted her away.

Come, Anne, and to the Ranger, You haven't heard the last of this.

They moved forward through a small crowd, which parted as they approached. Ladies and gentlemen – Nigel had a deep round voice, not what you expected – this man belongs to an organisation that wishes to drive the natives of this woodland from their habitat, this lady among them. How long before we are all driven from our homes, I ask you? Think on it, ladies and gentlemen. I shall be making a statement to the local press. Think on it.

No one answered. No one held them back. And they bumped arm in arm, awkward couple, bizarre, stale-smelling, out of the café clearing and disappeared. Thin behind them Anne heard, Riiight! drawn out for comic effect. Laughter.

CHORUS OF TREES

The sun is not set, although it is late and in the thinning sky the suggestion of a moon hangs. Waxing or on the wane – we weren't counting. A pale disc, almost rubbed through with daylight.

We're still growing.

We're still working with light and what water there is. We're selectively porous. Breathing with many mouths, we're not telling. We have secrets, hidden in our rings, shed if you like, in the autumn, from twigs that are stiff with forgetting.

Here is Anne, for instance, not much different from the moon, barely there, meandering back and forth at a loss. For the first time in how many years, she is purposeless, ricocheting wearily about her old haunts, keeping a shocked silence. Like the moon, she is almost erased by the time.

Spreading wide, enjoying the cool, we canopy the car park, where the Ranger, unusually late for him, is sitting in his truck, with the engine ticking over, worrying, worrying. He doesn't like it, all the same. He shakes his head and wonders, puts his hands on the wheel, thinking to drive to Anne's clearing, isn't sure of finding her, drops his hands and wonders again. Anne's owl crosses in front of him, its bright white advertising its position in the food chain. I'm white. Look at me. I have no predators. Wide wings sweeping away into dusk as soft as themselves. The Ranger puts his hands wearily back to the wheel. He's a kind man after all and he has no stomach for the job, but what can he do? He turns the truck out of the car park. Goes home to little Matthew and his pregnant wife.

Across the top of the wood, trees holding hands, connecting the different parts they shelter, roofing over the predator and the prey, equally and without prejudice. The trees don't care. It doesn't matter. There's always another time, for someone else if not for you. We see a wider circle. We see rings and rings.

Night fallen and Anne is turning back now, one foot in front of the other, automatic. She is going to the walkway. She's going up into its dark order, its promise of space for everyone, its distant, uncluttered perspective.

And if that fails, there is the dark chute from its top. There is the Mother Earth, which holds us all, which will pull Anne into her embrace and keep her there. In some ways Anne has been falling for a long time. And she doesn't want to leave the wood.

Bending our tops by the unfinished walkway, as Anne approaches, breaking the circle of hands, in this new space, what is this?

Boys, a gaggle of them, sitting on top of one of the big machines, swinging on the scaffolding, loud-mouthed. Two of them have bags they are holding. They hold the bags out over their faces, breathe into them and reel. See. That one there. Opens out his bag and, as he bends towards it, his head glints in the light.

What is it Anne wants, as she stands in the shadows watching? We don't know. What is it that, given another time, she would do or say, as instead, she turns away to wander back through the tangling undergrowth of her mazing mind?

We don't know. We can only witness, witness, witness.

DEAD WOOD II

Night deepens. Stars intensify and a wind gets up. Anne still battling on.

Remembering her beginning now, as though this life in the wood had been a breathing space, a pool outside time, measured in never-ending rings. She thought of her dad. She can't see the wood for the trees, he'd said. And I can't. I still can't.

On through Rollesmere Coppice and she stumbled, despite the moon, and put her hand out to the cool bole of an oak. Oaks are resilient. It's in every ridge of their bark. How do you manage? Anne asked it. I'm supposed to be a survivor. Then, looking up into its branches, she said, I don't think I can do it, Steve.

And lazily, through a half-closed eye, the moon looked back at her from the other side. Oh well.

I can't do it, Anne said again, louder this time, I can't do it after all.

One more time then. One more time to the walkway.

Anne set out on her little pilgrimage, stumbling continually now, scrabbling at hopes as she went. Maybe with sun-up the trees would show her a solution, surprised by first light and the far fields fuzzy with mist. Maybe.

But she was confused. It took a long time, past Smarty's old fields, the chicken sheds, the poaching grounds, as though she were swimming black water. Slow limbs and her own breath loud in her ears. It was deep into the night when the walkway rose up before her, deserted at last, with its clean, man-made lines saying, Order, Clarity. Anne stepped towards the ramp.

Something gleaming there, at the foot.

His eyes were closed when she picked him up. His eyes were closed and he still smelt of fear. White face almost translucent, and did she imagine it or was there a pulse beating at his neck? She carried him. Thistledown boy, gold hair new-grown. But he was heavier than you expected, a dead weight, and she thought she might break before she got him to her hut. Stumbling, back on fire across her shoulders, and maybe she made a high noise in the back of her throat, a keening, or maybe she didn't. Was he warm against her – or was it her own warmth she felt?

She carried him through the dark, to her hut. She laid him on her bed and she looked, as best she could in bad light, for damage. She bathed what she could see. She laid her head on his chest, but her own heart was making such a noise it wasn't possible to hear.

She held a feather to his lips and when the feather moved – and moved – and moved – she couldn't help the words or the sounds that came out of her, unbidden and for the first time. That choking rush of human things. What she did, what she said to him, they were just the limited words and gestures, just the ordinary things that a woman can do for a child. We don't have anything else.

But the length of that night.

The vigil in the hut, with the night noises outside. Holding the thin hand. The dirty nails. The smoothness of the skin. And the dust in the hut, the smoke from the stove. Do they bother you, Peter Parker? Are you warm enough? She bent over him continually, in the hopeless candlelight, and checked for his breathing. Thank God. Thank God. And the moon slid, cold and ancient over the wood, and the owls called.

Just a woman and a child after all.

At dawn, in panic, she took his shirt off. She laid him across her lap and she studied the miraculous map of veins across his chest and arms for movement, for any indication of life behind them. She dropped the feather among the dust and fumbled for it. Held it up. Couldn't see. Holding her big hands, now together, now apart. Oh please. Oh please. Touching, the amazing hair, the pale skin of his chest. Finding he was warm. Rushing to cover him with everything she could find, in case he got cold.

But it was so hard to know.

A long finger of light stretched across the floor, and in the canopy the birds were singing up another summer day. But Anne was shaking now and Peter Parker's head lolled.

She carried him in her arms, to her doorway, to the sun that he most reminded her of, to wake him. And in its light, his hair did wake, and his eyelashes, and the fine down on his cheeks. But the dew was on everything and the cold came out of the ground. And Peter Parker didn't shiver.

Then Anne caught him against her, rocking. Rocking.

And a cry convulsed her, as she lifted her face to an empty sky.

Oh my boy. My boy.

Peter Parker.

Where have you gone?

*

His arm hangs down and his head slightly back and his body drapes itself across her open knees and on his chest now a slow and bitter salt rain falls. Anne sits holding him and the sun lifts up through the branches of the trees, and the white duck takes to the water and in the distance there is the barking of dogs and voices that call, Simon!

Another beautiful day. The world and the wood roll on the same. A horn on the road carrying across, and the light slanting into the clearing. The small birds hopping closer and closer, wondering why Anne is not eating her breakfast, fluttering back and forth, perching on branches of the nearest hazels whose leaves shine translucent in the first light of this morning. Anne and Peter Parker sit on. Dew on the webs on the moss at the foot of the trees. And now pigeons clap upwards and the wood echoes with the barking of dogs and shouting.

Simon! Simon!

A helicopter stutters and Anne still sits with the boy across her lap. She doesn't look up, or call. She has no instinct for flight. She feels no connection to the people approaching. She looks at the moss and even in her agony she thinks, clear-headed, that it is so green, so dew-spangled, even today. Nearer and now nearer, and the undergrowth splitting.

She is still looking at the moss when the men in black and white, with dogs straining at the leash and Ranger with them, burst at last and with violence into the clearing.

Now everyone is shouting and Anne's mind is dark. The little birds have all gone. Stay where you are, someone keeps saying. They hold her as though she was going to move. They pick up Peter Parker. They bring a bed for him, a flat bed, and they strap him on it with blankets over and straps.

They cover his face and they carry him away, a different way from Anne.

In light and shade and shade and light again, Anne watches the thin shape of him, out of sight.

The little room smells wrong. It is hard-edged and white. No shade here. No filtered light. Every surface is flat like a knife. Difficult to find your way around a cell, if you've been used to a whole wood. Often Anne gets as far as the shelf-bed and is confounded. Up again and round.

There is a moon in the room, or a pale sun, square and very high up, barred. You can see the weather sometimes as if it were a swatch, not the whole thing, just a sample. When it rains at last, it is sample rain. Neither really sound nor smell, in the room at least.

Elsewhere, if you shut your eyes, it plops on the mould of memory, riffling and sliding through layers of less and less resistance, leaf, twig, leaf, leaf, air, and smells come up to greet it and the sound and the taste of it is absolution.

Like it is raining now, on a big man, walking up a track, head down. Raining on an empty hut when he gets there, the ground turning to mash. Leaves and blown twigs and sticks fallen, and the pool brown and swelling to flood. Silt and brash have pushed it up and over the stones and into the clearing, and on its surface now, among the giant gouts, are bobbing plastic bags. He watches the bags gyrate. A slow dance, under the drops, until they saturate and sink. Full bags, tied at the tops like rabbit ears. And in the bags is purpose.

And that is something.

EPILOGUE

There is still the wood. More or less. Just about.

Hard to eradicate, because wood is the fifth element after all. Closer to our own in some ways, although we have lost the knack of living in it. More human than air, or fire, or water. The only one to know, like we do, youth and death.

And it is an element, if you brave it alone, coming at its bulk slantwise, across a clagged field, with only half-intent to enter, and nothing to tell you whose wood it is, or if it only belongs to itself. And it won't help, despite its affinity, should you swing crazily for a moment, balaned on the top barbed wire, and lurch down and up the other side of the boundary ditch, all mud and brambles. It will just swallow your light with treetops, up and over your head, hiding birds and whispering.

But it will take you, if you let it, like it took Anne. Standing for the first time alone in that glimmer, it will be surprising if you don't prick alert with some forgotten sense. Listening – for what?

Something it knows, that you've forgotten maybe. Some story it absorbed. The distillation of a particular life, lived against the grain of the time. It doesn't matter where you start. You could pick any ring, reopen it at any point, and find it looping back on itself forever, still innocent of the end. A life lived in the wood, for instance, starting with the misfit at its centre, working outwards, counting down the rings that it took for her to become native, because survival doesn't come naturally to us any more.

Or something in the tree's heartwood, when the wood had made her, and where she'll always be, pacing the round of the same inner rings, gaunt, after a particularly hard winter, raging like the fox, eyes burning.

Then stand, like she did, at the wood's edge, by the field corner maybe, on a day when the sun stares milky through the mist, as if through cataracts, and the trees are ghosts and the breeze spins out its airborne droplets into threads of light, so you walk through a storm of glitter. Then you'll have some idea.

That's her. That's how she was.

Acknowledgements

I would like to thank the following people for their kind help and encouragement: Caroline Dawnay; Philip Hensher; Penelope Hoare; all the Keens, including the ones called Oswald; William Sieghart.

Grateful acknowledgement is made to Faber and Faber Ltd, for permission to reprint an excerpt from 'Trees' from *Collected Poems* by Ted Hughes, copyright © 2003. Reprinted by permission of Faber and Faber Ltd.

www.vintage-books.co.uk